Max's Folly

Essential Prose Series 128

Canada Council for the Arts
Conseil des Arts du Canada

ONTARIO ARTS COUNCIL
CONSEIL DES ARTS DE L'ONTARIO

an Ontario government agency
un organisme du gouvernement de l'Ontario

Canada

Guernica Editions Inc. acknowledges the support of the Canada Council for the Arts and the Ontario Arts Council. The Ontario Arts Council is an agency of the Government of Ontario.

We acknowledge the financial support of the Government of Canada.

Max's Folly

Bill Turpin

GUERNICA EDITIONS

TORONTO • BUFFALO • LANCASTER (U.K.)

2016

Max's Folly is a work of fiction. All the characters and situations portrayed in this book are fictitious and any resemblance to persons living or dead is purely coincidental.

Michael Mirolla, general editor
Lindsay Brown, editor
David Moratto, interior and cover design
Guernica Editions Inc.
1569 Heritage Way, Oakville, (ON), Canada L6M 2Z7
2250 Military Road, Tonawanda, N.Y. 14150-6000 U.S.A.
www.guernicaeditions.com

Distributors:
University of Toronto Press Distribution,
5201 Dufferin Street, Toronto (ON), Canada M3H 5T8
Gazelle Book Services, White Cross Mills,
High Town, Lancaster LA1 4XS U.K.

First edition.
Printed in Canada.

Legal Deposit—Third Quarter
Library of Congress Catalog Card Number: 2016938887
Library and Archives Canada Cataloguing in Publication
Turpin, Bill, 1950-, author
Max's folly / Bill Turpin.

(Essential prose ; 128)
Issued in print and electronic formats.
ISBN 978-1-77183-075-1 (paperback).--ISBN 978-1-77183-076-8 (epub).--ISBN 978-1-77183-077-5 (mobi)

I. Title. II. Series: Essential prose series ; 128

PS8639.U773M39 2016 C813'.6 C2016-902174-2 C2016-902175-0

To Lindsay Brown,
the love of my life
and my indispensable editor

NOW

To the Edge of the Abyss

MAX SET HIS smartphone on vibrate-plus-tone and slipped it into his breast pocket so he could "feel the buzz". Then he put his wristwatch on the same settings, plus a beep every minute. The phone was set for 1:40, the watch for 1:45. Failing to be at the office by 2 p.m. was not an option, and Max's formerly excellent relationship with time was no longer reliable.

He was walking around downtown Halifax, something he did religiously when he had problems to solve, and he had three of them. Big ones. He struggled to focus on the most urgent, but his issues with time had gripped him hard and would not let go.

Until recently, Max had paid little attention to time, even though it had been kind to him. (He looked young for his age, everyone said.) On the rare occasions when he thought of time, he pictured himself on some sort of rocket-sled; the future and the present blurring by him, the past a short, bright rocket-flame pushing against his back. And, sometimes, Max could see just enough of what lay ahead to give him an advantage. So for decades he had been secure in his rocket-seat, content but not grateful for time's gifts to him. He was untroubled by the time paradoxes that so tortured other people.

Lately, though, time seemed like a neglected friend who had finally left Max's life, creating an unexpected hole in his cosmic view and causing him to think about it constantly. Worse, time had taken to leaving him ominous messages. Once long ago, after a disastrous high school prom, his date scratched a note on his car door: "You'll be sorry, psycho!" That's how the messages from time felt. Just the other day Max was wholly engaged in thinking about time (and boiling an egg) when he felt someone squeezing his right elbow.

"Ground control to Major Max ... ground control to Major Max ..." the Wife sang, her voice affectionate but artificially bright. "Ground control to Major ..."

"I get it, Cactus, I get it," he said as reality — for which he also had a newfound respect — flooded the room.

The Wife said she had been all but hollering at him, trying to get his attention, but he was just staring at the stovetop. She thought he might be having a stroke. "Headache? Vision problems ..."

"No. Nope. I'm fine."

"Well, pay attention, then. You scared the hell out of me."

"A watched pot never boils," he said. "I was watching this pot until you interrupted and now, look, it's boiling."

"You going all inscrutable on me?"

Max tried to return the hard look she was giving him, but couldn't. Instead he kissed her left cheekbone and grabbed her right buttock, one of his favourite moves.

"Don't even think about jiggling my butt-fat," she said.

"What fat?" he asked, squeezing a little harder. "This is all muscle. You could crack walnuts with those glutes."

The Wife leaned into him: "That's more like it, Maxie."

Watching the water simmer, it had occurred to him that you need more than heat and a copper-bottomed pot from La Cucina to get water ready. You have to have time. You have to allow the pot to move through time. Time is a critical ingredient for boiling water. Does that mean the cook and the pot move though time at different speeds? Does "turning up the heat" really mean speeding up time for the pot? Jeez, what if you could really do that?

Could this be an insight? Max tested the idea in his usual laboratory — an imaginary, gas-lit, 19th century lecture hall where he stands before a learned but rapt audience. "And so, ladies and gentlemen," he says grandly, "I submit to you that time is ... an INGREDIENT!"

Alas, no one in the audience gasps in astonishment. Instead they arise as one and file out of the hall in an orderly fashion. So, *not* an insight.

Max's grandmother once told him that time is a river. The metaphor was lost on him because he imagined himself on the riverbank, watching dark water slide by. Now Max realized he should have been on the river, paying attention to what he saw on the banks. Damn, he thought, is it possible for someone to be so wrong about something for so long?

Now — walking downtown — Max was worried about losing time's greatest gift of all: his ability to travel it. Time travel was getting harder to control.

To his mild surprise, Max had already reached one his favourite stops — a flower shop. Its most colourful blooms spilled from the front entrance onto the sidewalk display from the earliest days of spring until autumn snatched the last of the leaves from the trees. Max admired the owner for his determination to ignore the weather despite the toll this took on his product. He stopped and bought his customary discounted bouquet of whatever was about to become unmarketable. Tulips, on this occasion.

"How are you doing?" the shopkeeper asked, bowing quickly at him, like a bird bobbing for insects at the beach.

"If I were any better, I'd be dangerous," Max replied brightly.

Time-jumping had been helpful in all aspects of his life except, maybe, family. At work, though, where Max was his firm's head of communications, it was critical. He always seemed to know what others at meetings were going to say a few seconds before they uttered the words, and he was ready with the right response before they even completed their sentences. Clients were in awe of his ability to know what they were thinking before they thought it.

Max's enemies were aware of it, too. He once overheard their take on it while walking past the smoking shelter. "If you think you've got a bright idea about how to cool the fucker's jets, forget it," one of his victims was complaining. "It just means he's set a trap for you. He does it for sport."

Well, that was true, but Max focused those efforts exclusively on the shitheads the CEO liked to hire.

"It's always good to keep a shark in the tank," the CEO liked to say. "It keeps the other fish alert."

But Max enjoyed a happy workplace. He admired and loved his younger colleagues — almost everyone — so when a shark showed up, Max would wait patiently until the moment he had foreseen occurred and the big bully-fish exposed a flank. Then Max would casually fire a political spear into its vitals.

The CEO hired the sharks, and Max got them fired. It was part of the rhythm of the office. It kept all the fish alert and happy.

Max passed the drugstore, a key landmark, which displayed a large sign declaring "your health matter's". The owners imagined this to be a clever pun, but it earned only derision from Max because of the egregious use of the apostrophe. But health definitely mattered these days. Max had heard through the family grapevine that the Brother was having "difficulties", and he suspected these, like his own troubles, involved the same ability to travel through time. Why *wouldn't* time-jumping be an inherited trait?

He felt terrible. Time-jumping had been critical to his life but his head had been so far up his own backside that he never really noticed. Now — and this felt like a premonition coming on — it might even be too late to talk it over with the Brother.

The need to talk was urgent because time-jumping had begun putting Max out of sync with the rotation of the Earth, and sometimes he would find himself east or west of a destination without any recollection of how it happened. This was because during the jump Max would continue to "rotate" from east to west, while the planet and its inhabitants stood still.

Max attributed these difficulties to his metabolism changing as he aged. He adapted by buying the latest in wearable "smart" technology. This brought most of the jumping outcomes under control. He dealt with the rest according to circumstance. If his trip took him west, he would compensate for rotation by walking faster. When headed east, he set his watch for 10 seconds less between beeps. This kept him out of the harbour. Walking north or south, he would subtly walk to the east by leaning that way to resist the rotation. He could not imagine how it looked to passers-by, but it seemed to work. On the other hand, it might explain why the CEO had been urging Max to ride with him to meetings in a taxi.

Max stopped at the newsstand which, as usual, was festooned with *Cosmopolitan* magazines that were in turn festooned with images of women who lacked pores and apparently knew gazillions of sexual techniques: *The longest weekend: Blast His Roman Candle to New Heights, Six Ways to Make His Star Burst, How to Make his Cracker Fire.*

Sex was another facet of Max's life affected by time-jumping, although with results that were more agreeable: the marital bed, mostly lukewarm since they hit their forties, had re-ignited.

Until recently the *Cosmo* surveys the Wife left lying around indicated that she was "not at all interested" in sex and "almost never" had an orgasm "with a partner". Max concluded that he must be at fault for this. Faulty time-jumping, he deduced, was causing him to "arrive", as the French say, early.

But now Max sometimes arrived later. This development might well be what shifted his wife to "somewhat interested" in sex, and it got Max thinking. He realized that if he could point the Wife due east, he would finish inside her no matter when he arrived. So, the next time he came to bed and found the Wife nude under the sheets, which meant that sex was on the table, Max seized the opportunity.

He climbed into bed and kissed her while sliding his hand over her abdomen, his customary opening move. "I want to try something," he said. "I want to line you up a certain way before we do it." To his surprise, instead of rejecting him, she smiled a little sheepishly and flushed. Her nipples perked up.

"Okay," she said, her voice croaking ever so slightly, whereupon she threw off the bedclothes and lay naked before him with her arms stiffly beside her. It had been a long time since she displayed herself like that. Max had earlier made a small mark on the wall that was due east, so he quickly grabbed her ankles and swung her around. She actually giggled as he took sightings along the length of her bare body. When everything was set, he eased between her legs to her centre, where he found a warm welcome.

Even better, the eastward dislocation had the effect of making his thrusts seem harder and increasingly rapid. That, combined with his newly late arrivals, eventually moved her along *Cosmo's* continuum to "very interested in sex" and "almost always" having an orgasm "with a partner". She began to suggest new positions and methods for lining her up. Once, breathlessly, she suggested that she go on all fours. It took Max far longer than usual to line her up, in part because she seemed to be resisting while at the same time insisting that the task be accomplished with absolute precision. By the time he had them both arranged, the Wife was urging him in the frankest terms to begin the final act. Max accomplished it easily, she being wildly wanton and he stiff as a flagpole. His last memory before the time-jump was her lovely long back extended out before him, her spine precisely in line with the rotation of the earth.

When he caught up in time, he found she had cuddled up and was looking at him softly. "It's been a long time ...," she said.

"We married young, started a family," Max said quickly, "and we had busy careers. There's hardly been time. But now we're in a new phase of our lives."

Max was back on the street, relieved and grateful that his mind had turned to the business problem at hand. He checked his watch. Five minutes to go. He felt the countless ideas that had been teasing him for days coalesce into a solution. Time to get to work. The remaining item on his mind, the mystery of his secret admirer at the office, would have to wait.

• • •

Max was at the head of the agency's long table, which he knew was little more than a glorified piece of Plexiglas skilfully designed and polished to look expensive.

Paintings, rented from the government art bank, tastefully lined the tasteful walls. They were well-done and interesting, but not so much that guests would be distracted. The Company Values were inscribed on a plaque: "Kindness, Kindness, Kindness." When asked about it, the CEO would explain that it was at the insistence of the company founder.

The CEO was to his left, flesh spilling over his collar. Nose hairs were visible, poised to become the leading feature of his physiognomy.

Next to the CEO was Max's Communications Director, playing the foil to the CEO's iconoclastic genius. Dressed in spotless casuals, she was calm as a cat enjoying a sunbeam, charming the clients and patiently awaiting her day as head of the firm.

The clients — two men and two women, one in a wheelchair — seemed out of place but he couldn't put his finger on it. Max fished his notes from his jacket pocket, gave them a quick glance and started in.

"Thank you for coming today," Max said. "Out of respect for your time, I won't beat around the bush: people love your product."

Max's Communications Director was the first to signal alarm, pushing her note-book away and firing her deer-in-the-headlights look at Max.

Christ, only four words into it and already she's bitching. Max moved on.

"And they love your employees ..."

Suddenly the CEO looked like he was about to drive his new Mercedes into a concrete post. He stared at his notepad and muttered something like "For the love of ..."

"... But they hate your company," Max said.

The clients' eyes widened as though Max had pulled out a gun. The CEO jumped to his feet and escorted Max to a corner. "They'll just be a second," the Communications Director said casually, making it clear it was all part of the creative process.

"Maxie," the CEO whispered. "The power company was yesterday."

"Yeah," Max said neutrally.

"Today it's the Abilities Bakery. Their bakers are all mentally or physically challenged and they have to lay off four of them. You're giving them the presentation we did for the power corporation."

Max pursed his lips: "It just seems like that. Let me run with it." Worst time-jump ever, he thought.

"Please, no," said the CEO.

"It's all good," Max replied.

He returned to the head of the table and paused for effect.

"Ladies and gentlemen, my partner has reminded me that you're not 'suits'." He looked at each pale face in turn: "A teacher, a retired engineer, a former elite athlete and an accountant with a private practice. You are a volunteer board.

"Sometimes I like to show clients how bad things could be if they don't take action. It's a shock tactic. But I can see I've done you a disservice. You've invested heart and soul in the Abilities Bakery. You are not complacent."

More pause for effect while he ransacked his memory for the correct talking points.

"And I don't need these notes," he said, tossing the power company index cards into a wastebasket. He picked up a brief from in front of the CEO and held it up.

"I've read your recovery plan, and what we communications folks call the 'key messages' are already written — by you. Here's how it works:

"When asked about layoffs, you simply say that no one is jobless. Instead, four people who've proven their skills at the Abilities Bakery have found jobs working side by side with abled people.

"When asked about the bakery's future without government funding, you show them your business plan and say that you will *double* the current staff in five years.

"When asked why you think your plan will work, you say that it was inspired by the courage, determination and *resourcefulness* that your staff demonstrate *every day.*

"You say that your staff have taught you to see opportunity where others see adversity."

Jeez, this is good stuff, Max thought.

When he spoke next, his voice was subdued but strong.

"You can say that, because it's the truth. You tell them that the Abilities Bakery has *a new future*. That your product is the best in town because your employees understand their *abilities* and they are ready to *compete* for their share of the market and on an equal footing. In the past nine years, no fewer than 14 people have gone from the Abilities Bakery to the mainstream workforce. A remarkable record."

Max concluded with: "My admiration for your company knows no bounds." And he meant it.

Half an hour later there were smiles all around as he escorted their satisfied clients to the elevator. By God, Maxie, you've pulled it out of the fire again, he thought as he watched them disappear behind the doors. But things weren't quite as rosy at the debrief.

"You can't keep doing this," his Communications Director said even before they got back to the meeting room.

"What do you mean? We've been through dozens of scrapes like this."

The CEO spoke up next. "But, Max, it's always been because the client wasn't buying the pitch, not because ... not because you forgot it."

"First time it's happened," he replied. He understood how others could interpret a bad jump as a memory lapse.

"No," said the Communications Director, with a gentleness that unnerved him. "There was Pike Video, the Archdiocese ..."

"The Archdiocese, those sons of ..."

"Nobody likes them, Max, but you gave them the Boy Scouts pitch."

"Well, they were very similar." But Max had no recollection of that pitch. Buried memories usually leave a thread, something you can gently grasp and tug on until the whole thing comes free. But here, there was nothing. Not even a gap where a memory had once been. Max felt his heart picking up speed.

"We're with you all the way, Max," the CEO said.

With me all the way?

He stared at the CEO's manicured hands and the elegant gold ring on his middle finger and felt self-conscious. They were partners, they were friends, they made the same salary. Why did Max feel so out of sync?

"What do you mean 'with me all the way'?" he asked. "This sounds like the prelude to a buyout offer or something."

"No, Max, nothing like that."

"Well, like what then?"

Now the Communications Director put her hand on his forearm: "It's just a misunderstanding."

Of course, it was, Max thought on his way back to the office. I'll never get them to understand the vagaries of time-jumping.

Still, even though the details of the incident were fading, Max had difficulty shaking off his unease. Then, as if to add to the confusion, he walked into his office and discovered that the secret admirer had struck again: there was a bouquet of tulips on his desk.

Max had lost count of the times he had strolled into his office and found flowers, chocolate and sometimes even cigars on his desk, just sitting there, without wrapping paper or even a note.

Whenever it happened, he was careful to be seen taking the gift home that same day, so that no one would think he was engaged in something improper.

"Your wife is a lucky woman," his Office Manager would say. "So many flowers."

But the Office Manager was his prime suspect, so to speak. Without question no one had more access to his office. And he was certainly attracted to her. She had a way of smiling at him and a gallows humour that kept him going through assorted crises. Max trusted her completely. She looked great, too. Sometimes he imagined a wild encounter in the stairwell, and then quickly suppressed the idea. He was loyal to the Wife to the point of ditching the flowers before he got home. Even though she would have been thrilled with them, it just wouldn't have been right to bring gifts from a would-be rival for his affections.

But now it's time, he thought, to bring this matter to a close. Max asked the Office Manager to come into his office.

"Waddup," she said, as usual. They kept it light when working together, no matter what.

He took both of her hands in his. In their long association, he had never touched her. "These gifts, the flowers and chocolates and such, they're from you, aren't they? If they are, I understand, but ..."

Her tears were sudden and ferocious. She sputtered out a "No!" and fled the room. Alerted by her ultra-sensitive radar for emotion, the Communications Director peered in from across the hall. Max headed out, down to the street, where he resumed walking. But now the streetscape seemed sinister and made him wonder if his time-jumping problems were permanent. He should phone his brother to ask if he, too, was a time-jumper, and see if he had some advice.

• • •

The male voice at the other end was unfamiliar.

"Just a minute," it said.

Max heard agitated conversation in the background. Then he heard the staccato of high heels nearing the phone.

"Max?"

It was the Sister-in-law.

"Who was that who answered the phone?"

A sigh. "My new husband."

In some part of his mind, Max knew what was coming next, but he asked the question anyway.

"You're divorced?"

"No, Max. Your brother died. You've got to stop making these calls."

The dark wave of awful news threatened to sweep him away; and yet it felt familiar. Another bad jump.

"Yes, that's right, he's dead, isn't he?" Max said quietly.

"Yes."

"Max, you've got to stop this. It's breaking my heart. Can you get home okay?"

The question startled him almost as much as the bad news. "Yes, of course I can get home. Just tell me one thing ... was he a time-jumper?"

It was a long wait for her reply. Max could hear water somewhere near him, gulls squawking and the traffic rumbling. When she finally spoke, he could barely hear her.

"Yes. Just like you. Go home now. Goodbye, Max." And then she hung up.

Max took a moment to get his bearings. Good thing because, looking down, Max saw that he was one step from a

20-foot drop into the black water of the harbour. The only barrier was a four-by-four railing at foot level.

In a day of bad jumps, this one took the cake. Max headed for his bus stop, his mind resolutely focused on the act of walking, lest he set off another, perhaps final, time-jump. By the time he boarded the bus, he could feel the pull of home and safety.

As the bus rolled on, the harbour-scare slipped from his mind. Instead, he began to wonder if his increasingly complicated time-jumping theory was some kind of denial, like guys who explain away their chest pains as poor digestion until they collapse on the street.

NOW

Present But Not Accounted For

MAX SAT CALMLY beside the Son and listened to the conversation with the specialist. He could feel the Son's distress and wanted to be glad for it; wanted the Son to be a villain. But there are no villains in this piece, he thought.

"It's happening faster than we expected," the Son said. "Last week, he took down every picture of my mother and threw them in the garbage." The Son's brown eyes were wide as they always were when he was upset. My eyes, for sure, thought Max. But the rest was the Wife's — firm chin, prominent forehead.

Max noted that people now talked about him as if he were not present in the room. More of that to come if he didn't do something, he suspected.

"The images of her were torturing me," Max shouted, as if volume finally might break through the Son's inability to understand. "I see her picture sometimes and I don't know whether she's alive or dead."

The Son asked the specialist if it was possible the sudden death of the Wife had hastened Max's memory problems. The doctor said it was impossible to know.

"Sometimes the healthy spouse will cover it up," he said. "People don't realize how bad it is until a crisis occurs."

Max did not care. He was no longer onside with all this nonsense.

"Sorry, but you're both full of it," Max said. "I've got some memory problems that are perfectly normal for someone my age. The real issue is time-jumping. I've just got to adapt a bit."

"Dad, I thought we agreed on this."

"I was pressured into agreeing. Anyway, carry on talking. I know nothing I say will change your mind."

Meaning that he would soon lose his freedom. Further, he worried the incarceration would be a long one; he figured he had many years to go before time's river returned him to the ocean. So, rather than rot away in an institution, he had resolved to become a full-time time traveller. He would find the Wife in the right place and in the right time — a snug spot along that river's bank — and stay there.

But even time travellers — perhaps especially time travellers — needed reference points.

Max interrupted the meeting to ask for some paper (he already had a pencil stub).

The Son failed to hide his irritation as he passed him a sheet of paper from the doctor.

"What for, Dad?"

"Just making some notes for the journey, Son."

Max isn't sure how to begin the journey. Maybe click his heels a few times, or ...

1975

Your Friendly Local Junta Cracks Heads

***Max can only** stare when the Photog appears before him. The two of them are sitting in a classic Spanish-American plaza that Max hasn't seen in 40 years. The Photog, on the other hand, continues talking exactly as he did back in the day without missing a beat.*

Max understands that he has made an enormous time jump, but the insight has the lifespan of a shooting star, gone almost before it arrives.

"So, Max. What eez our RAY-cord as freelance foreign correspondents so far?" the Photog asks.

Out of habit, Max pushes his hand deep into his left pocket, fishing for the familiar feel of the thrice-folded sheet of paper that he's kept there, along with a pencil stub, since his first reporting job. They provide a rudimentary way of taking notes when he isn't carrying a notepad. Also, when he is confused or has a problem to work out, the feel of the objects helps keep him grounded.

"So, Max! What eez our RAY-cord so far?"

The Photog is initiating their daily ritual of self-ridicule over their miserable record as freelancers since they quit the Sunday Tabloid and left Montreal to make their reputations. He comically exaggerates his Spanish accent. His tone oozes curiosity, as if he has no idea what the answer to his question might be. His face is obscured, as usual, by long black hair, some kind of floppy army hat, and cigarette smoke.

Max is into the game. He liberates his notebook from his back pocket and pretends to stare thoughtfully at the blank pages before taking a pull on his beer. The Photog raises his eyebrows in bogus expectation.

"We have been to four countries in four weeks, arriving in each case a day or so after the story we were chasing suddenly clutched its chest, keeled over, and died before hitting the ground," Max says.

His friend who, even at 25, looks like a genial plantation-owner — minus the expensive clothes and Panama hat, but with the bushy moustache — exhales a fresh blossom of blue smoke around his head. Max takes a sweet-potato chip from a bowl on their café table, which is leaning under the weight of the Photog's bulging bag of cameras and lenses.

The interior of the bag features a homemade prow of quarter-inch plywood built into the lining and designed for pushing through scrums. A wad of dubious identification cards is attached to the bag by a chain. The one on display reads: "*Prensa Internacional.*"

They are in the shade of a balcony that extends the entire length of the long, wide-open plaza. Shops and restaurants line the ground floor. Above are three storeys of colonial-style apartments.

"And ... today, Max?" Again, an eyebrow is raised expectantly.

"Today, we are in YOUR country, waiting for a student

demonstration. This is because of something that successful correspondents call a 'tip'. We are relaxing with beer and snacks because we expect, as per usual, that nothing will happen."

"*Es verdad*," says the Photog. "I am a FOUR-een corr-eez-POND-ent ... een my own ... CONN-tree. My mother's house ... eez 10 blocks a-WAY. Tell me, Max, what will we do if there EEZ a demonstration?"

"We will file a story and pics to an international wire service."

"Aha! A big payday at last?"

Max pretends to consult his notes again. "For our efforts we will receive bylines and photo credits. Oh, and four rolls of film."

"But this time, lots of money as well, no?"

"It seems not."

Max can see the presidential palace across the plaza, directly behind the Photog. It is a large baroque affair no doubt, somehow, celebrating the vicious exploits of the Conquistadors. The area in front of the palace, as well as the plaza itself, is paved with stones and devoid of anything that might interfere with a defensive line of fire from the presidential guard. A rugged iron fence forms the perimeter of the palace grounds. Max can easily picture bodies piling up against the bars.

He hears engines belching. The noise heralds a phalanx of motorcycles that careens into the plaza from Max's left and turns sharply toward the palace.

"Ahh," says the Photog, now doing an Ed Sullivan impersonation. "Ladies and gennulman, please welcome ... *El Presidente*!"

A black Cadillac limousine shoots into the plaza and tilts drunkenly toward the now-open gate. More farting motorcycles follow. A waiting honour guard decorated in feather-topped helmets and silver Conquistador chest-plates convulses to attention with salutes snappy enough to dislocate elbows. In dark civvies, El Presidente jogs up the steps, turns to wave to a non-existent crowd, and disappears behind massive wooden doors. The entourage roars off to someplace behind the palace.

Max nods in their direction. "A good time had by all, it appears," he says.

"He thinks he's the Patton of Latin America," the Photog says. "But he is the chicken president. He has never fired a single shot in anger. I doubt he has even been to a practice range. He is not even in the Army. He's a policeman. He should be writing parking tickets."

Max is only half-listening because he can feel a different mood taking over the plaza. The silver-breasted guards have disappeared. A pigeon nosing around the centre of the square thinks better of it and flaps away.

"He is the 'chicken president' because he got his job the same day Army Command came to work at headquarters and found a basket of eggs in front of their gate. It was a gift from the Navy, where the sons of the rich do their military service dressed in spotless white uniforms."

Max notices the sun has slipped behind the cathedral. It casts a wide shadow over almost the entire length of the square.

"The eggs, of course, meant the Army was afraid to execute the coup that the Navy had demanded ... oh, shit."

An armoured personnel carrier marked *Policia* slips

quietly up to the edge of the plaza to their right. Ten yards behind it is an open Army truck with nervous conscripts sitting on benches on either side. They are uncomfortably clasping and unclasping their rifles. They have the bronze skin and prominent cheekbones of mountain boys.

Max hears the Photog's motor-drive bang off three quick shots behind him. The mountain boys stare at the Photog. Max stares at the worn muzzles of their rifles, waiting for the worst.

"Don't worry," says the Photog, glancing at the troops. "They're not dangerous. They're pretending to support the police. Those boys just want to get back to their mamas and their alpacas. The real problem is the police."

The waiter is suddenly beside them: "*Senores*, come inside. *Muy peligroso*. Very dangerous."

"*Momentito*," says the Photog, who begins measuring light levels while talking earnestly with the waiter in Spanish.

Max sees four snipers take positions on the palace roof.

A water cannon painted a flat carbon black lumbers in from another side street. The driver sits behind a window made of heavy wire screen. A large fire-hose nozzle, also painted black, swings back and forth, anxious for a target. For some reason, Max is surprised to see the Mercedes Benz logo on the front, above the word *Policia*.

The waiter is getting frantic. "*Senores, por favor ...*"

There's nothing to see yet, but Max hears chanting from the end of the plaza, where there is still sunlight. It is timed to the beat of a deep bass drum.

"Max," says the Photog. "Our waiter he says it's very dangerous here. He says we can watch from the balcony above his shop."

"Fuck that. I didn't come here to watch it all from box seats."

The Photog looks up at the balcony overhead and back at Max. He reluctantly waves the waiter away.

"You idiot! You're going to get me killed," he says to Max.

Whereupon the waiter clears the table and retreats.

Max finally sees the reason for the excitement. Led by the drummer, a group of young demonstrators march boisterously into the square, chanting *"Abajo con la junta"* — *down with the junta.*

The ranks are four across on average, Max thinks. He counts the ranks as they enter the plaza, 40 of them — so maybe 150 people or so. Max tries to make notes, but his hands shake.

As the last batch of demonstrators crosses into the sunlight, another police APC blocks the street behind them. All but one of the six exits from the plaza are now blocked. Max sees the trap; the remaining exit will be allowed to fill with fleeing students and then sealed off at both ends.

Max points to it. "Do you see it?" he shouts to the Photog.

"Yes. It allows the police to beat their captives at a leisurely pace before arresting them."

The line turns right, marches up to Max's side of the plaza and then wheels left in a spirited but poor imitation of a military drill. They stop a few feet from Max's café table. Still shaking, Max begins making notes: *Bass drm ... 150, teens, erly 20 ... wl drssd ... 1/3 girls ... no wy out ... 2 police APC ... wtr cann Merc–troops ...*

The Mercedes' water-pumps start spinning. Someone among the demonstrators blows a bugle and they all sprint for the palace gate. The Photog has somehow manoeuvred in front of them. On one knee, he's taking pictures as they stampede past him.

But instead of following, the Photog runs, hunched over, to a spot behind a balcony post.

"Gotta keep the cameras dry," he bellows, looking at the water cannon.

The cannon lurches forward and lets loose. Its power is stunning. The kids tumble like stick-men. The water knocks the feet out from under them and they land hard. Max thinks he can hear bones cracking on the paving stones. The lucky ones are screaming and running. The water cannon operator gets the bass drum in his stream and sends it hard into a cluster of fleeing kids.

Cops move in, swinging black batons as if they are clearing jungle. Some kids fall, others run in spite of bruised muscle and shattered bone. A motorcyclist with a sidecar is cutting through the throng while the passenger whacks their victims on the backs of their thighs with his baton.

Max tries to make more notes but realizes, a moment too late, that smart reporters keep their eyes up during riots. An explosion in his head brings everything to a halt. The only sound is a loud hissing somewhere in his skull. He sees a swirl of sunlight, shadow and cobblestones and struggles to pull it into a picture of where he is and why. He gets that done just in time to see the ground rushing toward his face. He twists and lands on his shoulder.

Max dimly concludes that he has been hit by a baton. But that doesn't explain why his eyes and lungs feel like they've been bathed in acid. He tries to take a deep breath to douse the fire in his chest, but that makes it worse. Great gouts of mucus in his nose and throat make it hard to breathe, so Max just lets himself sink the rest of the way down and lies on the side of his face. From his worm's-eye view, he sees the Photog near the café door, curled around his camera bag.

"Tear gas!" the Photog yells. These are the first words Max hears since being hit. He searches for something sarcastic to say, but comes up empty.

His head feels like someone has driven a spike between his eyes, but he manages to crawl under a table. He peers through the pain into the plaza.

Tear gas canisters smoulder everywhere. A girl holding a bloody hand over the ruins of her mouth stands frozen. Another girl and a boy grab her elbows and usher her away. Some of the shop owners have opened their doors, and a few demonstrators make it inside. The rest run toward the trap. One of the APCs seals it off.

Empty transports arrive in short order to haul prisoners away. The water cannon begins sweeping the blood and debris toward a drain. Max can only watch while he waits for the pain and fire to let go of him. He cannot understand how quickly and easily chaos conquered the sunny plaza. He is shocked, not by the power of the police but by their willingness to use it against the bones, skulls and faces of unarmed students.

The truth of this story is in the details, he thinks, not the big picture.

When Max finally achieves something like full awareness, he realizes that he and his friend are surrounded by four men in cheap grey uniforms bearing plastic *Policia* badges. They point their Uzi sub-machineguns at the "foreign correspondents".

The Photog is the first to stand. Max, who is close to throwing up, can't find the strength to join him. Besides, the ground is shifting beneath him and his lungs are still burning. He can hear the Photog and the cops arguing, but has no idea what it is about. Finally, a cop gestures with his gun to suggest it's okay for the Photog to help Max stand up.

"Stay calm," the Photog mutters. "I'm putting two rolls of film into your jacket pocket. They want us to get into the APC. We can't do that. No matter what."

"Why? The bureau will get us out, won't they?"

"If they know where to look. But once the police brass realize they've arrested a foreign journalist, they'll do anything to avoid trouble. These are stupid men. That could mean dumping us in some backwater prison. After that, anything is possible."

"Fuck."

"Yup."

Max vomits with force and conviction before falling to the ground again. The cops back away a little.

"Great idea," says the Photog. "Keep it up."

The initial eruption was spontaneous, propelled by nausea and fear, but Max now puts his heart into it and manages two more upheavals. When the cops finally venture closer, Max convulses wildly, being careful to spray the vomit around with his flailing arms. They back away again.

"Excellent!" whispers the Photog, hoarsely. "Nobody wants to be the cop closest to you if you croak in public. Bad for the career."

"These idiots have careers?"

But the Photog isn't listening. He's watching the soldiers, who have driven their truck up to the police APC.

"*Ola, ejercito! Soldados*!" says the Photog.

Max's "convulsions" ease enough to allow him to take things in. The mountain boys seem to be interested.

Max hears the Photog say something like "these city pigs want to take us to jail" before the Spanish becomes too rapid to follow. He pauses and turns to Max.

"I am telling them I was an officer in the reserves providing relief during the big earthquake in the mountains. It was a terrible thing," he tells Max before resuming in Spanish.

Max picks up the words food, water and medicine, but that's all.

However, it's evidently enough to win them over. One soldier, with tears in his eyes, chambers a round in his rifle and swings it toward the cops. The sound causes the cops to turn their Uzis toward the soldiers, which causes more Army rounds to be chambered, which finally brings a sergeant out from the passenger seat of the truck. The Photog displays his plantation-owner smile. "Things are looking up."

The sergeant and the cops begin arguing furiously over who will arrest the foreign correspondents. The cops beckon their own sergeant. The Army guy gets on the radio. The rival sergeants stare silently at each other for a full minute before two more Army trucks arrive. A captain hops out.

"We are saved," says the Photog.

"*Ola! Hermano!*" he yells.

To Max: "He's wearing the patch given to those who served during the earthquake. Everybody agrees it was the best thing the Army ever did in peacetime."

Everyone is watching the captain, who is instantly recognized by all as the most competent person on the plaza, cops and foreign correspondents included. Max can hear Photog establishing his Army credentials.

They talk for a minute or so before the officer turns to what are now three trucks of mountain boys.

"This man," he says, extending his arm toward the Photog, "volunteered to serve during the earthquake. He worked for days without sleeping. He brought food, medicine and water." His troops nod enthusiastically.

Now he turns to the police. The Photog translates: "If you attempt to arrest these men, my soldiers will kill all of you. I will have to explain the incident, of course, but I will think of something." His troops adjust their rifles and nod matter-of-factly.

Another argument breaks out. The cop is demanding the Photog's film.

The Photog says something that provokes another round of swearing and gun-cocking.

The Photog says to Max: "I told him I left it in his mother's ass. It is a *very* bad thing to say in this part of the world."

"Not surprised," Max managed through the sour taste in his mouth.

"Give it to him," says the captain.

The Photog hands over a roll of film from his pocket and another from his camera. The cop triumphantly unspools the film from the canisters, tosses it on the paving stones and strides off with his men.

The Captain takes the Photog aside. Max and the soldiers, out of earshot, can only nod encouragement to each other.

The Photog walks over to Max. "He says we have to go. He says this operation was ordered by a Secret Police commander called *El Mago* and there'll be a battle right here if everyone doesn't clear out."

"Not that I'm complaining, but why is the Army even here?" Max asks.

"They are not yet ready to throw out *El Presidente* and his thugs. They pretend to be co-operating, but they are really ensuring things don't get out of control — arresting or killing foreign correspondents, for example."

So Max and his friend hobble out the way the Army came in and head for the wire service bureau.

"You got the film?"

"Right here," says Max, patting his pocket. "That's a great trick."

"I learned it in your country. The cops always want your fucking film."

• • •

Forty minutes later, Max is pounding out his story when the Bureau Chief comes by, glances at Max's six-take story and keeps the first page.

"This'll do," he says. "But you can't say the cops attacked children. It's editorializing."

"But they *were* children," Max says emphatically.

"Like I said, this will do. You smell like vomit, by the way."

"But I've got five more takes already written."

"I see that, but this is all I need. It's just a brief for the Latin America wire."

"Christ, we almost got killed out there," Max says, his voice still rasping from the tear gas.

"Bullshit," says the Bureau Chief. "Nobody from this bureau has ever been killed. Furthermore, nobody who's seriously hurt can type six takes in 20 minutes. More importantly, people want to read about the riot, not about how you almost got hurt. Do you see the distinction? It's important in this business."

"Sarcasm? That's what I get?"

The Bureau Chief looks like a nice guy; early forties, ancient tweed jacket and wide-set eyes. His hair, though, is the colour of a nicotine stain, and his soul is not gentle.

"Yep. And I've got more sarcasm: cover riots, yes; but don't stand in the middle of them. That space is reserved for cops and rioters."

"I gave you 600 words and you're only taking three paragraphs?" Max says.

"It doesn't take long to write about a riot, especially when no one dies," the Bureau Chief says. "A riot is just a riot."

"But the cops were going to kill us."

"See? THAT would have been a story. But they didn't. So it's a brief."

"Fuck me."

"On the other hand," he says thoughtfully. "Maybe I'll get the teletype guy to paste in the political background — something that you omitted — and put a longer piece on the regional wire."

"Background?" Max says, instantly wishing he could take the word back.

"Yes," the Bureau Chief says, relishing the moment. "You see, riots are not like spontaneous combustion. They don't just arise out of nothing. Typically, rioters are *upset* about something. In this case, they don't like the repressive government of *El Presidente* and his police henchmen. Torture and killings, that sort of thing."

"Why are the police running the country?"

"Another question that your six takes didn't answer. The *junta* should be the Army which, although reasonably popular, was run by incompetents when their moment came ..."

"The basket of eggs?"

"The kid does have a brain!" he says. "When their moment came, they hesitated because they had too many troops in the wrong places. But the *policia*, which is really a militia, had all kinds of people in the capital and took the Presidential Palace without firing a shot. Correction: one shot — into the head of the democratically elected incumbent."

"But ..."

"But people put up with them for a while, hoping they could clear the back-country of wild-eyed Maoists who, just to pass the time, will cut your dick off and stuff it in your mouth."

Max just stares at the guy, struck dumb by the realization that through bovine stupidity he has travelled thousands of miles to cover a story without understanding it.

"Just the same, not a bad job," the Bureau Chief says, scanning the copy again. "Too bad I can't use much of it. Let's go for a beer and wait for your buddy to finish in the darkroom — he's printing up some great shots of the kids coming right at him with a water cannon in the background. And dinner's on me. I want you guys to go to the mountains, where the real action is. *El Mago*'s home turf."

"You gonna pay us?"

"I'll buy your train tickets and give you a byline."

"I heard about *El Mago*. How much for an exclusive on him?"

The Bureau Chief sticks his forefinger in Max's chest. No one has done that since he was six years old.

"He's out of your league, sonny boy. Stay away. I shouldn't be sending someone like you up there in the first place. If something happens to you, I'm finished." The Bureau Chief thinks for a moment. "Tell you what. You leave that *El Mago* prick alone and I'll find a way to pay you."

"You mean you'll pay me if I *don't* get a story," Max says.

"Exactly. What does that tell you?"

It tells me I'm going to do a story on El Mago, Max thinks, and all the vicious fuck-heads who work for him.

1983

The Nature of Horse

SPRING HAS ARRIVED late in Halifax, but is no less welcome for it. In a downtown park, tall oaks, beeches and maples sway in the breeze. The sun has shaken off its veil. Its warmth is stronger, but still mild. Winter is forgotten and everything is soft. The leaves are a light green that yields easily to the eye, the breeze as gentle as a lover. Even the concrete sidewalks seem soft underfoot. Max and the Son sit close together, munching fries. Max is surprised by the growing muscularity of the Son, who stops eating occasionally to nuzzle his dad's arm. The boy inhales his father's scent and snuggles closer.

They've been staring at a huge chestnut-coloured horse harnessed to a tourist buggy across the sidewalk from their bench. The animal is peaceful, but not oblivious.

Max says: "Watch! Watch! He's going to do it again."

The horse snorts and shakes its head, sending a great string of snot arcing into the traffic, to the delight of the Son. And then, seeming to use the clamour as cover, the animal subtly pulls the carriage ahead until its head emerges from the shade into a patch of sunlight. As the beast executes the movement its hooves, big as dinner plates, land on the asphalt as delicately as flower petals.

"Oooh!" the Son hollers, apparently overcome by the controlled power of the animal and his father's omniscience. They have been watching the animal edge toward the sunlight for a quarter of an hour.

"The driver hardly noticed, did he?" Max says.

The boy shakes his head for emphasis. "No!"

They continue to observe in silence.

"What are we going to do with this apple?" Max asks.

"Mommy gave it to us," the boy replies, as if that's all that needs to be said.

The Wife had packed an entire lunch for them, but it was supplemented when Max spotted Bud the Spud's french fry truck, so neither of them has any appetite left.

"But horses like apples, too," Max says.

"They do," the Son says gravely, as if he has known this all along.

"We can give the apple to the horse."

"Yes!"

They hear leather creaking as the animal turns its massive head toward them. Bizarre, Max thinks, it's as if it knows it might get the apple. But the Son takes it in stride: "He wants the apple, Daddy."

The horse is edging toward middle age, but still on the right side of it. Strong, straight, and alert. He returns his calm gaze to the human parade in front of him, but his posture suggests he has not forgotten the apple.

Max and the Son walk toward the carriage owner. The horse watches closely.

Max asks the driver if they can give the apple to his

animal. They talk. Max wants assurance that the horse is gentle. The driver wants assurance that Max knows how to feed it safely. Max and Son walk forward and the horse lowers his head toward the boy who, with a little help, holds the apple out with his fingers awkwardly splayed to ensure they aren't accidentally caught. The animal makes a near-circle with his lips, like thumb and forefinger, and carefully plucks the apple from the boy's hand. There is a satisfying "pop" as the big jaws crush the fruit.

The horse, his head now fully in the warm sun, closes his eyes as his jaws begin grinding the apple into pulp. Juice flows from the animal's mouth as Father, Son and carriage owner look on intently. They are captives. For just a moment, they can smell the horse's oaty odour, feel him savouring the apple, and see the bright force that binds together the countless molecules of his body.

The Son turns to Max.

"Horse, Daddy!" he says, bending at his knees and pointing. "It's horse. HORSE!"

Max picks up the Son and hugs him with one arm: "Do you want to say goodbye to your new friend?'

"We already said goodbye," the Son says. "He said he liked the apple."

1981

The Smiling Cobra

The link between Halifax and Montreal in the journalistic telegraph is a weak one. Max has been able to learn but three facts before his arrival from Montreal:

1. *The city is served by two bad newspapers — a hoary old province-wide broadsheet and a "low-class" tabloid upstart — of which Max is now the editor;*
2. *In Nova Scotia, it is highly irregular for even a low-class tabloid to be edited by a CFA, short for "come-from-away", i.e., someone born outside Nova Scotia;*
3. *His new publisher and boss is known to all who work for him as the Smiling Cobra.*

"Max," says the Smiling Cobra. "We don't mind CFAs visiting here. We love visitors. We're happy to see them come and even happier when they go. So, if you want to stay you need to adopt our ways, because we're not going to adopt yours."

Max strokes his chin to show that he's taking it in. "How could it be otherwise?"

"We're tired of central Canadians coming here and telling us what to do."

So much for Maritimers' famous reticence, Max thinks. "Wouldn't dream of it," he says. "I'll just observe."

The irony is lost on the Cobra.

"Well, there's work to do, too," he replies.

Max agrees. The morning's front page features a huge photo of a dead man's torso. There are three holes in it. The first two are highlighted by small trails of blood running down the man's chest. The third is plugged with a screwdriver. The headline is *Cops seek killer with loose screw.* On Max's arrival, the receptionist remarked to him that she was busy taking cancelled subscriptions.

No surprise there. Max's reaction was to begin estimating the cost of returning his family to Montreal.

The Smiling Cobra places his hands on his desk as if to stand, but remains oddly still. Max finally spots the iron ring of the engineer on his pinkie. The Cobra sees that his ring has been duly noted and offers that he is a mechanical engineer, recently hired from a bankrupt government-run factory.

The Cobra stands. His torso is weirdly long which, combined with abnormally short legs, means that the effect of his standing up is almost negligible.

"Do you have any experience in the newspaper business?" Max asks.

The Cobra backs away. He inhales deeply and straightens up to fully display his towering torso. He moves his gaze down, causing the tissues of his neck to flare out — hood-like — and almost merge with his ears. The black eyes beneath his narrow forehead somehow line up with his nose and hold Max's gaze. He maintains that position for several seconds. Then he smiles, his mouth a perfect semicircle. He licks his upper lip.

"Yesss," he says. "That remark confirms what I have heard about you. A nattering smart-ass. Someone with no respect for authority. It doesn't matter. I plan to fire you at the first opportunity. I know the Owner in Montreal likes you, but eventually you'll fuck up so badly that it won't matter. As for my qualifications, I've been an engineer for 10 years and a newspaper is just another system. People are just more parts. I know how to make them run."

Further, the Cobra explains, the Paper's readership is based in a fast-growing Halifax suburb, and therefore its miserable circulation numbers will improve on that basis alone.

"Give me a bright cocker spaniel for an editor and a hundred pounds of puppy chow, and this paper will grow," he says. "You, on the other hand, worked for a crummy Sunday tabloid in Montreal — "

"*This* is a crummy tabloid," says Max.

The Cobra talks over Max — "and then bummed around Latin America for a while before getting fired by the only daily you've actually worked for, until now."

And that's why Max has to be fired soon, he explains. If the Cobra waits too long to shit-can him, then Max will get credit for the growth and may become impossible to fire.

Max agrees in principle but doubts he has much support in Montreal. Further, it's clear no amount of market growth on its own will overcome the Paper's ludicrous content.

He looks around the windowless office, which is on the second floor of a business park strip mall. Below is the newsroom. The floor is bare concrete, the desk is an oak veneer piece obviously rescued from a second-hand store. Bays of cheap fluorescent fixtures provide the lighting. The only acknowledgement of the Cobra's high station in life is a private bathroom. Its hollow, unpainted door is open, so Max can see the toilet. The drywall hasn't been finished.

"Okay," says Max. "I'm onside. Let me get to work."

"Just one more thing," the Cobra says. "This province is run by 14 prominent families. You'll learn who they are. Don't get in their way."

"El Salvador," says Max.

"What?"

"El Salvador is run by 14 families, not Nova Scotia."

"You see," the Cobra hisses. "This is what we mean about CFAs." He displays his fleshy hood again.

The Cobra turns away from Max, signifying the end of the meeting, but suddenly plants a heel and lurches stiffly back in the direction of his new editor.

"I almost forgot," he says. "There is an Indonesian guy out there in the newsroom. Your first act as editor will be to fire him. I know you don't want to do that. You don't have the balls."

"Of course. May I ask why?"

"You'll see. He's from a hot country. It's October and beginning to get cold. Already I can see his blood getting thicker, making him slower and slower. I want him gone before winter."

Max and his publisher engage in a staring contest. Incredulity versus dead certainty. Dead certainty prevails.

"Just to confirm," Max says. "The blood of people from hot countries thickens in the cold, making them slow down in Canadian winters? Is my understanding correct?"

"*Nova Scotian* winters," the Cobra stresses.

Max feels a black hole of fatigue take root somewhere

in his head and begin sucking at his energy. He now knows that, for the sake of the Wife and Son, he must don the infamous, imaginary kneepads that hang in the newsroom of the Montreal Daily, and make the Cobra happy. How bad can it be? A few years of "Yes sir. Right away sir" and then they can all return to civilization.

Or, at worst, Toronto.

"Of course. It shall be done," Max says to the Cobra.

Two steps out of the publisher's office, though, he knows he won't do it. Technically, newsroom staffing is his call but, in practice, publishers meddle when they can get away with it. Max is sure Montreal will come down on his side if he forces the issue, but the incident will be recorded as evidence that he cannot "manage up" or "find common ground". When word of that gets out, as it certainly will, his former colleagues will begin circling high overhead, waiting to swoop down on Max's new job.

Perhaps he should stall for time. Perhaps the Indonesian will be hit by a bus before Max has to do anything. "I was just about to sign his termination papers when I heard the ambulance pull up to the bus stop," he'll tell the Cobra. "Poor guy. At least I won't have to fire him now. His family will be rich, though, because he's in our insurance plan, right?"

In a way Max is relieved. He's long been worried that his lack of emotion in tight situations means he's a psychopath, but his decision to spare the Indonesian is evidence that he actually has a heart. Or lacks "the balls".

No matter. Job One now is to send a message to his publisher.

• • •

Max steps into his newsroom. There are the usual teetering pillars of yellowing newsprint, which is reassuring. So is the sputter of the single police radio. But all that separates the staff from their adoring public are double-paned floor-to-ceiling windows supported by thin metal frames. Max loves the general public, of course, but prefers to do so from a safe distance and two or three storeys up.

Newsrooms are designed to manage the flow of a lot of information in a short time. Instructions originate from central points and information flows back, provoking revised instructions. The cycle continues amid a miasma of profanity and ego until, many hours later, the presses roll.

But here the desks are scattered like marbles. There is no discernible city desk or business desk or anything indicating that someone is in charge of something. Next to one desk, a white Scottish terrier is lowering its butt into position for a bowel movement. An hour earlier, Max would have been surprised.

"So help me god," says a low voice to his right. "If that dog craps in here again, I'm going to punt the fucking thing onto the cocksucking freeway."

This would be a sight worth seeing, Max figures, because the speaker is wearing a bright, flowered summer dress and looks like the mother from The Brady Bunch, only nicer and with better elocution.

The terrier looks at her, apparently getting the point. A guy with a Farley Mowat beard and pipe picks up the beast and carries it through a door leading to the parking lot.

"Och!" he says before exiting.

Max turns in the direction of the female voice. She's maybe 20 years old, sitting at a desk two rows back. She's sifting through piles of light brown paper that originated from a loud dot matrix printer. Max surmises that each pile represents a category of wire stories. To her right is the only authentic piece of newsroom hardware he can see — a shiny, four-inch spike with a lethal point at the top. These are standard in newsrooms everywhere. Any story that doesn't make the cut gets slapped on a spike. This makes it easier to find on a slow news day when, hours later, there's still a hole between the ads of the next day's paper and any story, no matter how bad, will do.

Max figures the woman is the wire editor. He judges her to be a pro from the way she curls rejected copy so that she can snap it on the spike with one hand. At the highest levels of the craft, this is accompanied by a sneer and sometimes a muttered "piece of shit." Max walks over to introduce himself, while at the same time scanning the room for an Indonesian.

His divided attention is a mistake: he catches his foot on a random extension cord and stumbles. He reaches out with his left arm to balance himself, but it lands on another spike sitting on an empty desk.

The pain is blunt at first and then sharp, but mild given that the spike has penetrated halfway into his left forearm. Max continues on to the Wire Editor, extending his good arm to her. She has a nice handshake.

"You must be the new Editor-in-chief," she says with a British accent.

"Call me Max," he says. "You from Fleet Street?"

"Winnipeg."

"Winnipeg?"

"Winnipeg. Born and bred. I needed the accent to get hired. Anglophiles everywhere around here."

"Is there some guy here from Indonesia?"

"Yup. The Cobra thought his accent was British, too, but he figured out the guy comes-from-away and doesn't like him anymore."

She continues to scan wire stories and snap them onto her spike. "He's over there, on the copy desk."

Max cannot see anything resembling a copy desk, which is normally several work stations arranged in a U-shape with the news editor in the middle. There is, however, a darker than average man hunched over a computer. Max notes with approval that he's working on the computer while simultaneously spiking stories.

"Is he any good?" Max asks.

"He's a star in our small firmament. He's actually worked at real newspapers — Singapore and Hong Kong."

"And you?"

"I'm a quick learner."

There is an awkward silence while Max tries to think of his next question. The Wire Editor breaks the silence. "It's early in our relationship for personal questions, but I was wondering about that spike in your left arm. Will you be removing it?"

"You noticed, eh?" says Max. "I was thinking of pulling it out right away, but I'm worried about making things worse by grazing tendons and such. Not to mention dealing with bacteria."

The Wire Editor agrees, noting that this newsroom is more soaked in deadly microbes than most. "Best not to wait too long. There's a walk-in clinic right in this mall just three doors down. I had a Pap smear there last week. Very efficient."

"Good to know," Max says. He says he'll walk to the clinic

with the spike in place, not the least because it will likely get him in to see the doctor faster.

"That gives me a better chance of being back in time for the news meeting," he adds.

"I've heard about news meetings," she says. "But this has been a weekly for three years and a daily for one. We still haven't had a news meeting."

"Who decides what stories to use and where to put them?"

The Wire Editor can barely hide her glee. She smiles sweetly: "The fucking composing room."

Max gapes.

"Yep, the folks who set the type. Welcome aboard."

This news causes Max to move the Indonesian problem down on his priority list. He heads for the clinic.

1981

How to Piss Off a Living Saint

MAX BEGINS HIS second day with a call from Desmond Tutu's office in Cape Town. The caller says an unidentified reporter from the "Halifax News Collective" rang Tutu's direct line at 2 a.m. to confirm a story that Mother Teresa was dead.

"Now tell me, does that reporter work for you?" asks the scratchy voice at the other end of the line.

Max says it's entirely possible, but there's no Halifax News Collective that he's aware of. "I apologize and assure you — if this has anything to do with this newsroom — it won't happen again."

There's a knock on the door just as Max is hanging up. A rotund, smooth-skinned kid likely barely out of high school introduces himself as the Police Reporter.

"I know you're busy, but I want to say how pleased I am to have someone with your reputation heading up the paper."

"You've heard of me?"

"No, but that's my point. I promise to really suck up to you in the years ahead. That was just a sample."

Max begins to formulate a rude response when the reporter stops him with a hand gesture.

"Think about it before you reply. I'm really good at it. If you give it a chance, you may find you like it."

Point made, the Police Reporter squeezes past a tiny woman on his way out the door. She's pixie-ish, possibly the angriest-looking pixie Max has ever seen. She hands him a long list of "issues that have be resolved immediately" and leaves without introducing herself. Top of the list is a high-end air purifier, followed by hiring a columnist writing exclusively for people with allergies.

Max's office is a fish-tank — long and narrow, with a glass wall on one side. He stares balefully through the window at his newsroom. There's no sign of the terrier, but little else to rejoice in. He has never seen so many people gathered together with so little evident purpose.

He brightens a little when the City Editor takes the stage. Today she's wearing a businesslike skirt and snug but acceptable blouse. The silver bone in her nose is less reassuring. She walks past his office and then quickly looks back, as if she were trying to catch him in the act of checking out her backside. But Max knows that move.

He motions her into his office.

"Who was that guy yesterday with the dog?"

"That's Big Mac, the Visual Arts Editor. How's your arm?"

Best not to react to this too quickly, Max tells himself.

"Let's take these one at time," he says. "My arm is fine, thank you. No offence, but there are grocery store flyers with tonier content than this newspaper. What are we doing with a Visual Arts Editor? Why is he called Big Mac?"

"No offence taken," she replies. "Glad you're healing well. The Cobra hired him. Word is, it was some kind of political favour."

"And the name of our Visual Arts reporter is Big Mac," he says, putting the political issue aside for the moment. "Shouldn't he be in Sports with a name like that? Why is he called Big Mac?"

"Because he's not big," she says. "It's a Cape Breton nickname. Sometimes they're ironic."

"Seems like average height to me."

The Wire Editor looks straight at Max. "It's not about his height."

She reaches down, opens up a copy of the Paper and points to a staff contact list on Page 2. Above her fingernail are the words "Amhuinn Maolmuire Maceachthighearna".

"That's his real name," she says.

The heaviness that accompanied Max to work evaporates, a sign that a solution is about to surface.

"You know, that name looks Indonesian to me," Max says, staring at the jumble of letters.

She ponders that. "I can see how you would make that mistake. It could be Welsh, for that matter."

"No," Max says. "I think it's Indonesian."

"But that's his legal name — it's Gaelic. He adopted it when he became a 'Cape Breton radical'."

Max has known about Cape Breton since he was a kid, but the Wire Editor's tone is his first indication that the island has a special identity within Nova Scotia.

"Nobody could pronounce his new name," she says. "So they dubbed him Big Mac, based on the last name, I guess. And he knows nothing about the arts."

"Dare I ask what the Indonesian's name is?"

"Peter," she says. "Some Indonesians only have one name."

"Like Suharto."

"Yeah!" she says.

Max makes a steeple with his fingers.

"Okay, let's review," he says. "I've got an Indonesian whose name is Peter of all things—"

She interrupts. Her tone is a tad defensive, Max thinks. "His father was a missionary."

"—and I've got a Visual Arts Editor who knows nothing about the arts. And he's from Cape Breton, but his name looks Indonesian. They call him Big Mac but—"

The Wire Editor interrupts with a forceful, rapid-fire burst. "Because his cock-sucking terrier is supposedly better hung than he is."

Max raises his eyebrows.

"Sorry. Potty mouth. I couldn't hold it in any longer. Whew!"

"Okay," says Max. "But you say the guy with the Indonesian-looking name is actually from Cape Breton. You're sure?"

"Yeah. But it's really Gaelic."

"And our friend Pete is from Indonesia?"

"Peter."

"Where is Lewis Carroll when you need him?" Max murmurs.

"Pardon?"

But Max is too preoccupied with the solution that has finally presented itself to him.

"So, how would you like to move to dayside and be the City Editor?"

She looks at him sideways.

"Men are pigs, I know that," Max says. "But I think I'm entitled to the presumption of innocence."

"We can try that," she says quietly. "By the way, I curse a lot. My shrink—my cock-sucking shrink—says it helps me relieve stress."

Max hasn't noticed anything abnormal, but then she has been "holding it in." He looks through his fish-tank window at his newsroom again. It's like the zoo primate enclosure at high noon out there, he thinks. The inmates are too lazy even to brush the flies away.

Max turns to his City Editor-designate.

"Again, let me summarize," he says. "I will continue to refrain from making sexual advances or comments to you, and promote you to City Editor. In exchange for this, you will utter lewd remarks and profanity according to your needs." She nods. "All you have to do is this—the next time that terrier starts to take a dump on the floor, don't stop it."

"That's all?"

"Get a picture and report the atrocity to me, of course. Can you handle it?"

"Sure. Who gets to be the new wire editor?"

"Don't know."

"What about Peter?"

"The Indonesian? I have other plans for him."

The new City Editor blanches. "Are you going to fire him?"

Max is heartened by her casual insubordination.

"You don't fire competent people—that's right in the editor's manual," he says. "But, for reasons I won't discuss, I don't want the Cobra to see him for a few days."

"But you fire the *incompetent*, right?" Her tone is hopeful.

• • •

Max just has enough time to swivel back to his desk when he hears a knock.

The rangy man at the door, slovenly even by newspaper standards, sneers briefly at Max's surroundings and introduces himself as the "class-war reporter". He describes the dog's breakfast the paper produces as a revolution in journalism — "a reporter's newspaper."

Max agrees it's exactly what a reporter's paper would look like, except that it's not edited by reporters, not even by editors, but by compositors, the guys who glue the stories to "flats" so they can be made into printing plates.

"So it's actually a compositor's newspaper," Max says. "Possibly the world's first."

"That's the power of the Collective," the guy says. Max notes that he can see the man's nipples through his threadbare white shirt. "We are able to tap into the abilities of the working class in a way that capitalists will never understand."

"Enjoy it while you can," Max tells Mr. Nipples. "Because as far as you're concerned, this isn't a reporter's paper, and it's not a collective in name or otherwise. It's *my* paper. Think of me as Stalin."

Max is surprised by his own words, but they feel good. And, thanks to his interlocutor's use of the word "collective", he makes the connection with the call from South Africa. Max keeps going.

"Here's how that works," he says. "If you ever call Desmond Tutu again to enquire after Mother fucking Teresa or anything else, I'll make the Gulag look like summer camp to you."

The young man needs time to process Max's words. "I'll take this up with the Collective."

"Based on my recent experience, you shouldn't bet the farm on a collective, so to speak," Max says.

Mr. Nipples departs and, for the first time today Max is alone with his thoughts — three of them, as usual:

- One, it's again time for him to actually contribute something to society, i.e., change the Paper into something worthy of its readers.
- Two, he may be the wrong man for the job but, if he fails, he's going to fail by making his own poor decisions, not by letting others impose them on him.
- Three, he's going to throw every ounce of blood, sweat and tears he can muster into the task.

Max calls the Wife to tell her the news. She's thrilled: "Good job, Maxie."

The Wife is and always will be his ultimate editor.

• • •

Max closes his office door and shuts the blinds of his fish tank. He gets 30 minutes of uninterrupted think-time before someone knocks on the door. He ignores it and calls the Cobra instead.

"How do you feel about unions?" he asks.

"Hate their guts."

"Ever seen *Alien*, Sigourney Weaver?"

"Loved it," says the Cobra.

"Well, there's something trying to burst out from the insides of the Paper and it looks a lot like a union."

"Fuck."

"Exactly. But I think I've got a plan."

• • •

A few hours later, the Indonesian drops in. He's tall, thin and good-looking. His eyes are alert; they are on the dark side, like his skin. He shows no signs of nervousness at meeting his new boss, but he's leaning forward in his chair and watching Max closely.

Max decides to administer the irony test right away.

"Are you aware that your blood thickens up in the cold weather, causing you to slow down?" Max asks.

"It's news to me. Is there a procedure I can have?"

"Science is powerless against this sort of thing," Max says, eliciting a smile. "I want to be sure you start late enough that the Cobra doesn't see you for a day or so."

"I know."

Max makes a mental note: his City Editor-designate doesn't keep things to herself and may have a thing for the Indonesian.

"You know, there was some concern you were going to fire me," the Indonesian says.

"Yes, well, I know where you got that idea. You guys an item?"

"Just friends."

"Hmm. In any case, as near as I can tell, you are the only staffer here who has ever worked at a fully functioning daily newspaper. What's your strength?"

"I'm a desker — copy editing, news editing — love it," he says.

This is the best news of the day. A competent, engaged

deskman gives Max a big head start in reorganizing the Paper.

"I presume you already know who the new City Editor will be."

"Yes."

Max wants at least two people he can trust as soon as possible, one on nightside and another on days. His gut has decided they will be the new City Editor and the Indonesian. Others will have to earn their way onto the trust list.

He explains this to the Indonesian, who's shocked by the speed of the decision.

"I'll know soon enough if you're no good, and then I'll move on to someone else," Max says. "It's faster than using some cock-eyed human resources bullshit."

The job Max has in mind for the Indonesian is the slot man, also known as the night news editor. This is the person who oversees the melding of pictures, stories and headlines, not to mention quality. It's one of the hardest jobs on a daily paper.

"Okay then. How would you like to work the slot? You'll also have to look after the wire for a while."

The Indonesian clasps his hands together and shakes them like he's just rolled seven at the craps table.

"I'll start right away, if that's alright," he says. "Brace yourself for complaints."

"Wouldn't have it any other way. Why aren't you working at the Other Paper?"

"I thought you knew," he says, smiling. "My blood thickens up in the cold weather."

• • •

Wednesday.

Amhuinn Maolmuire Maceachthighearna — Big Mac — swaggers in and makes himself comfortable at the long table in Max's office. He's wearing a tartan tie and a tweed jacket.

He leans back in his chair and ostentatiously taps some tobacco into the bowl of his pipe, clearly at pains to demonstrate his job security.

"Dew ya mind if I smoke, laddie?"

"Quite a bit," says Max.

"Och." He proceeds to light his pipe with a Bic lighter. When he's done, he curls the left half of his lip and looks Max in the eye.

"I see you've detected that I'm a CFA," Max says.

"Aye," says Big Mac, spitting a shred of tobacco off his tongue. "You've got the look of a true wanker about you."

Max peers through the man's nicotine-stained thicket of reddish-brown facial hair and sees that he is barely past his mid-twenties. The hair on his scalp is blondish. It starts out straight near the part, but then degenerates into short waves and then clownish curls.

Max pointedly fixes his gaze on the ascending mushroom cloud from the faux-Scot's pipe. At the ceiling, it spreads out and thins, along with any doubt that Max should fire him.

"Well," Max says, still watching the smoke. "That brings me to the purpose of our meeting today."

• • •

Thursday.

Under Max's direction, the City Editor and the Indonesian have started organizing. It has the same effect as whacking the side of a henhouse with a two-by-four. Three people quit before word gets out that Max is accepting all resignations on the spot, no questions asked.

There is a bounce in his step as Max trots up the stairs to see the Cobra, who greets him with his now-customary distaste.

"Ah, Max, How nice."

"What do you want?"

"Did you fire someone?" he asks.

"Fucking right I did," says Max, his tone clipped and firm with false pride. "I nuked the Indonesian, as per your request. Caught him letting his dog crap on the newsroom floor."

The Cobra's eyes widen.

Max then adds his best rendition of a conspiratorial chuckle: "And let me tell you that beast was a Great Dane among terriers."

The Cobra allows the bottom half of his face to smile. "Fucking Indonesians," he says, shaking his head. "Letting livestock shit on the floor must be a cultural thing."

Max nods in the affirmative. "Yep. I nailed him dead to rights. The photogs got pics."

"What was his name, anyway," asks the Cobra.

"I couldn't begin to pronounce it."

Har-har. Their enmity is absent for a moment.

Then the Cobra goes quiet. He moves his torso slightly from side to side and he tongues his upper lip a couple of times. His eyes focus on Max's throat.

"Terrier?"

"What?"

"Did you say he had a 'terrier'?" he asks.

Max nods. He forces his facial muscles to go slack before his expression gives the game away.

"You didn't talk to him?"

"Sure did," says Max. "Very heavy accent."

"And that accent sounded Indonesian to you?"

"It was impenetrable, just like his fucking name, eh?"

But there's no collegial har-har. The Cobra rises abruptly and glides into his private washroom. Max hears the door lock and the faucets being opened. He returns a few minutes later and resumes his seat, folding his hands on his desktop.

"The sound of running water calms me," he says, adopting the quiet tone of a PGA colour commentator.

"Are you upset about something?" Max asks helpfully.

"That's wasn't the Indonesian," he says. "YOU FIRED BIG MAC! Everybody in the Party loves Big Mac."

"Whatever do you mean? That was Big Mac, the visual arts editor?"

"You fired Big Mac, you idiot. And now I've got to smooth it over."

"Sorry," says Max. "But really, anyone could have made that mistake."

• • •

Friday.

The end of Max's first week at the Paper.

He has invited the Indonesian to meet him for lunch. They're sitting at a Formica table, surrounded by the comforting smell of hot deep-fryer fat. They each face a paper plate heaping with fish and chips. Each has been awarded five Kraft tartar sauce packets. Two kinds of vinegar are available in bottles.

Max hands him a signed letter on the Paper's stationery.

The Indonesian sighs: "So you're firing me after all."

"On the contrary," Max says. "Put your signature under mine and your job is bulletproof."

The guy takes a closer look: "You're putting me on probation?"

"Yup. Until winter ends. If you can prove by March 31 that cold weather doesn't thicken your blood, then probation's over. If not, you're fired."

The Indonesian smiles.

"So, if I ever get fired for real, all I have to do is go public with this probation notice and ..."

"See? Bulletproof."

"But you don't even know me."

"I didn't know you when I was told to fire you, either."

• • •

There is a busy highway between the Paper and the fish and chips shop. Max is too excited to walk back to the intersection to cross. Instead, he does it Montreal style, jay-walking into the traffic as if he's suddenly lost the power of sight. Tires squeal as drivers in both directions stand on their brakes.

In the newsroom, he pauses long enough to appoint a new entertainment editor before bounding up to the Cobra's office. The publisher is lining up his collection of model Formula One race cars on his desk.

"You fucked me over, didn't you, Max?" he says without looking up.

Max sits and crosses his legs at the ankle.

"I hope so, yes," he says pleasantly.

"You did something to protect the Indonesian, right?"

"It depends on how you interpret these things. He's got until March 31 to prove his blood doesn't thicken up. In principle it's a formal warning, but I can understand how you might see it as protecting him."

"Not bad," the Cobra says.

"Thank you. Oh, and for good measure, I told Big Mac that Cape Bretoners' blood also thickens up in the cold. That should keep you busy with the Party for a while, you dickhead."

This earns Max a pained look from his adversary.

"You did? Jesus. Why? Why couldn't you leave him out of it? Why not just go running to your friends in Montreal in the first place?"

Because Montreal might have told him to pound sand, Max thinks.

"Because I don't like being underestimated. And you need to know that if you bloody my nose, I'll break your arm."

The Cobra purses his thin lips. Max sees that he's won this round.

"Being underestimated can be useful," the Cobra says. "But I promise I won't make that mistake with you again."

On the way back to the newsroom, Max recalls interviewing a Peruvian colonel in charge of a dismal yearly ceremony marking his army's worst defeat. "If you want victory, then defeat me," he said bitterly. "But if you want peace as well, then be careful not to add humiliation to my defeat."

• • •

Max picks up an expensive bottle of Cabernet-Sauvignon on the way home.

"It's been a great week," he tells the Wife as he fills their glasses to the brim.

The wine isn't as good as he remembers it.

NOW

Welcome Back to the Dungeon

Max developed a feel for what non-time travellers call the "present." First, he noticed a pervasive hollowness because, in the present, the Wife was not alive. The present also featured causality: if Max did A then B would (or might) follow. When he was time-travelling, however, he was a helpless prisoner of experience. Even his awareness that he was travelling was fleeting and occurred only at the beginning of each sojourn and the first few moments of his returns.

But that gave him the knowledge that he was indeed travelling in time — like never before — and full confidence that he would eventually encounter the Wife in the right place and time, and find a way to stay with her there.

This took the fear out of returning to the present, but not the effort. There were large pieces of the present that had to be relearned. This, he concluded, was the price he paid for visiting the past.

On this occasion, he found the glass and aluminum frame of an institutional entranceway resolving in front of him, as if he were emerging from a fog bank. Beyond, Max could see a rock-lined path and sunny colours. The path led to a broad street lined with a jumble of closely packed buildings. Inside, there was an elevator to Max's left. A vase of bright flowers stood like an exclamation mark on a small table next to it. To his right, a reception desk. On the wall above that, the words The Beacon Arms.

Welcome back to Halifax, Max thought.

An elegant woman in her sixties was addressing him. A nametag on her chest read: Registered Nurse.

"Max, have a chair. I'm sure he'll be here in just a few minutes."

Max was wearing baggy corduroys that he had never seen before and — to his dismay — a short-sleeved shirt. An old girl pushing a walker ran over his foot on her way to a bank of mailboxes. It could be some kind of hospital, Max thought, but likely worse.

Palliative care? Fuck!

The Registered Nurse recognized his surging anxiety. "Max, would you rather wait in your room?" Nothing in her tone suggested another option, such as walking out onto the street and "waiting" in the sunlight.

Weird as the situation was, Max sensed that he'd been through it before. So he squeezed down his panic and played it cool.

"Hmm," he said, indicating that he was thoroughly engaged in the decision.

A second woman, much younger than the nurse, smiled at him from behind a reception desk to his right. She was sporting purple hair and a nose ring apparently stolen from a shower curtain. "You're welcome right here with me, Max. I need some male eye candy to greet people as they come through the door."

"Eye candy," he scoffed, instantly fond of Purple Hair. "If I'm eye candy then you, my dear, are a five-course gourmet meal."

To Max's delight, she blushed.

Max thought hard. Whatever was going on here, he was likely better off in his "room", where presumably he'd be able to reflect. It was important to hide his confusion, though. The less they know about his difficulty, the better. What would happen if they knew he had a snowball's chance in hell of finding his "room"?

"I would prefer my room," he said to the nurse. "But perhaps you could come with me. My throat has been bothering me. Maybe you could take a look."

"Sure." But she offered no directions to his room.

Max detected a light breeze pressing against his back, thought quickly, and gambled there was a hall to his rear. He turned 180 degrees and immediately started down the "hallway", which he intensely hoped was actually there. Striding confidently into a wall would seriously undermine whatever credibility he had in this particular junction of space and time.

Happily, there was in fact a hallway. Less encouraging was its length, so great that it actually seemed to have a vanishing point. There were countless doors, each bearing an object of some kind: a teddy bear, a toy cat, a crucifix, cloth flowers, another crucifix (almost certainly made from sticks by a grandchild) and so on. Max got it — the adornments were there to help the inmates find their cells. He was in some kind of "home".

Not good.

He spotted a pewter plaque depicting a newspaper

press. Max didn't remember it specifically, but noted that it provoked a sense of familiarity. That could be mine, Max thought. Still, he couldn't be certain. Never assume.

Registered Nurse was slowing down, preparing to let Max lead the way. He needed a distraction while he confirmed where his cell was, so pointed to the award and spoke, careful to ensure his tone was neutral as to the ownership of the plaque.

"Looks like King Kong kicked over an office tower," he said cheerfully.

"Oh, for heaven's sake," said Registered Nurse. "Where do you come up with stuff like that, Max? You should be proud of that award."

Hah! My door it is!

When they got there, Max pretended to look closely at the award.

"Well, I guess you're right, it's not a building," he generously acknowledged.

"That's a relief," said Registered Nurse.

"Yep," said Max. "It's clearly an action figure of five executives screwing a newspaper reader. Must be an award from a newspaper chain." Now he could make out an inscription on the newspaper bag: Lifetime Achievement: Editor.

"Do you know when I got this?" he asked.

"Yes. It came in the mail last month."

"I presume I have a file here," Max said. "Have you read it?"

Registered Nurse nods in the affirmative.

"When did I retire as a journalist?"

"Must have been a long time ago," she says. "Your file

said you were a communications consultant. It barely mentioned journalism."

"It was only most of my career," Max says.

The worst thing you can do to a journalist is give him a lifetime achievement award. It's like a bullet in the back of the head. But whoever sent him this award waited until he was jailed for having memory problems. Can this get any worse, he wondered.

The only recognizable object in his closet-sized "room" was the king-sized marital bed, in a sleigh-style frame worthy of a tsar. The Wife's inflated salary as a university flack had paid for that. There was barely room for end tables between the bed and the walls. There was a window, but another building across the alley blocked most of the light. Max needed only a quick look around to confirm that the Wife was not with him, so there was no comfort in seeing the familiar piece of furniture. It merely reminded him that he was lonely.

The nurse patted the edge of the bed.

"Just sit here for a moment and I'll check your throat," she said.

The throat was quickly pronounced healthy.

Max chose his next words carefully. "Sometimes it feels like palliative care around here."

"No," she replied. "We'll be sorry when you leave here, but I'm sure you'll do it under your own steam."

"You mean as opposed to feet-first."

"Dear lord, you're blunt," she said and, with that, Registered Nurse left him alone.

Two steps from the end of his bed was a bathroom, tiled completely in white and lit with a high-contrast curly-bulb bright enough to belong in a football stadium. The bathroom had all the charm of a freezer chest. Max slid his hands into his pockets. In the right, where he always kept a few bills and change, there was nothing. But in the left pocket he found a pencil stub and a piece of paper, the feel of which told him that it was old. He pulled it out and in the surgical light from the bathroom he could see that in a former life it had been an envelope. Max recognized his own handwriting.

"Check socks drawer, end table," it said. The numeral three was also scrawled on it three times.

Beside the bathroom door was his dresser and in the top drawer were socks and underwear. Max dug down and found an envelope labelled *Welcome back to the dungeon.* Inside was a note — to himself.

> *Do not delay: make sure there are backup copies of this note in each end table.*

He was tempted to go on reading but summoned the discipline to confirm the presence of the other notes.

> *Bad news first: if you're reading this again, there isn't a lot of good news.*

Reading it *again*, Max thought. Why?

> *You have lost control of the time-jump. There is no telling when a jump attempt will work or where you will land when it's over. Sometimes they occur spontaneously. Worse, your recollection of previous jumps is fading. That's why you've written this note. This room seems to be a base of some kind. You keep coming back to this*

situation, but DO NOT STAY here if you can manage it. You're not dead yet, my friend. Find the Wife in a good time/place and figure out a way to stay there. Be friendly with the people here — most of them are kind — but jump if you can. Otherwise, in time, you'll get comfortable and you don't want that.

The Wife is not here. Check the wall for updates. ESPECIALLY THE CORNERS. When you've got a number in each one, you're good to go. You'll know what I mean.

Max snapped his head up to look at the wall, heard an alarming crack in his neck and felt something like a shard of glass slicing into the top of his spine. Evidently he was getting older.

The wall was covered with terse notes written in crayon. Max was horrified to recognize his own block printing, the style he used to mark proofs for compositors, printers and assorted ad agencies. He'd spent his adult life honing his prose to be precise and full of meaning, but these scrawls were Neanderthal grunts:

Purple Hair OK.
Max gone. Bye-bye.
Pesto yes; SpaghettiOs, no.
Big nurse steals pocket change.
God? Hah! Not here.

The meaning was obvious: in this location in time, lucidity was not guaranteed. Just the opposite, actually. Thus, his task was to get out of this time and place as soon as he could.

He looked at the four corners. Two of them bore the number three; the others were blank.

Max stewed over his own cryptograms until Registered Nurse returned. She had in tow a familiar-looking, athletic man with closely cropped black hair. He wore a wool jacket that carried in a whiff of cool fall air.

"Max," she said, "your son is here."

He looked too old be the Son, but Max was catching on: stay vague until you figure out who they are and listen carefully for clues.

"Oh! What a surprise! It's good to see you ... son. How was the drive?"

"The drive was fine, Dad," he said. "I'm only 10 minutes away."

Max parried: "With the traffic in this city, nothing is ever 10 minutes away."

The nurse asked: "What should I tell the kitchen? Are you two eating here or going out?"

"Don't get me wrong," Max said, guessing that he praised the kitchen regularly. "I love the food here. But nothing beats a meal that my son's paid for."

Everybody laughed a bit too hard, and Registered Nurse departed. Max walked to his dim window, then turned partway toward the Son. He gave him a cagey, sideways look.

"What do horses eat?"

"Apples," was the reply.

Only the Son would answer that way, of course. Max's heart opened and, suddenly, his head was clear. Where was I when this fellow became a man, he wondered.

"How are you, Dad?"

"If I were any better I'd be dangerous."

Max feels a question gnawing at him, but he can't articulate it. The Son comes up with one of his own first.

"Your gout okay?"

Gout? "Not a problem," Max said.

The Son was silent. The journalist in Max knows that he can wait him out, force him to break the silence. Long silences are often followed by useful information.

"Dad, we may have to start looking at a new place for you, a place with more services."

Max attempted a menacing tone. "Now why would that be?"

"It's your ... memory ... sometimes you forget things ... get confused ... yesterday you peed in a potted plant."

"That wasn't me," Max said. "It was years ago. The fisheries minister got so drunk at a fundraiser that he mistook the champagne fountain for a urinal."

"You're in denial, Dad."

Max had to concentrate. How do you refute the allegation that you're in denial? Deny it?

He was about to make this point when he remembered the notes in the drawers. Stay cool.

He looked the Son confidently in the eye: "Let's say that's true. Do you have a better strategy than denial?"

Max didn't wait for a reply because the question that had been nagging him had finally gnawed its way to his consciousness.

"I need to confirm something. How long has your mother been dead?"

"About five months."

"That fits," he said.

"What?"

"This is my base station in time," he said. "Not a problem. It's all good. I'll find her. How about your sister? How is she doing?"

The Son deflated a little. Max felt sorry for him.

"Dad, I don't have a sister ... never mind. Time to eat," the Son declared.

Max didn't want to hear anything more about why there might not be sister. "Good. I could go for a big glass of draft, too."

"The doctor thinks alcohol's a bad idea."

"Bad for who? Bad for the doctor's theories, I expect. But not me. Anyway, if you're right about what you say, it can't do me any harm, can it? I mean, the arse is already out of 'er, right?"

The Son smiled. "We'll get something deep-fried, too, with extra salt."

Max's core warmed and softened.

"And I'll get a new ball for you," Max said, recalling a different time-space junction where he and the Son were walking home from a school event, snow crunching under their feet. The Son pointed to the half-moon burning high and white surrounded by pinpoint winter stars. He said it looked like a father walking home, with a new ball for his son poking part way out of the pocket of his greatcoat. The Son said it made him feel safe. Max hoisted the boy onto his shoulders and that's the way they walked the rest of the way home.

The grown Son placed his arm on Max's shoulder and they walked out to the glass door. The Son waved to Purple Hair and punched a four-digit code into a security pad. Max couldn't see it all, but was pretty sure it started with a 3.

Inside his pocket, he found the pencil stub and, pinning the paper scrap against his thigh, scrawled an awkward 3 on it.

1969

Friday Night at the Strip Club

***Max had no** doubt he was jumping to Montreal. The grey concrete of the Metro tunnel flashed by inches from his window. When the train stopped, he stepped out of the car and into, of all places, a strip club named Goldpussy's.*

Max is embarrassed by the rapt attention his three roommates are devoting to the spectacle before them.

It's Friday night with nothing happening on campus, so they're all downtown drinking beer at the 007-themed club.

His friends have cajoled him into sitting near the stage, which Max hates because it costs a lot in tips and the view is better suited, in his opinion, to medical texts. Max loves looking at naked women; he just prefers to do it with a degree of decorum.

But two beers into the evening, a naked dancer in red sequined heels strides over, turns her back, and offers them the Holy Grail of the strip club experience. The Roommates go nuts and toss money on the stage for her to pick up. Max averts his gaze, but discreetly, because he doesn't want to hurt the girl's feelings. He pretends he's turning away because he has to sneeze, and finds himself looking right into the face of an attractive older red-head sitting alone a few tables away.

And she is looking right back at him. No question about it. And she is beaming at him, the way his high school algebra teacher used to beam at him when he solved quadratic equations. (It occurs to Max that his former mentor would probably be disappointed to see him in a crummy nightclub with his face just a couple of feet from someone's bare behind. "You were such a promising student, Max, and now this!")

A while later Max is gazing toward another part of the club when he sees the red-haired woman again, still beaming directly at him. He tells himself to stop fantasizing. The woman is easily 10 years older than him and 'way out of his league. But, not long after, Max sees her smiling warmly at him again, this time sitting alone on the other side of the club, her round face A-framed by the legs of a stripper.

Max has to search the room to find her the fourth time. He spots her near a corner, much farther away, but this time she nods slightly and holds up her beer glass to him. Max's friends don't even notice when he abandons them and gingerly walks to her table. As he does so, he envisions the gas-lit lecture hall: "And so I submit gentlemen, the straightforward approach is best in these situations. Just walk up confidently and ask: 'Excuse me, have we met?' 'Eureka,' the audience yells. 'Hear hear! Well done, Max!'"

Thus prepared, Max instead circles behind her and says to the back of her head: "Do you come here often?" As is his habit, he realizes the words are wrong, but not until he's in mid-sentence.

"Well," she says, turning to him and still beaming. "I work here some nights, so I guess you could say that."

Up close, Max can see that she is without question the most beautiful woman in the world. Hair the colour of copper, bright green eyes; her expression open and curious. But Max, his ears burning bright red, is the biggest clod in the world. He wobbles under this clash of insights.

"I think you'd better sit down," she says, motioning toward the chair right next to her.

Max sits and clears his throat: "So, are you one of the bartenders?"

"No."

"A cook?"

She shakes her head.

"Umm, dancer?"

"The word you're probably looking for is 'stripper'," she says. "And part owner."

It seems only natural to Max that strippers should have the same power of speech enjoyed by other humans, but Max himself is mute while his brain works to process the reality of it and deal with the assortment of hormones and other complex molecules flooding his bloodstream.

"So, whoever you are," she says, "I'm feeling kind of lonely tonight and want to know if you'll go out for a drink with me."

"My name is Max," he croaks.

"Maxie! That's a great name. I've always wanted to know a Maxie. Shall we go?"

Max glances at his friends, who are busy contorting their necks, and decides not to bother saying goodbye.

He and the Dancer step carefully down a dark, uneven

stairway with a landing at the halfway mark. It features a crude spray-painted "X", reputedly marking the farthest a bouncer has ever tossed a patron for touching a stripper. For Max, it feels like a point of no return on a journey into the unknown.

As they step onto the sidewalk, the Dancer turns, causing them to bump into each other front-to-front. She kisses him quickly and lightly on the lips, like a teenager on a first date. Max is surprised to see that she is shorter than he is.

"I suppose you think you're going to get laid," she says.

By now Max can barely stand up. Thoughts and emotions whirl around him like a midway spinning wheel. The wheel stops at 'urbane and expansive'. Max says: "I'd rather imagined so, yes."

Fuck! Why on earth would he answer like some kind of B-list Bond? He knows these words will echo in his skull for the rest of his life.

The Dancer laughs, which Max interprets as confirmation of his error, but she saves what's left of his self-esteem with a smile that says he has just made himself more interesting, not less. She looks into his eyes and forces him to hold the gaze for an eternity.

Max feels like his psyche is undergoing some kind of scan and wonders if she's a crazy-woman or on drugs.

"If you want to sleep with my pussy," she says, "I can promise to make that happen in the next 30 minutes. But sleeping with *me*, that's not guaranteed yet. Do you get the distinction?"

The wheel spins again and lands on witty. Max begs himself not to utter the words, but as usual there's nothing to be done.

"Is your pussy detachable?" he asks. Max's mind is blank, as befits someone who once again regrets his words before uttering them. The reptilian part of his brain instantly downgrades its sexual expectations for the evening to a solitary act.

The Dancer pulls him close by his lapels and gives him another crazy-woman look. Her breath smells like strawberries: "As a matter of fact, in a way that only a male could understand, that's *exactly* what mine is. Detachable. You can have your way with it, but my mind will be miles or years away. But, if you want to take a shot at sleeping with *me*, we need to spend more time together. You've got 10 seconds to make your choice."

As a university student without money or a girlfriend, Max's standards for a wild night are low. So having sex with an actual female sexual organ, detached or not, is something he's loath to gamble away. On the other hand, despite the Dancer's advanced age (he can see tiny crow's feet now), Max finds her intriguing. He doesn't want to part company in just 30 minutes.

"I rather enjoy your company," he says.

"Please don't say 'rather'," she replies.

She takes his arm and slides her hand half way up the inside of his bicep, pulls his shoulder to her and rests the side of her head on it. For a moment, there is no Max, just an extraordinary sensation of lightness from the soles of his feet to the top of his head. A cool breeze on his cheeks returns his senses to him. He sees that the street is full of people and cars.

The Dancer nudges him forward without loosening her grip. "I can spot potential a mile away," she says.

She guides him to an ordinary wooden door on a dim part of Guy St. It opens onto a long narrow stairway with, of course, a landing halfway up. This gets Max thinking: he is going to be mugged or hustled for cash.

"I've never paid for it," he says.

She tops at the landing and turns to him: "Oh Maxie, you *do* have some rough edges. I don't doubt what you said for a second. But how does that make you a better person?"

"Well, I rather thin ... I mean, I think that's obvious."

"Oh, is it? Are you a better person when you're making love to your fist? Or maybe a girl at a party who's so drunk she may not even remember you the next day?"

"I would never do that," Max says.

"Which?" the Dancer asks with a mischievous smile.

"The second thing."

"But you do the first, right?"

Maxes flushes bright red and, despite his rich vocabulary, can't find the words to admit that he has remorselessly spilled his seed unto cold, barren ground.

The Dancer relents: "Now listen, Maxie, we're going upstairs for some nice food and music, during which time I'll decide whether my instincts about you are right. I don't want to talk about 'paying for it'. In fact, I don't want to talk about it at all. Deal?"

Max agrees and they walk the rest of the stairway. The Dancer doesn't hold his arm.

At the top, she opens the door and leads them into a restaurant with a small dance floor and three-man band jamming blues and jazz. A dignified, fatherly maître d' strides up to the Dancer and embraces her affectionately, followed by the ritual double air-kiss preferred by Montrealers.

"Welcome, monsieur," he says to Max after introductions. "I am pleased to say we have a wonderful table available. Not too close to the music, and in a spot where you will enjoy the breeze."

Max sees the point. Even though it's autumn, the heat from the two storeys below has risen to the top floor and settled in. Their table is near an open fire-escape door where they can feel a light breeze from the outside. There are about a dozen tables boasting gingham cloths and candles set in raffia-covered Chianti bottles. Max is without doubt the youngest and poorest person in the room. The men, all 40 and up, have a scrubbed, self-satisfied look that he finds vaguely irritating. The women are all spectacular.

Max isn't sure what to do next, but the maître d' rescues him by appearing out of nowhere. He's careful not to ignore Max, but makes it clear that the Dancer is in charge. He presents the menu with a flourish.

"Would *mademoiselle* and Monsieur Max like an aperitif while you discuss our offerings tonight?"

"That would be lovely," she says. "Maxie, have you ever tried Campari?"

Max mumbles in the negative.

The Dancer looks up at the maître d', displaying a highly kissable neck.

"That would be lovely. Max will have a Campari and soda, and I will have *pastis*."

"*Parfait, mademoiselle*," he says as he departs.

"His style's a bit too formal," she says. "But he's a lovely man and he always waits on me, even though it's not really his job."

Silence. Max is relieved to see that she is beaming at

him again. It's clear, though, that she is not going to carry the conversation for him. The drinks arrive as if my magic. The astringent taste of his Campari surprises Max. The Dancer's drink, a transparent yellow, is accompanied by a small container of water. The Dancer smiles at Max and pours a dollop into her drink. He tries not to react like a bumpkin when the drink turns cloudy. Max catches the eye of the guitar player, who is riffing on *Honky Tonk Woman.*

"So," says Max. "How did you come to be part owner of a successful club?"

The Dancer rewards him with an encouraging nod: "The previous owner owed me some money, so he gave me a twelve per cent interest in the club in lieu of cash. When he sold it, the new owners were gracious enough to let me keep five per cent."

"Well," Max says. "I rath- .... You'd think they'd be legally obliged to let you keep the full twelve per cent."

"The owners can be very kind to people they like, but hard on people who interfere with their business interests. The 'X' you saw painted on the landing, that's not a myth. I am happy with my five per cent."

The maître d' reappears to take their order.

"For an appetizer, we'll have the *escargots aux fines herbes.*"

"Excellent choice. For wine, may I suggest a Sauvignon that we just got in this week?"

She turns to Max. "I don't know much about wine, but he never leads me astray."

"Mademoiselle is too modest. Your knowledge of wine has become most impressive."

Max asks what *escargots* are.

"I believe they are related to snails, monsieur."

"How closely related?"

The veteran server raises his eyebrows, expels a breath and shrugs, as if to say that no one really knows: "And for the main course, *mademoiselle*?"

"I was thinking of the *Coquilles Saint-Jacques*."

The maître d' stops writing on his pad and stares into space. He patiently clears his throat.

"On the other hand," the Dancer says, "maybe the *coq au vin* would be better."

"Excellent choice." He turns to Max. "Your friend is a remarkable woman, yes? How could she know that the scallops have been sitting at the back of the freezer for a week? *Formidable*."

"Remarkable does not begin to describe her," Max says, surprised by his own grace and sincerity.

"I *knew* it," she says, beaming at him again.

Max is unused to being demonstrably liked by a woman. He has long assumed there are simple rules, so far unknown, for achieving that state of grace. The Dancer, however, now has him wondering if there might be something more to it. He takes another sip of Campari and finds the taste is growing on him.

"Why me?" he asks. "Why did you pick me out of all those people at the bar? Is it because I wouldn't look up the dancers' backsides?"

"Close, but why shouldn't people be curious about body parts?"

"You're saying there's more to it than not staring," Max says.

"You're on the right track. Look, you're awfully good-looking ..."

"I am?" he says, unable to contain his surprise.

"Sure. You've got great hair, your features are well-proportioned — large, but not too large. Great skin. You would make a great girl, too."

Max flushes, having no idea what to make of that.

"But I like men whose looks match their character."

Max gets the penetrating gaze again. She's waiting.

"Okay. How do I look?"

"You look a bit self-centred, but honest. By honest I mean that when you look like you're interested in someone, it's not an act. You might also be kind, something I intend to find out."

The *escargots* arrive along with a bottle of wine in an ice bucket. Max notes suspiciously that the *escargots* are served in snail shells, but doesn't care. He and the Dancer toast their new friendship. The wine is cool and crisp. It is the first white wine he can remember with no hint of paint thinner. The wine and the snails cooked in garlic and butter go together so well that he is light-headed.

They linger over the appetizer. Magically, just as the last drop of wine is consumed, the *coq au vin* arrives with another bottle of white.

"I hope mademoiselle does not mind," the maître d' says, "but I did not want to interrupt your conversation to ask about wine. I took the liberty of choosing a Chateauneuf-du Pâpe on your behalf. Of course, I will take it back if you prefer."

"You know I would never do that," she says, laughing. "But you're not worried that it's a little pricey for a girl like me?"

He offers a slight bow. "That is not something you need concern yourself with," he says, and glides away.

"Is he a friend or something?" Max asks.

"No. He is just a regular acquaintance. But it makes him happy to be kind and generous to people he likes."

Max only sort of understands but, rather than reveal his ignorance, he tackles his *coq au vin*, which turns out to be chicken. He's caught on to the idea of matching food and wine. The succulent chicken and taste of berries and spice from the wine inspire waves of pleasure from head to foot.

The Dancer tells him that not long after arriving in Montreal she got into speed and started stripping to pay for it. She was headed for disaster when an out-of-town bar patron pulled her back from the brink. Now she's a part-time "mature" student getting a degree in commerce.

Max tells her that he is studying physics and expects to make it his career.

"Tell your mom and dad not to bet the farm on that," she says. "I can read the signs."

"Oh, really?"

The Dancer points to his left sleeve. "Just for example, even a student physicist will buy a button rather than fasten his cuff with a stapler."

"I was in a hurry," Max says.

"Of course you were, Maxie. I don't know where you're going to land, but it won't be physics. I know men. You're the kind of guy who wants to *do* something, but doesn't know how."

Max is okay with her assessment of him, even likes it a little. He looks past the Dancer at downtown Montreal, in silhouette and light, past the fire escape. The vision is inseparable from the intoxicating rhythm of the band. Max is reeling under the exquisite influence of the wine and food;

transported by the beauty and warmth of the woman sitting across from him.

Max is also aware that sex with her is almost a foregone conclusion although, for once, sex is not dominating his thoughts. Which is unnerving.

How can something this great be happening to me, of all people, he wonders.

NOW

The Great Escape

The Dancer faded away to be replaced by Purple Hair, who was walking into his dungeon with a fresh cup of coffee. She wished him a good morning, patted him on the shoulder and left.

He filled his lungs with the aroma and reverently savoured the first sip. The effect was a call to action. He looked around for inspiration and spotted two piles of crumpled bits of paper on his night table. The sight of the two lumpy pyramids, each large enough to fill a trouser pocket, set off a soothing wavelet of familiarity. Max smiled to himself and began pawing through them.

Purple Hair = A-OK.
Scrambled eggs = dry.
DIY plumbing ≠ OK.

The one that got his attention was *3333 ≠ exit code.* So 3333 did not equal the exit code.

Max looked around and noticed that each of the four upper corners of his space bore the number "3". Four 3s. Max had no trouble recalling what "exit code" meant. It was the electronic number pad that stood between him and freedom. He spent hours by the reception desk every day watching visitors punch in the exit code and hearing the lock's well-oiled snick as it slid open. But Max could not figure out the code.

Other balls of paper documented earlier attempts to crack it.

First code # = 3. There were a lot of those.

Get 2nd #. No shortage of those, either.

3333 = exit code. Yes! Max gone soon! Goodbye!

3333 ≠ exit code.

So which is it, Max thought, 3333 = or "3333 ≠? Hah! It can't be 3333 or he would be long gone.

If not 3333, then what, Max asked himself. The Son will know, but won't tell.

There was an overlarge phone on his table, each key the size of a Scrabble tablet. Jesus Christ, a phone for the armless: Headline: *Man dials Queen with nose!* No, better would be: *Armless man has world at his toe-tips!* Hah! Max cackled at his own jokes.

Beside the gargantuan dial pad was a column of pictures, none of which he recognized. Each was accompanied by a button and a name in large print. One button, however, had the word "SON" beside it. Max picked up the handset and pressed SON.

"Hi Dad, how ya doin'?"

"If I were any better I'd be dangerous!" Max said. "How are you and your good lady?"

"We're fine. Did you enjoy supper last night?"

Who knows, Max thought. "You bet," he said.

"What's up?"

Max summoned his most relaxed and engaging tone of voice. "Well, it's the damnedest thing, but I've forgotten the exit code."

Max watched the silent seconds go by on his wristwatch.

"Exit code?"

"Yes," Max said evenly. "That would be the code for exiting this building, I believe."

More seconds of guilty silence ticked by.

"Well, Dad. They change the code every day. You should ask the front desk."

"Oh, I should, should I?"

Maybe my memory's a bit creaky, but I'm not an idiot, Max thought. The staff couldn't spend their days handing out fresh exit codes to every visitor.

"Uh, yes. You should ask the front desk."

"Okay. Thanks. Bye."

As he cradled the phone, Max struggled to hold onto his intent. He imagined it as a presence in his frontal lobe that was slipping away. He turned his attention to his breath, hoping that by concentrating on it he could beat back the thoughts that were competing with ... with ... EXIT! The exit code. Max surveyed his desktop and there it was, the clue: *3333 ≠ exit code*. He was back on track. Max wanted to kiss the bit of paper.

Let's assume the code is just four digits, he thought. That much seems likely. Does four digits indicate they are serious about security? No. And, if they are not serious about security, how likely are they to make the number easy to remember? Very likely indeed.

Max felt his excitement before he even realized he had the answer. On the phone dial-pad the number 3 corresponded with the letter E. "E for EXIT". Hah! EXIT corresponded to 3-9-4-8 on the dial pad. Max ripped a large piece of paper from his pad scribbled the solution down before he could forget: *Exit code = 3948.*

Max jumped up and did the Dance of Joy, the little two-step he used to do whenever a truly juicy story crossed his desk.

"Thirty-nine forty-eight!," he shouted. "Thirty-nine. Forty-eight! Hut-hut! Hike!" Then he clammed up. If Purple Hair heard him, she'd come running down the hallway.

Max knew he had to act quickly. He put his coffee cup down and headed for the hallway. He turned right and there it was: daylight at the end of the tunnel.

"Good morning, sexy." Purple Hair was behind the reception counter, grinning at him like he was the only man on Earth.

Max's focus escaped like a fish from a hook — a flash as the underbelly reflects the sun, then it's gone.

"Haven't been called that in a while," Max said expansively. "And it's always a pleasure to hear it from someone as beautiful as you."

"You know you're the only man here who likes purple hair."

"That's because they don't know anything about women."

"And you do?"

"Well, I know what I like."

She smiled.

"Your *Globe and Mail* is waiting for you in the lounge."

"You're very kind," he said, noting sourly to himself that for some reason he knew the way to the lounge. Been here too long.

Max was deep into the newspaper, enjoying another coffee, when one of the kitchen staff walked up to him holding an envelope.

"Hey Max," the kid said. "You gave me this and told me to give it back to you this morning."

Max stared at the friendly-looking kid who, judging by his weight, clearly wasn't stealing food from the kitchen. "Really?"

"Yep. You said it was top secret. I haven't shown it to anyone. You gave me 15 copies and said to return one to you at random about every week or so."

Max looked to see if the kid was just humouring him, but no. Apparently he was an ally. The return address on the envelope said *The Beacon Arms.*

"The Beacon Arms?"

"Yeah. That's where we are. The Beacon Arms."

Max tore off the end of the envelope, blew into it theatrically and said: "And the winner is ..."

There was a handwritten letter inside, in Max's handwriting, the salutation of which said: "Dear Self."

"Anything interesting?" the kid asked.

"Apparently it's a blast from the recent past," Max said.

Dear Self,

If you're reading this, the kid from the kitchen should have interrupted you while you were reading the Globe.

Correct, Max thought, impressed with his foresight. Hind-sight, not so much.

With luck, today is the day you'll find a note in one of your pants pockets explaining how to escape this place. If it's there, ACT RIGHT NOW! Don't worry about Purple Hair. They won't fire her.

Max checked his pocket. Bingo! There it was.

Good work! First, there are tens and twenties in your shoes, underneath your orthotics. Put one bill in your pocket.

Max slyly slipped a twenty from his right shoe, put it in his pocket and returned his attention to the note.

Go up the stairs to the second floor. The fire alarm should be to the right of the door. Set it off and wait 30 seconds. Then go back downstairs. Purple Hair probably won't be there, so she won't be punished for your escape. Punch in the code you found in your pocket and Go, Baby, Go! DON'T WAIT. GO NOW! LEAVE THE BLOODY GLOBE AND MAIL *BEHIND!*

Except for a little indecision about leaving his newspaper behind, Max's thoughts were clear and laser-focused. At the second floor he opened the door and looked right. There was the fire alarm. He'd always wanted to snap one of those glass bars and so he did. The alarm rang out loud and clear.

School's out, Max thought.

He got to the main floor just in time to look through the safety glass and see Purple Hair marching purposefully down the hall, wearing a hardhat and a vest that said "Fire Warden." No one was at the door. The number pad beckoned.

Max looked at the note: 3948. He punched in the code. Nothing. Behind him he heard Purple Hair reassuring folks that everything was all right. He punched it again. Nothing.

Just as panic seemed inevitable, Max's mind cleared. He was calm, calm like a crocodile drifting with the current toward a fat shorebird. He carefully punched in 3948 and finished it off with #. The door buzzed. Max leaned on it ... and he was out.

He slid the paper back into his pocket, hurried along the path and turned randomly, which was up a small hill leading to a large supermarket. A good place to hide while he figured out what to do next.

Max didn't look back, but he did worry that his escape would hurt Purple Hair's feelings. He hurried toward the store, hoping to ensconce himself somewhere inside before people started looking for him.

1981

Talks with Collective End Well

Max looks down the length of his scarred meeting table. Mr. Nipples — the class-war reporter — and three compositors are sitting two to a side. This is the entire Collective. In deference to the inherent equality within collectives, no one has taken the spot directly opposite Max.

Nothing distinguishes the three compositors from one another. They all wear blue work clothes and all are ruddy with anger, although nothing has happened yet.

Mr. Nipples opens the discussion.

"The Collective has discussed what you said to me yesterday," he begins. "We've concluded that you lack the authority to give direction on reporting assignments and we are issuing a reprimand for the unprofessional way you spoke to me. To wit: the phrase 'Mother fucking Teresa'.

"Furthermore, this meeting is to inform you that the Collective will not take direction from you and will issue an advisory to all staff that you have no authority over them."

Meeting apparently concluded, the four arise as one to leave.

"Wait a second," Max says. "Let's chat."

The Collective members exchange glances and arrive at consensus: they will stay.

"I was looking at your personnel files ..."

Mr. Nipples interrupts: "You have no right to those files."

"And yet, I have them right here," Max says. "The short version is that not one of you has any of the skills required for your job."

"This is typical of the ruling class," says Mr. Nipples. "You know full well that the so-called qualifications are just a façade enabling employers to pick and choose who they hire."

Max nods solemnly.

"You are absolutely right," he says. "And I hereby use the powers vested in me by 'the façade' to fire you immediately. Your severance is waiting for you at the front desk."

"You can't do that."

"Yes, I can. You haven't passed your probation, comrade. I can fire you just because I don't like your haircut. Even the severance is an act of generosity. You are four incompetents who've spotted an opportunity to acquire some power that you know will never come your way otherwise."

Max can see the three ruddy compositors thinking this one over.

Mr. Nipples stands up. "Do you have something against the Collective?"

"Well, the Collective and I have met a few times before," Max says. "It's never gone well."

Mr. Nipples is literal-minded, and Max can see he's having trouble recalling their previous meetings. But he can see the others got the point.

"If you'll excuse us, the Collective would like to caucus," Mr. Nipples says.

Max holds up his hand. "With great respect to the magical wisdom of the Collective, I feel I should say that it would be only slightly more difficult to fire the rest of the people in this office. More importantly, I have additional information that may prove useful to your comrades."

Mr. Nipples remains standing; the others sit like Easter Island statues.

Max turns away from them and starts perusing resumes. Finally, one of the compositors can take the silence no longer.

"What information would that be?"

"Glad you asked," Max says, handing out slips of paper to each of the compositors. "With the departure of your fearless leader here, the 'façade' has an extra salary to work with. We've divided it by three, and those bits of paper have your new salaries written on them, should you decide to stay."

Too late, the penny drops for Mr. Nipples: "Comrades, it is at times like these that solidarity is most important."

"Yeah, for you," says one.

"We're not going to listen to you if you don't deliver the goods," says another. "This guy — and I'm not saying he's a prince — just delivered them. From you, we've got squat."

Max turns to the third compositor: "Do you have anything to add?"

"No. Even after taxes, this raise is going to make a difference."

"Well, I guess we're done then," Max says, flashing a phony smile. "Lots of work to do before the day is over."

Mr. Nipples heads for reception to get his money. Two others head back to the composing room. The last waits just long enough for a private word.

"We'll never forget this," he growls. "You fucking prick."

"I understand your anger," Max says, oozing false sympathy. "But that's self-discovery for you."

1983

A One-Child Family

Max is uneasy about being at the Paper. He missed the birth of the Son because he had "one last story" to cover before closing the Montreal Daily's Latin America bureau and returning to Montreal to become the night police reporter.

Today, in Halifax, he hasn't the slightest idea what that story was.

Now, he worries that he'll repeat the mistake. With a hoped-for baby daughter on the way, even a hint of trouble with the pregnancy makes him want to stay home. This is such a hint. He and the Wife and Son went for a long walk yesterday and a few hours later she developed cramps. They had been through minor scares with the Son but those were later in the pregnancy and all dismissed as normal by her doctor.

By bedtime, the Wife was better and in the morning insisted that Max go in to work. The pull of the newsroom and the fear that he might miss something, combined with the Wife's insistence, won out. He calls her from his office for the fourth time in three hours, but now she says he should think about coming home.

"It's not the pain. Something just doesn't feel right."

Max says he's headed home and begins loading his briefcase with things he can work on. The City Editor, wearing a sharply-pressed Girl Scout uniform, knocks once and cruises in.

"Gotta go home," Max says. "I need you to take the news meeting. Don't worry, nothing's wrong."

The City Editor wants Max's advice. The Paper's business section wants a grip-and-grin photo at the chamber of commerce; Entertainment wants a shot of a busker who breathes green fire.

"You have to ask?"

"Business will be really pissed. They say you're always grinding them for pictures and then cancelling their assignments."

"Is that true?"

"Indubitably."

Max tries to walk past Sports on his way to the Business desk.

"Hey Max," says the dayside guy. "Did you see the typo those nightside assholes let through last night?"

Max's stomach lurches.

"Look at this: 'the Montreal Canadiennes'. What kind of idiot spells Canadiens like a girls' team? I don't know why I bother coming in if these guys are just going to fuck it up."

"Why are you here at all?" Max asks. "It's noon on a Wednesday. Who the Christ is playing sports at noon on a Wednesday?"

"Someone's got to plan the coverage."

"But you're claiming overtime at night for that because you don't have time to do it in the day."

Max senses the Cartoonist breathing behind him. He desperately wants to ignore him and leave.

"What have you got?"

He's got a nice drawing of the Minister of Education teaching an elementary class. The words "HOW I LIED ABOUT OUR SCHOOLS" are printed neatly on the board behind him. The caption is "Education Minister explains his actions."

"You can't call people liars," Max says. "It's hard to prove and it makes them determined to sue."

"But he's a liar."

"It's a bitch to prove. How do we prove he didn't just make a mistake, or misspeak, or was misinformed?"

"We'll prove it in court," the Cartoonist says.

"Spoken like a man who's got fifty grand in his pocket. It's not about losing, it's about the cost of winning. We have to pick our spots. This isn't one of them."

"Really? Fifty grand? OK. Can I change the wording?"

"Yes, but call me at home."

By the time Max gets out the door, it's been half an hour since he closed his briefcase. The drive home is reckless, but too late.

The Wife is sitting up in the big bed, looking drawn and teary.

"I lost the baby," she says. "It was a girl."

"You can't tell at this stage ..."

For the first time in their lives together, the Wife yells at him. Through her sobs.

"Don't tell me what I saw. I'm the one who flushed it down the toilet!"

Max climbs on the bed and spoons with her. He wraps

his arms tightly around her and lets her cry. When she's done for a while, she turns and faces him.

"Nature took something from you," he says. "It's not your fault."

"But I feel so empty and useless. And you wanted a little girl. I shouldn't have gone on that walk."

"The walk had nothing to do with it, you know that. And I have you and our son and I love you both so much. That's everything I want. Everything."

Max's guilt is an anchor chain around his shoulders.

"It's not your fault," she says. "I told you not to stay home."

"I knew better."

Just as he knew better than to stay that extra day at the Latin American Bureau.

• • •

Two mornings later, they are eating a late breakfast, having packed the Son off to school. Max, still shaken by the miscarriage, can't taste the food. But the Wife is cheerfully devouring everything on her plate, looking up at Max periodically to be sure he's getting the message: *I am moving on from this.*

"Maxie," she says. "I'm not sure we should try to have more kids. The miscarriage was a message."

"It doesn't work that way," Max says.

"Don't be so sure. There may be more going on in the cosmos than you think."

Max isn't prepared to believe that. But, although he was excited about the possibility of having a little girl, the truth is his feelings are more about guilt than loss.

"I don't think I'm an earth mother," the Wife says. "Besides, the Paper's never going to pay enough and we need to start making some decent money."

This is true, Max thinks. Newsroom salaries back home have been going through the roof, but not in Halifax. Max is definitely having more fun than his buddies in Montreal, but his take-home is a fraction of theirs.

The Wife wants to apply for a public relations job at the University.

"Actually, they call it communications now," she explains.

"But it's still the Dark Side," Max says, echoing the prevailing view among journalists.

"Yeah, well, Darth Vader pays better," she says. "Anyway, it's just journalism in reverse."

"Can flacks and hacks be married?" Max asks.

"Mixed marriages are more and more common," she says.

1983

A Column from the Editor

When nature decides on abortion

We had a miscarriage in our family recently, and I was surprised by how hard we took it. My wife and I already have a son who finds ways to make us happy every day, and we know that miscarriages are common. Our doctor says one in five pregnancies end this way, and lot more if you count ones that occur before the woman knows she is pregnant. Almost all occur before the foetus is viable on its own.

It happened at home and I was late getting there, so it was all over before I got to my wife's bedside. We called our son's school and left a message that we were out for a while and he should wait for us at his friend's house down the street. On the way to the hospital we decided to tell him when he's older, if at all.

After an examination the hospital sent us home, stressing how routine it was and assuring us that we could have another pregnancy if we wanted. Nonetheless, the drive back was lonely. At home we ordered a pizza, but before we could eat my wife hugged our son and left the table in tears.

Later that evening, as we were preparing for bed, I remembered what my wife said when she broke the news to me. "I've lost the baby," she said.

I didn't think anything of it then, but now I realize the words imply that my wife was somehow at fault for what happened, as if she had left a baby on a park bench.

We don't talk about miscarriages much, but they can be packed with grief. A woman whose pregnancy has suddenly ended in the death of the foetus not only has to deal with her sense of loss and guilt, but also the departure of powerful hormones that were preparing her for motherhood.

Phrases like "lost the baby" only reinforce a woman's sense of guilt.

My wife experienced one of the common risks of pregnancy, but there was never a baby. There was a foetus and there was a spontaneous abortion.

Nobody was at fault.

NOW

Minor Incident Blown out of Proportion

Max wanted to put distance between himself and the Beacon Arms as fast as his gout would let him, but he couldn't resist looking back for just a second. The street was placid. There was no sign of a search party or vicious tracking dogs angered by having one of Max's used socks rubbed in their noses. But it was early. Or was it? There was no way of knowing how long the time-jump had lasted in so-called "real" time.

Ahead, at the top of a gentle hill, was a large grocery store. A great place to get lost in a crowd. Max focused on the huge Canadian flag above the building and pressed on. By the time he made it inside, he wasn't sure why he was there. Whatever: it beat sitting in his dungeon.

There was a "Hot Snacks" area in front of him and to the right, hallelujah, a government liquor store. It was under the same roof as the groceries, but enjoyed its own entrance. Time for a beer, he thought. There never seemed to be any where he lived. Max plunged a hand into his right pocket, feeling the tight balls of paper within. One stood out for its size and texture. He retrieved it and found it to be a twenty-dollar bill.

"Did you find everything you needed today, sir?" the clerk asked as he slid a giant can of Foster's over the scanner.

"Yes, I'm very pleased," Max said as he handed over the bill. "This is quite the innovation, isn't it, having a government liquor store and food under the same roof?"

"I guess so."

"And yet, it seems calm. There are no rapes taking place in the aisles? No looters? There are no fires burning downtown?"

"No, sir."

Max warmed to his topic. He had written many sardonic editorials about government liquor stores.

"So, you're telling me that it's possible to sell food and booze in the same building and yet maintain order."

"That's $4.39," said the clerk, evidently a practising somnambulist.

"And suppose you were able to pay for food and booze both at the same cash-out. Would that mark the beginning of the Apocalypse?"

"I don't think so. But the union wouldn't like it."

"Ah, the Collective. Of course. What was I thinking?"

The clerk peered at the twenty as he prepared to make change.

"Hey! Is this legal? It's got writing on it."

Across the middle, written in ink, were the words "Max is free! Har-har!"

"First time I've seen it," said Max.

Next stop: the feedlot. Max bought a hot dog fresh from a greasy roller-grid, and a large bag of potato chips. He claimed a table and prepared for his first meal as a free man. Prioritizing, he cracked open the Foster's, which welcomed him with an enthusiastic gasp of recognition. Max had barely savoured the first sip when there appeared a security guard packing a Magnum Force walkie-talkie.

"Sir," he said. "You can't drink that here."

"What?"

"That," said the guard, pointing to the beer.

"You're referring to my can of Foster's?"

"Yes, sir. You can't drink that here."

"Why not?

"It's not allowed."

"Ah. I can tell you've explored the issue in depth. Can I eat my hot dog and chips?"

"Yes."

"But not my beer."

The guard's jaw tensed. "That's right, you crazy old bastard. Everyone knows that. It's just the way it is."

The guard nervously clicked the transmit button on his radio, which responded with a belching noise, which in turn prompted him to put the mike to his mouth and say "Clear". Max could tell the guy loved saying "clear" into his walkie-talkie. They stared at each other silently, sizing up the enemy. The guard grimaced, as if he'd stepped on something soft and foul, but he pressed on.

"I'm saying you can't do it under this roof. I'm saying they don't pay me enough to listen to your fucking sarcasm," said the guard, who then seized the Foster's, walked across the feedlot and poured it into the garbage from a great height, all the while staring at Max.

"Get it?" he asked.

Max wondered whether the guard had simply given up hope of salvaging the situation or was trying to intimidate him. In any case, he was surprised by the power of the epithet "crazy old bastard". Although often angry, Max rarely experienced it. But even as he felt the details of the incident slipping away, he kept the anger tightly in his grasp, like a lifeline.

"Got it," said Max, who understood that he was in the guard's territory, not the reverse. Max turned his attention to his hot dog. It was salty, greasy and warm. The bun fell apart in his mouth of its own accord. No chewing required, which could not be said of the hot dog. Perfect. It occurred to Max that it might be nice if his potato chips were warm, too. He recognized a microwave sitting on a shelf in the corral. What could go wrong?

Max sauntered over to the microwave, glossy chip bag in hand. He studied the control pad with various settings written on it. Helpfully, one of them said "Potatoes." Max tossed in the bag and hit the button. Initially, the process seemed to be going well, despite the popping sound the chip bag made as it exploded.

In for a penny, in for a pound, Max thought, and did nothing. Very quickly, the air inside the microwave turned black. He pressed the open button on the machine and the door swung all the way out. Being a former science student, Max realized, belatedly, that fresh oxygen was now rushing in to fill the vacuum created by the burning potato chips. After pausing for dramatic effect, the microwave erupted into a single deep yellow flame resembling a broad maple leaf in autumn. It gave birth to a column of tarry smoke that extended all the way to the ceiling. Not to be outdone by the smoke, the flame raced up the black column, achieving the impressive height of a dozen feet before the guard rushed in and killed the whole thing with a blast from a fire extinguisher. This was just marginally less impressive than the fire itself.

A shopper beheld the scene and screamed. Her husband pointed at the blackened microwave and yelled "Fire!" Thus alerted to the danger, the curious gathered around for a closer look.

"You piece of shit," said the guard. "I should have kicked your ass out when I had the chance." He jabbed his index finger at the ceiling: "I swear, if those sprinklers go off, I'll charge you with arson."

Max thought the security guard looked familiar and not especially likeable.

"There's no danger of a building fire," he said quietly. "You dickhead."

Max could hear sirens outside the store, growing in volume. He knew the sirens belonged to fire trucks, not police cars or ambulances, although the cops could not be far behind: someone had called 911.

Fuck.

Max left the building just in time to see a ladder truck screaming up the street toward the store. It had to brake hard at the entrance of the parking lot to allow a burgundy 1975 Lincoln Town Car to enter first. The vehicle, roughly the size of a compact British aircraft carrier, moved with majesty and serenity. It skirted a clump of confused drivers near the entrance, turned left and came to a stop in an area marked "fire lane". The front licence plate said "Antique".

Max gratefully seized the latch and pulled the massive passenger door open. Inside, seated comfortably in the velour driver's seat, was the Copy Editor.

"Jesus," said Max, "I *thought* I recognized your car. Don't ask questions. Let's just get the fuck out of here before they arrest me."

"You bet, Max," said the driver as he turned the wheel. The Town Car sprinted ahead just in time to make room for the much slower fire truck.

They slowed at the parking lot entrance and Max looked at the table-sized side mirror to see what was going on behind them. The guard was waving his hands at the firefighters, but it wasn't clear whether he was telling them to hurry up or slow down. It didn't matter, because people just entering the building were realizing that something was wrong and turning around to leave, crashing into firefighters bearing extinguishers.

"Not good," said Max.

"Which way?" the driver asked.

Max looked left and saw a patrol car cresting a hill. If they went right they'd look like they were fleeing the scene. In contrast, no bad guys ever drive *toward* the cops.

"Turn toward the cops, but not too fast."

Rocking gently on its springs, the metal behemoth eased confidently into the intersection and started up the hill as the cop car screamed by them going the opposite way.

"Good job," said Max as they came to the crest. "How did you spot me?"

"You're six-three with bright white hair," he said. "I was on my way to visit you when I saw all the ruckus at the store. You were right in the middle of it, standing out like a lighthouse."

He looked at the Copy Editor, who normally at this juncture would be reloading his pipe from a pouch in his left jacket pocket, and then fishing a wooden match from the same pocket and igniting it with his thumbnail. The guy looked and acted like the Copy Editor and the car was the same, but Max was sure he had died long ago.

A time jump would explain the contradiction, and the presence of the Copy Editor would mean the Wife should be around somewhere. He felt his chest flutter at that prospect, but the situation didn't feel like a jump. For one thing, the rest of the cars on the road looked like go-carts compared to the stately Town Car.

"So," Max asked. "You seen the Wife around?"

"No, Max, I'm afraid she's not around."

"You still working at the Sunday Tabloid?"

"I didn't have the honour of working there," he said.

The driver twisted toward Max and suddenly he wasn't the Copy Editor. His pipe was gone. His hair, which had always been slicked back on all sides, as if permanently styled by a fierce wind, was instead dark and unruly. He was a small man, maybe in his late fifties. He wore a blue blazer with elbow patches that clearly were not original equipment, and eyeglasses with thick dark frames.

Max realized the enormity of his mistake and flushed with embarrassment.

"I'm sorry," he said to the driver. "I thought you were someone else, and now you're aiding the escape of a grocery store arsonist."

"You set the place on fire?"

"Well, I have a vague memory of something like that. In any case, they're rude bastards and deserved it; for another, they might have put it out. I can't remember."

"It didn't look too bad to me," said the driver. "I'm sure it'll work out."

They went downtown and drove around until their pulses returned to normal.

"I'm very sorry to have put you through this," Max said. "I'm a time traveller and sometimes the transitions in time can be confusing. You've been very kind."

"I hope that doesn't mean you're leaving," the driver said. "We are friends in this time period."

Max asked what year they were in and was told 2015.

"That doesn't mean much to me, but I think it's home base," Max said. "When I'm jumping, I have very little control. Here, it's somewhat different, and you do look familiar. I'm awfully sorry, but I just can't seem to remember names. Relationships, but not names. It's a side effect, I think."

"I understand completely."

The giant balloon that seemed ever-present in Max's chest these days began to deflate. Being safe and in the company of someone who understood time-jumping allowed him to relax.

"You understand? That's a first. Help me remember who you are."

"Here's a clue: I was your first public relations client."

"The Guru!" Max said. "I remember you. But your name is still a mystery."

"That's okay. The Guru works just fine because — thanks to you — I *am* a guru."

"Well, fuck me gently!"

The Guru laughed. Max asked why he was driving a 40-year-old car.

"Antique cars are my hobby," the Guru replied. "Gurus are allowed to have hobbies. It's right in the handbook. You told me that yourself."

Max recognized that as something he might say: "But there isn't really a handbook, is there? It was my way of telling you not to worry about rules that don't exist."

"Exactly," said the Guru.

"Good for me. Is it a coincidence that this is just like the Copy Editor's car?"

"Nope. You told me about him and his car. That's why I own one like it."

The Guru went silent while he navigated a turn designed for a horse and buggy.

"What's it like, time-jumping?" he asked.

"It's never exactly the same. But in general, it's like driving through fog. Ever driven across the bridge when there's a fog bank sitting exactly halfway across?" Max asked, although scarcely a soul in the city hadn't had the experience. "At first the fog looks like a solid wall. Then, once you're a little inside, you can still see and you wonder if there was ever any fog at all. Then it thickens. But then, by the time you get to the end of the bridge, it's as if the fog bank had never existed."

The Guru drove on, apparently content with silence for a while.

"The thing is," Max said, "it's getting harder to tell what's 'now' and what's time travel. Even clear spots like this eventually become foggy." Max paused. "But just to confirm, the Wife has died, right? She's not just away?"

"Yes, Max. She has. I'm sorry."

"That's okay. I could feel that. I'll find her."

NOW

Girls in Their Summer Clothes

The Guru and Max cruised down Spring Garden Road, discussing what to do next. A young woman in a yellow dress walked into a beam of sunlight. The dress was incandescent, as was the wearer, who suddenly seemed to express all the beauty and possibility of life.

"Lord, she's beautiful," Max said.

The Guru murmured his agreement.

"*The girls in their summer clothes pass me by*," Max said.

"What?"

"*Girls in Their Summer Clothes*. Bruce Springsteen."

With one exception, being passed by was something Max understood well as a young adult.

And he knew blame for this lay at his own feet. Max was an earnest participant when his brothers-in-adolescence theorized about girls, but his heart was elsewhere because their obsession made no sense to him.

Oh, he noticed when girls in his last year of elementary school grew buds on their chests and curves on their hips. Boys and girls alike seemed equally startled by these developments and initially saw them as something that had happened to them collectively. Or so Max thought.

But it wasn't long before his former female playmates became inscrutable. And then his male friends went off in a new direction, with Max struggling to keep up. Their behaviour became as bizarre as the girls', though in a different way. Max's gang, as eight-year-olds, would never consider shooting apples off someone's head with an arrow. At 12, it made perfect sense to everyone except Max.

Then the disease hit Max full on. He went to bed one night still normal and woke up the morning longing beyond all reason for girls. The sight of one girl's damp lips and dark eyes was enough to stop his thought processes cold. Sometimes, when a girl brushed by him in the hall, he could barely remain standing after he caught a whiff of her hair.

Max's confusion was compounded by the arrival of erections, and he was slow to make the connection with his weird new feelings. Neither health class nor the book he found carefully placed on his pillow one night covered the problem effectively. At school, the official diagram of the female reproductive system could just as easily have been the interior of the poor girl's sinuses. The male diagram didn't even hint at erections.

In the eighth grade, Max would squirm during class as he manoeuvred unbidden and unwelcome erections (a.k.a. hard-ons, boners, woodies, throbbers, jackhammers, throbbing jackhammers, trouser snakes, stiffies, chubbies, diamond cutters, *ad infinitum*) until it lay flat, and therefore less visible, against his abdomen. For additional protection, he carried a three-ring binder and a couple of textbooks with him at all times in school. This arrangement could be held over his front at any time, sitting or walking, to hide his swollen "thing". Spontaneous erections weren't something he and his friends talked about (except for updates in terminology), but most of them carried three-ring binders.

Much too late, Max understood that the boners were not always spontaneous. All it took was an accidental flash of thigh from the science teacher or — oh dear lord — cleavage.

Adrift in this hormonal sea, Max could barely keep his head above the surface. Nor did he know with any certainty whether the girls were hip to any of it. At sock hops, they would spend most of the evening dancing with each other in circles to the fast songs while the boys looked on stupidly.

Every now and then a girl, usually someone he had known in elementary school, would ask him to slow-dance. Within seconds of their coming together on the dance floor, despite all the concentration he could muster, Max's thing would expand, like Godzilla rising from the sea to terrorize unsuspecting Japanese. For the sake of decorum, he assumed, the girl would press the beast against herself to hide it, just like his trusty three-ring binder. This was effective camouflage, but just seemed to feed the monster. At the end of the song, Max's only option was to casually thrust both hands into his pockets, creating a protective tent, and skulk back to join the male wallflowers.

Sometimes his dance partner would give him cover by walking with him to the wallflower chairs lining the gymnasium walls. Not a word would be said about the untoward event that had occurred on the dance floor. In Max's mind, he had revealed himself to be a pervert and was being discreetly escorted to the sidelines for the benefit of society. Much later it occurred to him that his dance partners might have known exactly what to expect when slow-dancing with adolescent boys.

The arrival of university women in Max's life confirmed for him that females were a different species entirely. They were terrifying, unlike anything Max could have imagined. To all their other confusing aspects, they now added an entirely new layer of inscrutability. He had no hope of understanding how they felt about him, good or bad. Some seemed to like being near him sometimes, but why? Because they had nothing else to do, or because they liked him?

When a girl he was walking with seized his arm for a second (sending his heart racing), was it because she wanted to be closer to him or was losing her balance? If there were signs to be read, he could not decipher them, a weakness made worse when he liked a girl a lot. He was sitting with a friend in the student union once when the object of his desire walked in on the arm of some idiot who styled himself after Jim Morrison.

"What is she doing with that jerk?" he asked his friend.

"Maybe she got tired of waiting for you to do something," was the reply.

At that moment, Max foresaw a long, perhaps indefinite, period of sexual purgatory ahead of him.

At the same time, he found himself drawn to the campus newspaper.

"Aha," said the Guru. "Finding yourself outside the tent, you elected to join a group of budding journalists, a group dedicated to assailing those inside the tent."

Max believed he had been lost in thought. Now it seemed he had been speaking his thoughts to the Guru.

"You're suggesting life is better lived inside a tent?" Max asked.

The Guru mulled it over.

"No. I guess not. On the contrary. Point taken."

1985

CFA Shows Flair for Halifax Real Estate

***A Montreal firm** is showing a flair for real estate in Halifax.*

Golden Cat Real Estate bought 17 properties in the last 18 months, sold half of them at a profit and financed apartment complex proposals with the proceeds.

But some Halifax councillors say the project violates community values and will oppose it even though it meets planning bylaws.

The feisty owner of Golden Cat, a national company, says she is undeterred by the opposition ...

"Hey Maxie, did you see this real estate story this morning?"

The Wife is eating breakfast while reading the Paper. Max is standing by the toaster with bated breath.

"I don't read advertorials," he says.

"And yet you knew it was an advertorial ... you don't recognize the Montreal woman's name?"

Max marshals his thoughts. Marriage has not diminished the Wife's power to tie his tongue in knots.

She smiles at him like an angler, waiting for him to tire himself out and be reeled in.

"It's funny you don't remember. She was arrested in Montreal for arranging sex parties in private houses. Maybe you were dodging Latin American bullets back then. Or maybe you knew her by her professional name — Goldpussy."

The Wife raises her head from the Paper and looks expectantly at him. She's wearing a peach silk blouse and a muted grey skirt suit. Max likes the way her legs look in high heels even while wondering how she can walk in them. A silver pendant glitters in the hollow of her throat. She is dressed like the consummate PR pro she has become. She exudes self-possession and competence. Moreover, her decision to abandon print reporter fashions has made her first impressions "easy on the eyes" as they say. Max figures he's lucky to have married her before the competition realized what a catch she was.

"Hmm. Goldpussy you say? Could be," says Max. "So, you say she was acquitted?"

"By golly she was. But I didn't say that. You did. Maxie ... do you know Goldpussy or not?"

Max raises his eyebrows, expels a breath and shrugs, as if to say that no one really knows.

"Well, yes and no," he says.

"How is that possible?"

"Well, 'yes' in the sense that I know her, and 'no' in the sense that I didn't know you ever heard of her."

The Wife flushes and her voice lacks its usual certainty.

"So, in all our time together, it never occurred to you mention that you have a friend who is a prostitute?"

"Prostitute? She's not a prostitute. She was a stripper, that's all." Max is horrified. He feels like he's in free-fall. "She's one of the nicest women I've ever known. She's my friend."

"She could still be a prostitute. It fits with lining up girls for the sex parties."

"That was never proven."

"Maxie, did you have sex with her? And, if you place any value at all on your marriage, don't say 'yes and no'."

"Once. Well, one night." Don't say it, he begs himself. Stop now. "Well — full disclosure — four times but ... one night."

She flies out of her chair, red-faced. "FOUR TIMES!"

Max briefly thinks he can control things by warning her that the Son could overhear, but the boy's at camp.

"FOUR TIMES! You've never done it with me four times in a row, but with some tramp — no problem."

"No-no-no-no," Max says. "I didn't even know you then and she wasn't a tramp. And even if she was, or is, she's still my friend."

"Four times? I worked hard to get you, to make sure you were the right one. Now I feel so cheap."

"She was my first time," he says. "I had lots of pent up ... energy. If it had been you, it would have been six times." He pauses: "You worked hard to get me?"

"You were my first time, Max."

"But ..."

"Yes, I know, I seduced you. It's the only way to get your attention sometimes."

"No," says Max. "It's the other way around. I seduced you."

"Oh, puhlease. How many guys with staples in their shirt-cuffs can seduce *anybody*?"

Max doesn't say it, but it occurs to him that his stapled cuffs have a pretty good track record.

Max makes a quick trip to the old lecture theatre of the mind. His unusually rapt audience clearly sides with the Wife. But an embarrassed young female student walks to the dais and silently passes him a note. Max reads it. Eureka!

"Okay," he tells the Wife. "But our count is five. We did it three times, plus that other thing you did — twice — so that's five. You're the world record holder."

"You should have been a lawyer, Maxie. You certainly know how to miss a point."

Max's special male instinct tells him that raising the Wife's count to five isn't having the desired effect. He tries another tack.

"If it was your first time? How ... ?"

"Research and planning," she says. "You may not have noticed, but it's not terribly difficult to seduce a man in his twenties. Any woman with a temperature above freezing can do it."

Now Max understands why the Copy Editor inexplicably left them alone in the bar on that momentous night.

"You set it up? You got him to leave?"

"Yes. I asked him to leave us alone if the second button on my blouse mysteriously came undone. He was more than happy to help."

The Wife looks nothing like the girl who seduced him that night. The reporter clothes — shapeless jean skirt, white blouse — are gone. Her eyes, which he once idiotically complimented as "probing", are in fact warm and inviting. She's blessed with what Max's grandmother called an "old soul".

"Nobody seduced anybody that night, Cactus," he says. "A smart, beautiful woman with a generous heart got my attention long enough for me to realize that I had been in love with her for months and always would be. It was the most important and unforgettable night of my life."

The Wife leans over and kisses him. Max is surprised to notice some dampness near her cheekbone. She smiles, blinking a little.

"Now you're talking, Maxie," she says.

1988

Bingo!

Max can't wait for the Paper to move to its new building. He is sitting in the same windowless room where he first met the Cobra, who is at this moment using the same jumped-up closet as a washroom. The drywall remains unfinished. The toilet is still flushing when he emerges.

"You said you wouldn't run the story about the bingo fraud," he says to Max on the way to his desk.

"No. I said I would think about it," Max says. "Like you, when I say I will think about something, I mean I will do what I want."

"Well, the Archbishop is pissed," the Cobra says.

"No problem. I've been condemned to Hell since the day I was born a Protestant."

"His Excellency says your coverage is irresponsible."

"I have the right and a duty to be irresponsible."

"He said to remind you that he sits on the board of the university."

"So what?"

"That's where your wife works, right? How would you like to be a one-income family?"

The Cobra coils into his chair and turns his attention to a specially-marked file from the Paper's accounting department. He holds up an invoice from the Lawyer with the bottom line highlighted. Max can see that the number is north of $10,000.

"I guess you also said you'd think about not opposing publication bans," he says.

"Yep."

The Cobra believes sending a lawyer to oppose a judge's publication ban is "interfering with due process."

The previous month the Paper's lawyer had to appear three times to lift a ban on the name of a city councillor charged with drunk driving.

"It cost us $12,000 and look what you've done to the man's reputation," the Cobra says. "He hasn't even been convicted yet and you're smearing his name. You don't see the Other Paper doing that."

"No, you don't," Max says.

"It's expensive and the Courts don't like it," The Cobra says. "It's not the way we do things in Nova Scotia."

• • •

Max is not worried about the legal bill because the Owner supports him on that issue, but he is concerned about the threat to the Wife's job. It would be easy to make that happen if his Excellency could find the right excuse.

He cuts through the composing room on the way to his office. The Collective, as usual, stare at him resentfully. Time does not heal all wounds, Max thinks. It's been seven years since he wrested away their God-given right to decide the content of the Paper.

The newsroom, now organized by newspaper section, finally has the quality Max wants most: intent. The people in the room know why they are there. Even the Sports department, a mulish group in a mini-wing set 90 degrees to the rest of the newsroom and ankle deep in fried food containers, is as good as he has a right to expect. Far better than the one across the harbour at the Other Paper.

Who was the opposing team when Jean Beliveau scored his last regular season goal? The Sports department knows. (The Rangers, of course.) In 1960, Mickey Mantle batted .400 in the World Series final. Who was the opposition? Sports has the answer. (The Pirates, of course.)

Who's hockey's brightest prospect? Why, it's this hardworking young guy born right here in Halifax.

The latest market study suggests the Paper is regarded as both credible and irresponsible. Or, as the marketing expert put it, people believe what they read but many think it never should have been written. At the meeting where the results were presented, Max did his best to appear disturbed by the news.

Two of the reasons for this seeming contradiction — "unprecedented" the marketing guy said — are within shouting distance of where Max stands. The City Editor, today wearing the mid-thigh black dress with a plunging neckline and Goth eyeliner, has a knack for hitting every hot-button in the region. So much so that Max sometimes wonders if there might truly be 14 easily-offended families running the province, primed to fulminate with every edition of the Paper.

Then there is the Cartoonist, who could pass for the lovechild of Jack the Ripper and Shirley Temple. A stocky guy with blond hair flowing to his shoulders, he lurks a few yards away, waiting for an opening. He wears the expression of the perpetually falsely accused; layered upon that is an expression of saintly forbearance for his accusers.

The Cartoonist is brandishing a fresh drawing. Max steels himself. He likes the Cartoonist and his work, which is brilliant and routinely provokes outrage — the kind of outrage that sells newspapers. The cartoons are well-drawn and clever. But Max knows that the greatest single threat to his employment is a single pen-stroke from the man with the hot stare walking toward him.

"Just wanted you to see this," he says, handing his work to Max as he pirouettes smartly and starts on the way back to his lair. Max recognizes the warning sign. The only reason for a cartoonist to leave before receiving the praise he so deeply needs but so routinely disdains is that he has drawn something he doesn't want Max to notice. It's also why the approval process is taking place in the middle of the newsroom: no editor wants to appear chicken in front of his staff.

Max does a pantomime of a cowboy roping a steer, dragging the Cartoonist back into the conversation. The energy of the room changes as reporters and editors quietly tune into the action.

"Let's see what we've got here," Max says.

It's a drawing of the Speaker of the House, routine except that he's not wearing anything except black knee socks and garters. Mercifully, his back is turned, although his buttocks look like two sacks of potatoes.

Max is okay with it, but a small voice in his head tells him to keep looking.

"You see?" says the Cartoonist. "It's The Emperor's New Clothes."

This is meant to distract Max's attention from the drawing.

Finally, Max sees it: an almost imperceptible pointy object dangling between the great man's thighs. Imperceptible, that is, to everyone except the Cartoonist's detail-oriented fans and rabid critics.

"What's this?" Max asks.

The Cartoonist peers at the drawing, clearly intrigued. "Well, it could be a smudge or a stray mark."

"Hmm, it could be," Max says. "But what is it actually?"

"Well, some people might think it's a penis."

They go back and forth like this until the Cartoonist admits that the object could be seen as a penis because he drew it that way.

Max admires him for having the gall to try something like that, but mostly he is angry. Max feels his face turn red.

The cartoonist notices: "It's just a small one. If it's about the size, I can ..."

Max cuts him off.

"Kindly erase buddy's organ and bring the drawing back to me for approval."

The Cartoonist looks stricken, a sincere working artist cut down by "the Establishment" in front of his colleagues.

"You know," he says sadly. "It's not my job to self-censor. It's my job to draw cartoons as I see fit and your job to spike them if you see something you feel is inappropriate."

Max doesn't disagree, but he's acutely aware of his audience, which now includes everyone present. Most are still green and need to know where the line is and not to cross it.

A macho declaration, he decides, is best for all, including the Cartoonist, who will soon be retelling the story of how he got Max to lose his cool.

"Well, take note, because this is an example of inappropriate," he says with all the menace he can muster. "And if you're so interested in dicks, I'll arrange things so you can use yours as an eraser."

Not exactly out of the *Modern Leader's Handbook*.

The eavesdroppers snicker. The City Editor wonders aloud if such a thing is possible.

"Eraser? How would that work?" She shouts at the retreating Cartoonist: "Oh, wait ... are you circumcised?"

The Entertainment Editor is waiting for him in his office. It seems HR wants to dock her new writer two weeks' pay on the grounds that he wasn't in the newsroom.

"You mean that prematurely bald guy? His father was sick in Vancouver?"

"Yeah. His father died," she says, near tears. "He's flat broke."

"But you and I decided we'd keep it off the books," Max reminds her.

The Entertainment Editor, it seems, is worldly in the ways of the arts, but not bureaucracy.

"Right. And that's what I told HR," she says.

"No problem," says Max. "But 'off the books' means we don't tell HR. We just unofficially let him work overtime to even things out."

The Entertainment Editor flushes and covers her face.

"I'm so stupid," she says, her voice muffled by her hands. She offers to let Max deduct the money from her salary, which isn't much better than the writer's.

"First," he says, "we don't hire stupid people here. So, you're not stupid. On the contrary, I would say. Second, your offer is very kind, but unnecessary. Just tell HR I said that I will look after it."

"You're going to pay for it yourself?" she asks.

"Good God no!" he says with theatrical emphasis.

"So, what will you do?"

"Nothing," Max says, smiling at her.

"Won't they bother you about it?"

"Maybe, but eventually they'll drop the issue. The longer I stall, the harder it is for them to explain themselves to Accounting. In the end, they'll decide it's better just to forget about it. Now, go in peace."

"Thanks. I feel smarter already," she says on the way out.

And so does Max, who is starting to feel like an old hand, and likes it. He is also fond of almost everybody on his staff. They are smart, funny and surprisingly kind for a group that works in a newsroom.

May I always love this job and may it always love me, he thinks.

1973

Smoked Meat Provokes Wild Encounter

The new lovers have spotted Max's roommate eating smoked meat at Schwartz's and have decided to go directly to his apartment on l'Esplanade because it's one place they can think of where they haven't "done it" yet and they know it must be empty. Turned on by the risk of the Roommate returning early, they've left Max's bedroom door open to heighten the excitement, stripped naked facing each other, and hopped onto his bed.

She's a busy love-maker, but Max doesn't really notice her attentions because he's been greedily consuming her. Smelling her shiny brown hair, tasting her mouth, feeling her skin against his cheek, teasing and tasting her nipples; simultaneously tasting and feeling and sniffing her long back. Max inspects the dimples above her buttocks, first with his eyes and then with his tongue. She giggles. He flips her over and, for the first time, considers a new frontier. He rests his chin on her *mons* for a moment, looking up the length of her torso and between her adorable breasts to see if his intentions are understood and accepted.

She raises her head: "Yes, Captain," she says. "You may boldly go where — incidentally — no man has gone before."

"Stand by, Ensign," he replies. "... engaging ... ." The starship shudders a little.

Some time later she draws him northward. Now, at last, he is poised above her, feeling her heat. His crazed erection beats time to an insane pulse. Her hand, surprisingly cool, takes control.

"Captain," she says. "We've landed on an Earth-like planet. I can feel a large, smooth cactus ... should I take it aboard? ..."

"A cactus. A *large* one, you say?"

"Oh, VERY large, Captain."

Max's voice is husky: "Very well then, Ensign ... proceed to bring the cactus aboard the ... ahh ... main cargo bay."

He yields to her firm pull. Her affection for him, so obvious when they entered the room, is supplanted by the look of a woman who has gone feral. Max is not far behind.

When they return to their senses, she rolls Max onto his back, and stretches out beside him.

Deadpan: "Max, I worry that you're repulsed by my body."

"I can adapt," he says.

He clears his throat.

"Max, don't say it," she says.

"Don't say what?"

"You know what."

"Don't say it ever?"

"Don't say it now."

Max obeys, silently and once again pondering the inscrutability of human females.

Without ceremony, she compresses the entirety of his precious male equipment in one hand and squeezes, more or less gently.

"Here are my terms," she says, her breath caressing his ear. "From here on in, you are mine. For greater certainty, this includes — but is not restricted to — what I am holding in my hand. Do you understand what I am saying and all that it implies?"

"Is this a relationship conversation?" he says lightly.

She squeezes harder. "Careful, Max. I want you, but I'm willing to let you go."

"I accept your terms. And all that they imply." Max pulls the blankets over them. "Now can I say it?"

"Later."

She settles her head on his chest and says "hmmm".

Max is alarmed and confused to hear his own voice in his head. He has the spooky notion the voice is speaking from another time.

"*Here. Let us stay here together*," the voice says.

But the weird sensation is short-lived. The football game, the open door, the smell of her, the feel of her and feel of his heart opened wide are escaping him. The more he wants to hang on to it all, the faster it disappears.

1981

Wife to Max: Don't Hurt My Baby

The Night News Editor at the Montreal Daily lights yet another noxious Gauloise and immediately jams it into his heaping ashtray, where it will smoulder for the rest of its foul life. The fan from his computer blows the manure-scented smoke into Max's face. The Night News Editor is the only person under 35 Max has ever met who could be described as ruddy. He scrolls through stories on the computer screen while he talks on the phone with the Managing Editor, nicknamed Pickup, who likes to be safe at home before any critical decisions are made, but never fails to call in before the night crew really gets going.

The Night News Editor has the demeanour of a Clint Eastwood character and a weird ability to track everyone in the newsroom without shifting his gaze from his computer screen. Thus you always have the sense he is looking at you, but you can never be sure.

This time, however, Max's reporter instinct tells him he is definitely the topic of conversation.

"He did?" the Night News Editor asks, with a level grin simultaneously conveying satisfaction and bloodlust. "Fuck me ... Jesus fucking Christ ... the cocksucker ... God, what an asshole."

The last epithet is the kiss of death in journalism. Max isn't sure how he earned it, but suspects he hasn't done enough to hide his disdain for his job as night police reporter after toiling in Latin American shitholes.

But the newsroom consensus was that the Montreal Daily never needed a Latin America correspondent and that Max should be happy just to have a job after the shocking round of layoffs endured back home. This despite Max's world-beating story on the counter-coup, which prompted the Montreal Daily to hire him in the first place, promote him, and then bring him back to Montreal to chase police cars, all in the space of a couple of years.

"Okay. Yeah. I'll tell him. Count on it," the Night News Editor says.

"Hey, Max," he says without, of course, turning his head. "You know the Owner and Publisher?"

"Yep. They're actually the same guy."

"Well, if I said the Owner and Publisher of this piece-of-shit newspaper has left a note for you in Pickup's mailbox, what would you do?"

"Ask you if the Managing Editor was supposed to have given it to me personally?"

"Correct."

"But Pickup didn't want to be around when I read it?"

"Correct."

"Pickup" is the name the Managing Editor earned during his glory days as the paper's Washington correspondent. He was so named by the very same Night News Editor, who at the time ran the foreign desk. Pickup was unloved for the way he handled all the major U.S. stories. He would phone in two or three ambiguous paragraphs to the foreign desk and then say "pick up the rest from the wires." This meant pawing through reams of wire stories printed on brown paper, gluing the best stuff together and sometimes rewriting around Pickup's lead before sticking it — and his byline — on the top. In time, the Owner realized that Pickup had lost the respect of his peers. He therefore brought him back to Montreal and promoted him.

"Correct," says the Night News Editor. "He's a Type B Asshole — doesn't want to be near the debris field before or after an explosion."

"Got it," Max says.

"Yeah ... Jesus Christ ... cocksucker."

As he leaves to retrieve the note, Max hears the Night News Editor say: "Max fucked up the Form Reduction Committee."

"How is that possible?" someone asks.

When Max returns, sealed envelope in hand, the half-dozen people around the desk have tears in their eyes from laughing. The Photo Editor is making a big display of rolling on the floor in mirth, supposedly unable to crawl back into his chair.

The Wire Editor walks over to the coat hook and performs the ritual pantomime of retrieving the newsroom's mythical set of invisible kneepads. "You'll need these for the meeting tomorrow, Max. The Owner's a delayed ejaculator. And don't forget to shave tomorrow ..."

Har-har.

"Yeah," says the Night News Editor, joining in the routine. "He hates getting beard-burn on his thighs."

Guffaws all around before everyone settles back into editing the night's copy.

"Hey Max," the Photo Editor says. "Somewhere in the distance, a dog is barking."

It's a reference to a favourite cliché of novelists and overreaching foreign correspondents, and sets off another round of guffaws.

"Ask not for whom the dog barks, Max, it barks for you." Apparently, this is even funnier.

Max opens the memo. He can tell from the pointedly restrained tone that it means real trouble:

> *Max,*
>
> *I'm disappointed by reports I've heard concerning your contribution to the Form Reduction Committee. Doubly disappointed because I thought you alone among the failed poets and fly-by-nights I employ understood that this company is a team.*

There are no fucking teams, Max thinks. Only gangs.

> *In addition to reporters, photographers and editors, newspapers also comprise proofreaders, compositors, advertising production people, ad salesmen, secretaries, executives, printers, truck drivers and delivery boys. It's really quite a long list.*
>
> *I thought you knew and appreciated that, and so I requested your participation on the interdepartmental team tackling the proliferation of forms — all 102 of them — in this company. We are buried in paper, like autumn leaves. I also believed this would forge a badly needed spirit of co-operation in our company.*

The Montreal mob co-operates brilliantly.

I am now informed that, after two meetings, during which you were quite voluble, the committee unanimously recommended the creation of a new form, the 'Form Reduction Form.' I'm sad to say that I was not aware of this development until 1,000 copies of the Form Reduction Form had been printed. And so, we now have 103 forms to contend with and a demoralized Form Reduction Committee.

I strongly suspect this is your handiwork, Max. It's the kind of lampooning of process that your father liked. However, I recall that he also delivered the goods as a reporter.

This is a serious matter, Max. I look forward, albeit pessimistically, to your denial.

Max is guilty as charged, but he's enraged by the reference to his father.

Below the Owner's typed message is a space reserved for replying. He gets to work with a ballpoint pen:

1) *How can we track the forms we eliminate without a form for that?*
2) *For the record, I produced more than 1500 stories for you as a correspondent often while covering my own expenses.*
3) *As a reluctant police reporter, I have produced several hundred more.*
4) *The only thing my father ever did was make the alkies laugh in the tavern across the street—during working hours—and drink himself into second childhood.*

• • •

Max and the Wife have managed to get the Son to sleep after a day of teething pain. Now, Max thinks, the boy's growing brain will process the experience and add it to the expanding list of painful mysteries that will someday constitute adulthood.

The family's "four and a half" room apartment is dim because its windows face the building's other wing, 25 feet away. Everyone's windows are open, allowing all to share their sounds and smells. Max notes that the Screamer and her dogged husband are at it early. "Whoa-OH-ho!" she moans. "Whoa-OH-ho! Whoa-OH-ho!" It's as regular and rhythmic as a handsaw cutting a two-by-four.

Max fishes his stopwatch from the kitchen junk drawer. He starts it, and saunters into the living room. The Wife puts down her newspaper and spots the stopwatch.

"Do you think they'll break the record tonight?"

"Don't know," says Max. "The heat has to tire them out. On the other hand, this could be their biggest audience of the summer. They'll want to make the best of it."

"Listen to her," the Wife says. "Is he screwing her or sawing her in half?"

The Wife points out that the copulators, like the other neighbours, have been listening to the Son cry for the past three hours: "You'd think it would illustrate to her the advantage of blow jobs," she says brightly.

On hearing the phrase "blow-job" Max perks up like a retriever hearing a gunshot. But the Wife just rolls her eyes at him and shakes her head.

Max has learned lately that women have to *feel* sexy before they'll do sexy things. The Wife loves her baby fiercely, but believes the pregnancy made her fat and unsexy.

Max disagrees. He's not even sure she's heavier now than she was before the baby — her actual weight appears to be a national security issue — but if she has gained, it's in all the right places.

She's let her light brown hair grow into loose curls. Her face is still well-defined. Her limbs are shapely. And, if anything, pregnancy has made her breasts even more enticing. For Max, this makes her "earth-mother-sexy". He tells her this often, but she doesn't buy it.

"I don't sit down to read anymore," she likes to say. "I just pick a landing spot for my drooping butt and drop. The rest of me arrives a few moments later to form a fatty cone with my head on top."

"Whoa-OH-ho! Whoa-OH-ho!" They both roll their eyes.

Alas, with early morning oral sex out of the question, Max concludes he might as well tell her about the memo from the Owner. He hands the Wife his copy of it. He is shocked to see her expression change from exhaustion to alarm.

"Max. This reply, did you send what you wrote to the Owner?"

He asks whether something is wrong with that.

"He's going to fire you," she says quietly.

"Why would he do that?"

"Because you're being a prick."

"That's crazy!"

"He's laid off 30 people but found a way to keep you, and this is how repay him?"

Max is exasperated. "Fuck! I was all over Latin America for him."

Now the Wife stands up. "Yeah, and I was alone here,

except for two visits to your bureau where, incidentally, you got me pregnant. And that was *after* you had six months as a freelance getting the correspondent thing out of your system — supposedly, that is."

"But it was a full-time job. You could have moved in with me."

"Then I would have been alone in a foreign country while you camped out with guerrillas," she says, angry now. "You were going to have to choose between your family and the bureau anyway. Luckily, the decision was made for us."

Max groans: "But I wound up as the night cop reporter."

"And your salary is the same as the Washington bureau chief's. How many cop reporters make that kind of money?"

"It's not about the money."

"Okay. What, then?"

"I dunno. It's just not enough," Max says.

"You're ready to throw your job overboard, but you don't know why."

Max knows where the Wife is going with this. He sees himself in the 19th-century lecture theatre, laid out on a slab in the cool air. The Wife — not Max — is giving the lecture.

"And so, I submit to you that there is an *overarching* problem here," she says, gesturing to Max. "This specimen is becoming an idiot."

The white-coated crowd is silent for a moment before breaking into furious applause. 'Eureka!' they shout, over and over.

"Max, you're turning into an asshole right before my eyes," she says.

If the Wife had accused him of having leprosy he would have been no less astonished. "Me? *I'm* not an asshole!"

She patiently explains that she agrees, but only because she is in love with him. Others merely have his words and actions by which to judge him. These, she says, have been tending toward "assholish" for some time now.

They hear the Son fussing and stop talking.

Suddenly the Wife is on him with "Spousal Warning Expression No. 11," known to the lay community as "you broke it, you fix it." It's impressive, but by no means the only arrow in her quiver. She wants to know if Max understands that her part-time salary at the Sunday Tabloid obviously cannot support the three of them.

"You know why I don't mind being fat?" she says, her voice low and even.

"You're not ..."

"Be quiet. I don't mind being fat because life is simple for me. Life is simple because only one thing — one thing — matters. And that is the well-being of our little boy. God help anybody — ANYBODY — who gets between me and his well-being."

"I know that."

"So get down there and fix this."

Max tells her "no problem" and stands at the open door, waiting for the ritual goodbye kiss.

It is not forthcoming.

From the apartment hallway, he hears a faint "Whoa-OH-oh! Whoa-OH-oh!"

• • •

Ten steps into Montreal Daily's newsroom, Max reads the signs and concludes the situation is already out of control.

The atmosphere is just not right. And there's more to it than the presence of a few straggling dayside reporters, most of whom are usually gone before Max arrives.

The Night News Editor raises his head from his computer terminal and looks Max directly in the eye. "It's bad, Max."

Oops. Fight-or-flight time, he thinks.

"Bad for who?"

"You."

"How bad?"

"Look," says the Night News Editor, "Pickup didn't even stay for the news meeting. He took off early, doing his busy-walk."

The busy-walk is famous in the newsroom, which likens it to someone whose buttocks have been sutured together.

"But I caught up with him at the elevators and he spilled right away," the Night News Editor says. "There's a memo in your mail slot. Pickup says you're fired."

"All this because of the Form Reduction Form?"

The Night News Editor looks around and then motions Max to join him in the Cage, Max's current work-station. It's a tobacco-stained, glass-walled room featuring half a dozen squawking police radio scanners and the lingering body odour of countless crime reporters. All "real" reporters have done stints in the Cage. Some, like budgies, won't come out even when you open the door and offer a better job on the outside.

The two of them settle in, taking a moment to savour the atmosphere.

"Actually," says the Night News Editor, "The Owner thinks your stunt was mildly funny—turns out he doesn't like the guy who started the committee, some idiot in Marketing. Pickup now agrees with him, of course."

"We have a marketing department?"

"Yeah. You should know stuff like that, Max."

Max asks if his recently-cited assholish behaviour is a factor behind his firing.

"You've been a borderline asshole, but you worked hard as a correspondent and filed real stories. And you still work hard. Everyone gives you points for that."

Max looks out at the newsroom, the biggest he's ever worked in. Now, contemplating unemployment, he's already missing the Cage, the piles of newspapers and clippings spilling from every desk, the ceiling tiles yellowed from cigarette smoke and, even, "Redundancy Row", the offices of the senior editors. Hell, he misses the legendary kneepads, and wonders if it would help if he strapped them on.

"So why?" he asks.

The Night News Editor looks around nervously. "The union. The union fired you."

"Fuck those Marxist dicks," Max says.

"Yeah, I know," the Night News Editor says by way of agreement. "They're pissed about the shipping reporter thing."

"Come on, everyone knows that cocksucker richly deserved it. A guy gets shot right in front of him and he does fuck-all because it's not about *ships*."

Max remembers the incident well because he was the union's shop steward at the time, a position to which he was elected *in absentia*. When Pickup presented him with formal notice that the shipping reporter was being dismissed, Max congratulated him on the decision and neglected to pass the paperwork on to the union. The dismissal sailed through the personnel department unopposed.

And when the shipping reporter got his walking papers, he was too indifferent to bother telling the union and just walked out, waving his middle finger high above his head.

Max thought the whole thing had gone rather well, but now he's hearing differently.

"The union went berserk," the Night News Editor says. "They felt you made them look bad."

"But I swear I heard applause when that moron walked out."

"Yeah, but you violated the union code: 'Leave no lazy asshole without a job.'"

"But now *I* don't have a job," Max points out. "And *I'm* in the union.

"They feel you have to go for the benefit of the collective interest."

"Of course, the greater good. Never to be confused with revenge."

Max is about to argue that unions can't fire people when the penny drops for him.

"You got it," the Night News Editor says, seeing the look on his face. "They told the Owner that if you didn't go, the new contract would be hell to negotiate."

"How do you know this?"

The Night News Editor shakes his head sadly. "Max, stay on top of things. I'm on the union bargaining committee. I'm learning how these guys think for when I'm in management, which won't be long because I'm getting to know the Owner pretty well from the committee-work."

"Jesus H mahogany comical creeping Christ on a bicycle," Max says slowly.

"I know," says the Night News Editor. "Don't rely on performance to get ahead, if that's what you want. Those kneepads are there for a reason. Alternatively, you could get onside with the union. They know they could use you."

But Max does not like people in groups larger than three.

Max hustles over to the mail slots. As he scans the memo, he recalls a mentor telling him about the "Southern Preacher" method of obtaining converts. First you take the heathen to the edge of the abyss and let him have a good long look. Then, and only then, do you show him the path to salvation.

Thus the Owner uses the first five graphs to explain why Max must go, ending with "there is simply no role for you in Montreal." The abyss.

But — oh thank you Jesus — the last graph says: "Through misadventure, I own a somewhat unusual paper in Halifax. They need an editor-in-chief and they'll accept you on my recommendation. My advice is to take the opportunity."

• • •

The Wife is still awake at 2:30 a.m. when Max returns home. He slides into bed and tells her the news while staring at the ceiling. It turns out the Wife's family used to vacation in Nova Scotia.

"Halifax is not bad," she says. "To tell the truth, I'd rather raise a child there than Montreal. Everything on Montreal island is either asphalt or lawn fertilizer." She turns on her side and nuzzles him, sliding a bare thigh upwards over his own. "You know, I could show the Screamer how *real* women make noise ..."

But Max, to his own disbelief, is not ready to engage. He's begun making a mental list of where else he could find a job in Montreal, especially with the Quebec sovereignty referendum coming up. No good Quebecois would miss that, regardless of how they intend to vote. With a little work on his written French, he might even get a job at one of the French-language dailies. *Le Devoir* might like an *anglais* like him as a columnist.

"You know, there may be other options."

The Wife rolls over on her back again and sighs. Max feels his skin cooling where her face and leg have been.

"I don't even want to hear about them," she says.

"Thank you for your support."

"Look, if it had been up to me, I would have fired you. Your behaviour shows zero promise. Instead, these guys are giving you a chance to keep your credibility. Don't reward them by turning your back."

"You think I failed?" he asks.

"Ever had a pet goat?"

"Lemme think," he says. "No."

"Well I did, briefly. He liked to push up against people with his head, so I would push back. He just loved that. There's a picture of me leaning into his head at a 45-degree angle. The goat was never happier. Some people, usually potential boyfriends, pushed back too hard, trying to beat the goat. The goat would fake a retreat and then butt the guy a couple of feet in the air. My dad loved it; he said it eliminated stupid genes from his daughter's dating pool."

So, I'm a goat, Max thinks. Not bull, or stallion or even a gazelle. A goat.

"How come I never got the goat test?"

"I was worried for my goat."

"So, I failed here, you're saying."

"No, I'm saying you're not happy unless you're butting up against something," she replies. "So now, you'll be running the number-two paper in Halifax and you can push against the number one and anything else that catches your attention. We both know you haven't done much since you got back to Montreal. And here's something else: you've been making all the big decisions since we got married. Well, it's my turn to make a call, and I'm saying Halifax."

Max knows the argument is over and he doesn't mind losing it because she's right. Their choices have been mostly about Max, at least until the Son arrived.

The Wife seals the deal by slipping off her nightshirt and focusing what he sometimes calls her "Gypsy" eyes on his. She smiles seductively and rolls back onto him: "Come on, Maxie, be my goat-man and take us to Halifax."

Perhaps it is the sight of unbridled breasts, but Max feels better.

He responds with his Groucho Marx impression: "You know, my dear, you're smarter than I look."

The Wife gently bites the magic earlobe. "Whoa-OH-ho," she whispers.

1975

Trout for Breakfast

The Wife is not here, Max realizes, just before the time-jump takes full control of his consciousness.

He looks up to get his bearings and is surprised to see the Photog snoozing beside him. The two have been asleep on a wooden bench thanks to a train ticket funded by the Bureau Chief. He and the Photog are on the road to journalistic glory, via the Mountain Express.

Although the symptoms of being clubbed and gassed persist, Max believes the experience has made him a seasoned journalist, a truth-seeker to be reckoned with, one who doesn't make amateur mistakes. His inner editor, however, begs to differ, noting acidly that he still hasn't bothered to learn the "political background" the Bureau Chief mentioned. Of course, that would have included asking why the demonstrators went to the plaza in the first place, something Max didn't really care about at the time.

Now, in the third-class coach on the Mountain Express, which features slatted wood benches, caged chickens and short women wearing bowler hats and layers of clothes that make them egg-shaped, he sees some possible "background" rolling by outside.

It's an outlaw settlement known as Pueblo Jovén, inhabited mostly by the same mountain folk sharing the train car with Max and the Photog. It appears to be built entirely of refuse and sits on smooth ochre-coloured terrain that Max and his high-school golf buddies called "hardpan".

Hardpan shows up toward the end of dry summers in spots the groundskeepers can't be bothered to water. Woe to any golf ball that lands on hardpan. There's a thin layer of dust — just enough to stop the ball from rolling onto the grass — and beneath it earth packed hard by rain-bursts and broiling sun. You have to pick the ball clean in that situation, of course, but that means no backspin, making it hard to hold the green.

But you don't have to be a sociologist, Max thinks, to know that the minds of the squatters of Pueblo Jovén are untroubled by rogue chip shots. Top of mind, after finding something to eat, would be keeping their fragile little houses from falling apart in the next rain or big wind.

Max can see open sewers that have carved their way deep into the hardpan. Packs of mongrels root for something to eat between bouts of humping. Max has met these beasts close up in other parts of his Latin American tour. They are absolutely unconcerned by humans and, unlike normal dogs, will look you straight in the eye if you get too close. They're like the scrawny little men who drink in urine-scented bars. They are no problem as long as you don't violate their secret code of conduct; if you do, they'll come flying at you like a tornado.

Max studies the houses. The sturdiest were built first, near the train tracks, and doggedly upgraded over the years. Some feature roofs of corrugated steel or fibreglass, and sometimes even glazed windows. Some, outrageously, have electricity running from the poles that run alongside the tracks. Do squatter electricians wait for an outage before connecting, Max wonders, or have they learned to handle live wires without being killed?

But the more he sees, the more he thinks the answer is ingenuity. These are — supposedly — 200,000 people somehow getting by without running water or sewage.

Yet, Max sees signs of order in Pueblo Jovén. Some streets and blocks have self-organized. Every now and then Max spots a group of school-kids wearing spotless white shirts and carrying ragged book-bags; or a man wearing the trademark black vest of a waiter. There are *bodegas*, and water tanks pulled by mules.

It is here in his stream of consciousness that Max understands what a jerk he is, riding through the worst slum he has ever seen, thinking about making chip-shots off hardpan.

The Photog is sleeping, hat over his eyes. Max grabs him by the knee: "Hey, you've got to see this."

"I have seen Pueblo Jovén many times, my friend," he says, without looking up. "They have no business here. They do not pay taxes. They live on land they do not own."

"They should go back to the mountains?"

"You think they are better off here?" he says sourly.

"I'm not sure, but obviously they think so."

The exchange ends right there. No debate, no banter.

The Photog should be in a better mood after their triumph on the plaza. He even sold two pictures to the Bureau Chief.

The train lurches and rolls on for another 30 minutes

before it leaves Pueblo Jovén behind. The last of it that Max sees is a tall man wearing a chef's hat. He gives Max the one-finger salute. Not to the train in general, but to him. Max is sure of that.

Thereafter, Max is conscious only of dust. Red dust rises from the floor of the car. Dust sparkles in the sunlight, sticks to his skin and invades his sinuses. Even when the train arrives in the mountains, 12,000 feet above the desert, Max is still in pain from the dust.

"Oh, it's not dust," the Photog says. "It is *la sorroche* — altitude sickness. It is like divers getting the bends — the drop in pressure causes gasses dissolved in your blood to vaporize. Not everyone gets it, but it can be very painful." A more detailed, mildly patronizing lecture on the topic followed.

Heavy clanking and banging jars Max from his uncomfortable snooze. The train is grinding its way up a hillside using switchbacks. The racket comes from the process of changing direction at the end of each cut. Max could taste "dust" all the way from his nose and tongue to his intestines. He feels grit in his teeth and between his toes.

He can see that a few of the locals are faring just as badly. Some are bent over, massaging their foreheads. A city-type suddenly stands and lunges up the sloping aisle, but vomits before he can make it to the washroom, which has a long line of people outside waiting their turn to use the reeking toilet. The odour of fresh vomit starts a slow chain reaction running through the miserable queue.

Max hangs on to his stomach contents with everything he has.

"That is most unusual. Maybe once I have seen this before," the Photog says, surveying the commotion as if he has just discovered a rare butterfly. "Far more common, as you may also have noticed, is the effect of the low air pressure on the intestines of our fellow passengers."

No, actually. Until that moment, Max has not noticed, perhaps because he is so busy dealing with nausea and a dusty headache. But now he can feel a distinct bloat building up under his belt.

The Photog is animated, like an enthusiastic science teacher. "If we had a balloon with us, we would notice it getting bigger and bigger as the air pressure outside becomes lower and lower. Because the air inside has no place to go, the balloon will eventually explode.

"Fortunately, for humans and their animals, there is release," he said. "Perhaps you can detect it."

He offers a smile, but Max isn't sure what lies behind it.

Max tries for the tenth time to open the window beside him.

The door at the front of the carriage opens and a copper-coloured man enters carrying some kind of large animal bladder under his arm, like a bagpipe.

"*Uno centavo. Uno centavo,*" he murmurs. Those who pay get a blast of air from inside the bag and inhale deeply.

"It is OXYGEN!" the Photog says, the same way he would say, "It is Mick Jagger!"

"Bullshit," Max gasps loudly. "It's a ..."

Max fights the rising tide in his esophagus.

"... placebo."

The Photog's amiable tone dissipates. "Maybe. But if I were you, my friend, I would not refuse even a placebo."

Max pulls a five-centavo coin from his pocket and holds it out to the vendor, who bends close to him with the bladder and locks eyes with him. But he stops there and waits until the very moment Max anticipates a blast of air. Then he hisses into his customer's ear in clear English: "Five centavos is a lot of money for bullshit. So fuck you, gringo. Enjoy your visit." He moves on without taking the coin or dispensing "oxygen".

The Photog sighs. "Well, anyway, we are almost halfway there."

During the walk from the train station to their hotel Max tries to control his pain by minimizing the movement of his head, like balancing a tray of brimming drinks atop a pole of rickety vertebrae. When they arrive at the hotel, despite his inexperience and his miserable condition, Max recognizes it as an economic development project that has never made a *centavo* in its history. It is meant to evoke a mountain resort, complete with log walls, even though Max hasn't seen a full-grown tree for hours. The wooden staffs that serve as door handles might qualify as rustic if their varnish hadn't been rubbed away from use.

The Photog leads the way in and almost collides with the Doorman, a moustachioed man in his mid-thirties wearing a train conductor's uniform adorned with brocade and the mandatory gold epaulets.

"*Bienvenido*," he says and launches into a torrent of Spanish that Max cannot even begin to follow.

"He is the desk clerk as well as the doorman," the Photog says. "He apologizes for the uniform, but his only alternative was lederhosen."

The Doorman turns to Max and says expansively: "Welcome to *El Palacio de las Montanas*—The Palace of the Mountains!"

He leads the weary travellers through a leather-chaired lobby to a short flight of steps flanked by two stuffed bears.

"You have bears here?" Max asks. But the Doorman apparently doesn't hear him.

Max looks around. The design has evidently been intended to reflect both the rich dignity of a backwater provincial capital and the adventure of a mountain lodge 10,000 feet above sea level. Time has been harsh, though, and now it looks mostly like a huge logging camp latrine. The Doorman checks them in, being especially careful as he records Max's passport number next to his name and room number. That done, he looks at Max and hands him a yellow soda from beneath the counter.

"*Para la sorroche*," he says. "*Muy bueno*."

"*Cuanto cuesta*?" Max asks.

"*Nada, senor*," the Doorman says, smiling and spreading his arms. "Courtesy of El Palacio! May I ask what brings you to our mountain paradise?"

Max takes a drink of creamy yellow soda and studies the man's broad smile, trying to see if he's joking. "We're journalists," he says. "*Periodistas*."

"Aha! Just 10 kilometres from here, there is a two-headed sheep. I can take you there. Just a small charge."

"We're not that kind of journalist," Max says, torn between politeness and the desire to stretch out on a bed. Even a bed of nails will do.

The Doorman looks shocked.

"What kind of journalist does not write about two-headed sheep?" he asks.

"*Prensa Internacional*," the Photog says.

"Foreign correspondents," the Doorman says quietly. "But there is nothing here for you. You should go home."

"I've been thinking that all day," Max says.

The Photog and the Doorman talk for a few more minutes in Spanish. Finally, they walk through an open door onto a wooden footbridge that crosses a wide stream and leads to an open door on the other side.

"They are very proud of this," the Photog says. "When the *Palacio* was new, guests would catch trout from the bridge and the kitchen would fry them up."

"And now?"

"He says not to drink from the stream because it is too close to the toilets, which are no longer connected to a sewage pipe."

"Jesus Christ. We can't stay here."

"Well, it seems my information was out of date, yes. But do you really want to start searching the streets for a better place?"

Max does not. Altitude sickness has lodged in the very centre of his skull and is expanding. Every joint aches. He wants to throw up. He wants to go home.

The Photog leads the way across the stream and into a room sporting two cots. They look kid-sized against the high-ceilinged room with its enormous windows, one of which was actually a set of doors opening to a balcony. The filthy ceiling features a filthy plaster *bas-relief* of some filthy satyr. The window frames are ornately carved. The bathroom door is boarded up and the floorboards are covered in oxblood paint where carpet used to be.

Max sits on the edge of one of the beds and begins to search his knapsack for his toothbrush. "How much are we paying for this?" he asks.

"Thirty-five cents American per night," is the triumphant reply.

"Jesus help me."

The Photog is angry. "You were the one who said we had to make every centavo count. I had to make expensive phone calls in a short time to find this place, which has an excellent restaurant. Besides, I do not think there is a Howard Johnsons nearby."

"Sorry. That wasn't very helpful of me," Max says.

The Photog is silent for a moment.

"You have altitude sickness and you are stuck in a strange place. Drink your cola—believe it or not, it will help."

Max is beginning to feel just a little better when the Photog pulls from his backpack a blade that looks more like a small scimitar than a hunting knife, and jams the point into the floor near the head of his bed.

"What are you doing?"

"There are no locks on the doors, Max. It's best to keep your knife where you can find it during the night."

"That's just asinine," Max says.

"I am not familiar with that word, but I get the idea. Do what you want, but remember, this is my country. You should do what I do."

Max recalls how quickly he was felled back on the plaza and reconsiders his position. He opens his puny Swiss Army knife and sullenly sticks it in the floor. The wood is heavily pocked by knife marks of previous guests. Max stares at them and makes the connection with the Bureau Chief's promise to pay them something because of the "danger". It makes his head hurt still more.

Max pulls the bedclothes over himself without further ceremony. "If someone breaks in," he says, "I'm going to let them kill me."

"That is just *la sorroche* talking," the Photog says kindly. "In the morning, you will feel better. We will have fresh trout for breakfast!"

1995

The Campaign: Drinking with the Fishes

Max is watching large goldfish swimming against a current below his forearms. He is drinking beer, sitting up at a bar that features a clear, four-inch, water-filled pipe that runs its full perimeter and disappears into an aquarium somewhere in the back. The club regulars include journalists and politicians.

In the history of the place, countless arguments have faded away as the drunken belligerents became engrossed in the fishy activity beneath their elbows. The bartender, a shadowy, mischievous fellow, has been known to stir things up by changing the direction of the current without notice. This prompts the fish to change direction. Eventually someone notices, which provokes loud debate about the direction the fish normally swim and why it might have changed if, in fact, it has.

At other times, the morose can look at the fish and contemplate the futility of their lives, which is what Max is doing. For him, it's a moment of quiet contemplation and self-loathing. For the fish, a circuit around the bar is likely the equivalent of space travel. On balance, a good arrangement for all, Max thinks.

Since the provincial election campaign began Max has been "drinking with the fishes" a little too often and too far into the evening. He is resolving to stop it when a youngish guy in a nice suit takes a seat next to him and stares into the tube.

"Fuck," the guy says to the fish.

"What?" Max says.

"The fucking campaign. I feel like those fish."

"Everybody feels like the fish," Max says.

The bartender evidently hears the conversation and feels the need for downbeat music. Wordlessly, he starts a cassette player and the room fills with the lugubrious lyrics of *Ruby Don't Take Your Love to Town.* Kenny Rogers is singing. It seems his lover has painted her lips and curled her hair. The sun's going down and Kenny's worried she's headed to town and takin' nothin' but her love with her. Kenny's on his own. "*Roooo-beee ....*"

Max looks the guy over. It's the Premier's executive assistant, his fixer.

"I know you," he says. "You're that prick who works for the Premier."

With some effort, the guy brings his gaze to bear on Max: "You're that asshole editor. Fuck. I'll buy you a beer."

"Sure."

Their mugs land heavily on the bar without another word being spoken. They clink their beers together, temporarily united in their distaste for political campaigns.

"The only good thing about this campaign is the pussy," the Fixer says. "It's everywhere this year. It's a bumper crop out there."

"We don't have that in my business," Max says.

"I know. You guys wear hair shirts and self-flagellate. Saintly hypocrites."

Max figures that's fair ball, but thinks the guy should know why he's drinking with the fishes tonight.

"Fine. But why can't you guys just let me do my job?"

"We are letting you do your job. Truth is, for my two cents, we should have you killed," the Fixer says. "Humanely, of course. We're not animals."

"You call what you're doing to me 'leaving me alone'?"

The guy orders two more beers. When they thump down before them, he begins his explanation in slow, measured tones.

"There ... is ... no ... conspiracy ... against ... you."

"Really?"

"Swear to God. I mean, according to your editorial page, we're just a bunch of half-wit buffoons who haven't even bothered to scrape the cow dung off our boots."

"Strictly speaking, I said horse manure."

The Fixer executes an exaggerated bow that would have toppled him from his stool but for Max's intervention.

"My apologies, your greatness," the Fixer says upon regaining his seat. "But if that's your opinion, what makes you think we can organize a conspiracy?"

A large goldfish is stationed between Max's forearms, calmly working against the current: "See, Max," it says, "that's what we've been telling you all along."

Max sighs. "Okay, if not the Premier, then who?"

"Nobody. You have to think of the Party as an independent, living organism."

"Like a low-grade virus, or foot fungus?"

"Oh, man, you *are* a fuckhead. On the contrary, it's a very complex organism. Its members join, participate and die off, like cells in your body, but the Party continues. It even has its own immune system. Right now, it's having a big immune response to you and your ratbag paper."

Ruby, Don't Take Your Love to Town segues into *You Picked a Fine Time to Leave Me, Lucille.* Kenny Rogers is clearly having a bad night. First Ruby takes off on him, and now Lucille is cruising the bars, leaving him to bring in the crop and feed the four kids by himself. The bartender shakes his head in apparent disbelief at the fecklessness of Kenny's womenfolk.

"Just ignore him," says the Fixer, motioning toward the bartender "It's his way of telling us to go home. Next, he'll hit a switch on the pump to get the fish swimming in the other direction."

"Can you prove he does that?"

"No. Many have tried, but none have succeeded."

Max looks around and sees there is exactly one other customer in the establishment, passed out on his table. He brings the conversation back to the non-conspiracy.

"But somebody has to *organize* the immune response," Max says.

"No. That's the POINT!" The Fixer is strident. "It's *organic*, self-organizing. When you get a cold — or maybe chlamydia in your case — do you command your immune system to mount an attack?"

Max's thoughts turn for a moment to his stomach problems, which the Wife says is stress. But he's wondering if it's cancer.

The Fixer drones on with his metaphor.

"No. Your immune system is self-activating. It's the same

with the Party. One member—an immune cell—detects an asshole like you and decides he's a problem. So he files, in your case, a defamation suit. Now, that's like a flag for other immune cells, and they just pile on. No one has to tell them to do anything. Same thing happens to Party leaders who fuck up. Even sitting premiers."

Max can feel his hangover starting already. The Fixer keeps going.

"The Party is saying to you: 'Stop pissing into our tent; c'mon in and piss out like the rest of us'. Make no mistake, we could use you. You could really make a difference."

Max looks at the fish. He is sure they were swimming in the opposite direction just a moment ago.

"I hear you," he sighs, "but why now?"

"Because you're pissing on the third rail of Nova Scotia politics. Everybody knows you're trying to get a story on that so-called runway."

"Jesus, you know how to mix a metaphor," Max says. "Now I'm pissing into the tent *and* onto an electrified rail?"

The Fixer offers to buy Max another beer. Max declines. The Fixer orders himself a Martini.

"My point is, the project is in *rural Nova Scotia*," the Fixer says. "Nobody cares what your crappy little paper does in Halifax. But the outback, that's another matter. That's offside."

"So you want me to kill the story."

"You do what ya gotta do. I'm just sayin'."

The Fixer's head is unsteady on his shoulders. He squints at Max: "You don't even know where it is, do you?"

"OK," Max says, ignoring the jibe. "You didn't start the immune response, but you can stop it, right?"

"We can, but why?"

Max can tell the guy's dying to say something else, something juicy. He decides ego is the right bait.

"I guess I'm in over my head," Max says.

The Fixer nods in agreement: "You don't know the half of it."

"What are you talking about?" he asks.

"Always ask yourself who's got something to gain, Max."

You pedant, Max thinks. Come on, spill it. You know you can't help yourself.

"Let's just say your publisher is a friend of the Party."

"He's a friend of whoever's in power," Max says.

This earns a smug grin from the Fixer.

"Well, the Party is in power. And therefore your publisher would love to see you on permanent stress leave. Or dead. That wouldn't break his heart. It's no big deal, Max. It's just friends looking after friends. And remember, the Party will look after you, too — if you ask it to."

1969

The Dancer's Proposition

MAX IS IN bed, his head throbbing like a broken thumb. He is pretty sure there's someone else's naked back resting against his own. His love life has been so dismal that his first thought is that there was a big party downstairs and some drunk guy has crawled into his bed. University has been an education that way.

Consequently, there is a mind-bending "Believe it or Not!" moment when he rolls over and sees the Dancer's fiery red hair spilling across the pillow. Max recovers quickly.

Heart beating madly, he slides down a little and spoons against the warm, dry skin of his new friend. It's a glorious fit and he feels his appendage beginning to explore what little space remains between their bodies.

"This is nice," she murmurs. "Let's stay like this for a while. You would think four times would be enough."

Max doesn't know the frequency protocol for one-night stands, but four times does seem sufficient. On the other hand, he doesn't feel he should be held accountable for one headstrong organ, or be a slave to convention. Nonetheless he repositions. By way of compensation, he starts feeling around carefully with his free hand and finds a soft breast. He cradles it gently and is rewarded with a low "hmmm."

"Good enough," he thinks and drifts back to sleep.

Max is awakened by the sound of the Dancer opening his bedroom door and walking into his room naked from her flaming hair to her purple toenail polish. Except for her sunny girl-next-door smile, she is every inch a Vargas drawing from *Playboy*. Everywhere he looks — and he looks everywhere — Max sees pleasing curves.

"You walked to the bathroom naked?" he asks.

"So it would seem," she says. "I met one of your roommates."

"Who?"

"He couldn't remember his name."

No wonder. Max is now thinking it doesn't hurt his image to have this spectacular woman walking between the bathroom and his room without her clothes on.

She picks up on this line of thought: "I think your reputation was enhanced by the encounter. It's no big deal, you know."

"Well ..."

"Well nothing. We're all the same."

"I'd say you stand out a bit," Max says.

She smiles.

"You're very kind, but my body has a half-life, as I believe you scientists say."

She holds her breasts. "These babies are already starting to sag and my backside could fall at any moment."

"Sorry to be argumentative, but all the parts you've mentioned seem to be holding up quite well."

Pleased, she stretches hers arms above her head like a cat in a sunbeam.

"Well," she says. "I would agree, but modesty forbids ..."

Max laughs out loud, whereupon she leaps onto the bed and rests her head on his chest.

"After I got into trouble with speed, I finally quit after I met an economist at a private performance who said drugs would quickly destroy my only capital asset."

"Capital asset?" Max says.

"I believe you've become quite familiar with it over the past 12 hours. It's currently my only source of income and I have to maintain it long enough to build a normal business before my behind falls, which is what I think will happen first. Worst case, I'll use the money to have it hauled back up.

"That's why I became part-owner of the club, to build up some other capital. And now, I want you to join my advisory board."

"Your what?"

"It's a group of men I've met who've agreed to help me with business decisions," she says.

"Why me?"

"Because you have a certain kind of smarts that I'm going to need."

"I do?"

"Yup. There's just one thing. If you join my board, we'll 'do it' one more time to celebrate, and that's it. From then on, it's all real business and no funny business. You've been more fun in the sack than I expected, but rules are rules. And no falling in love. You're not in love with me, are you?"

"Well," Max says. "Our age difference is too big for me to fall in love with you."

Max is surprised to see the Dancer startled by his remark. She hesitates. "Like I said, a *certain kind* of smarts.

You've still got some work to do when it comes to women. So, are you in or are you out?"

"What's in it for me?"

"Non-voting preferred shares."

Max does not know what those are, but he likes the Dancer a lot and wants to be in her life. Incredibly, lust is going to have to take a back seat. Once again he hears himself saying the unexpected: "Okay. I'm in."

She speaks directly into his ear, a rapidly-emerging erogenous zone, in a way that makes him regret his decision already: "This is how I'm going to be rich. I know how to spot the right people. I'll make you rich someday, too, Maxie."

For lack of anything better to say, Max asks about the name of her business. She rolls off the bed, stands in front of the window and snaps opens the roller blind. The mid-morning sun illuminates a magnificent, coppery bush.

The Dancer sees him looking. She pats the general area affectionately: "See? Goldpussy! That's the business name. Welcome to the Advisory Board!"

Time to celebrate, Max thinks.

1996

Guru Likes Beer, Credit

Max is on a *pro bono publico* "communications" assignment organized for him by the CEO. He is still sufficiently newsroom-oriented that he regards *pro bono* public relations as an oxymoron. And, as a journalist without a newsroom, he has a new appreciation of the phrase "fish out of water."

He walks up two creaky flights in a building that appears to have been designed by Raymond Chandler. Each office door has a large frosted glass window emblazoned with a number, and sometimes a business name in a large fancy font.

Max knocks on the door marked 202 and half-expects to hear a hard-bitten voice say something like "C'mon in, sweetheart. Sit down and give those long legs a rest." But the words below the door number — *Bernie's Meditation Services* — don't quite fit with that. Even so, Max isn't ready for the short rotund fellow about his own age who opens the door, phone in one hand. He gestures to Max to come inside and then disappears into a side office.

Seating is problematic. The room has a single chair on a dais and about a dozen bright futon mats about two feet square. A small boxy cushion sits atop each mat.

Max tests a cushion and confirms that it's filled with dense foam. He parks his backside on one and settles in to wait. His client is soft-spoken, but Max can hear his end of the phone conversation. He thinks he detects a slight East Indian accent.

"Yes, that's right ... I owe you $18,235.23 ... that was my trip to Nepal ... no, I can't pay it back ... yes, I understand the terms of an American Express account, but that doesn't change the fact that I don't have the money ... no, I will not be sending you any money whatsoever this month ... you see, I don't have money ... not soon, no, but sometime in the future ... oh yes, I am willing to look at an arrangement ... uh-huh ... uh-huh ..." There is no indication in his tone that Max's client is in any way perturbed by the conversation.

When the client walks out, Max gets a better look at him. His greying black hair is unruly but not sloppy. His glasses have prominent black frames set on a bulbous nose. His clothing is unremarkable: shirt and slacks. Max sees humour in his eyes and senses he's in the presence of someone who is never surprised; that if he had found an alligator in the room instead of Max, he would have calmly called animal control and returned to work while he waited for their arrival.

The client extends his hand and Max rises from his cushion to greet the first Guru he has ever encountered. Max starts off the relationship by apologizing for overhearing the Guru's difficult conversation with American Express.

"I'm sorry to hear you're having difficulty."

"No difficulty for me, mate," the Guru says.

"Really?"

"It's all a matter of perspective. Let's say I spent $18,235.23

of your money on my trip to Nepal and can't repay it. Who's got the problem, me or you?"

"Me."

"Exactly. Same with American Express."

"What are you going to do?"

"No, chum, you still don't get it. The question is, what are *they* going to do?"

"OK. What are they going to do?"

With no apparent irony, the Guru says: "They are upgrading my account and working out a payment plan for me. Now, let's have a conversation."

The Guru sets up two cushions so they can sit cross-legged, facing each other. He bows to Max without ceremony, Max follows suit as best he can. "It's good to formally acknowledge each other at the beginning of the conversation," the Guru says.

The problem or "challenge"—which the Wife has explained is now the correct term—is that, after a year in Halifax, the Guru still lacks enough meditation students to support himself. He has studied meditation in India, Tibet, Nepal and Colorado for most of his adult life and is a well-regarded teacher. However, he has never adopted a religion or any of the many lineages associated with meditation. He believes he is the victim of "credentialism".

"There is nothing spooky or life-threatening about meditation," he says. "Still, you should know what you're doing if you're going to teach it. My problem is that the places where I've studied don't issue framed certificates."

Max is well aware that he is newly-minted as a "communications expert" and also lacks credentials. Further, this is his first consultation, so he resists the impulse to immediately suggest the Guru change the name of Bernie's Meditation Services.

The Guru also believes that his humble meditation hall is off-putting, but he can't afford to upgrade until he's paid for the trip to Nepal.

"Why don't you just put it on American Express?"

"Well," the Guru says. "Despite my upgraded status, I don't feel they are ready to offer me more credit right now."

The Guru switches the topic to Max's truncated career, which he finds hilarious. Max is still raw from the experience and finds it difficult to join the laughter. The Guru sees that and apologizes.

"I'm not laughing at you, my friend," he says. "I'm laughing at the predictability of it all."

"I didn't predict it."

"Really? You had no idea?"

"Well, in retrospect, it shouldn't have surprised me."

"Exactly. That's why it's good not to live in our heads. But you had a good time at the paper. Your new CEO said so. And now you're moving on. It's like you've done the roller coaster and now you're going to try the Gravitron."

"I'm not sure I can do communications."

"Don't be ridiculous. It's just like journalism, only in reverse, eh?"

They laugh at the use of "eh", which gives Max the confidence to say what's been on his mind.

"You sound Indian, which is probably good for your line of work, but 'Bernie'?"

Max is no marketer, but it seems to him that westerners wouldn't look for someone named Bernie for a meditation instructor.

"But that's my name. My father was from Toronto. He stayed in India after the war and married a good Indian girl. Both have passed away, so I decided to use my Canadian citizenship and immigrate. I don't want to change my name to boost sales. I need to be honest with my students. That's not negotiable."

Max is certain there's a solution to this somewhere.

• • •

A few minutes later, having ascertained that Gurus drink, Max has led his client to a bar he knows too well.

"Why are there fish swimming through this ...?" the Guru asks, gesturing to the clear tube surrounding the bar.

Max raises his eyebrows, expels a breath and shrugs, as if to say that no one really knows. "But they're here, so successive owners just keep feeding them."

"Do they have names?"

Max begins to ruminate on appropriate names for fish but catches himself.

"What's your full name?" he asks the Guru.

"Bernard Ashok Carruthers."

Hmmm.

"Ashok?" Max asks. "Does that name have a meaning?"

"Why is it that when people hear a foreign name they want to know what it means? Does anyone ever ask you what Max means? Do you even know?"

"It was a professional question, but the answer to your questions are dunno, no and no."

The Guru nods. "Ashok honours Ashoka, a great Indian emperor who one day realized that victory at any cost is actually defeat. Then he adopted Buddhist principles and instituted a reign of peace."

"That's good, but not great," Max says. "What's the name actually mean? Like Miller — everyone knows what Miller means."

"Let's see if I understand you. My name — my actual *name* — is good, but not *great*," the Guru says. "You seem to have an instinct for your new business."

"Irony is not lost on me, you know," Max says. "I'm fully aware that I'm staring at goldfish in a Plexiglas pipe with some kind of sarcastic guru. Are you going to tell me what Ashok means?"

"Well, it means something like 'without sadness' or 'without sorrow'."

Without sadness, Max thinks. Thank you, Jesus. This job is even easier than I imagined. All you have to do is buy your client a beer and get him to cough up the meaning of his middle name.

"Don't you think," Max says, "that 'without sadness' is a much better name than Bernie — no offence?"

"But meditation is not about driving away sadness."

"It's not?"

"Can't be done. You can make room for sadness, though."

Max is about to ask why it can't be done, but realizes that if driving out sadness was that easy, there wouldn't be any sadness. He thinks about ways to turn this obvious communications weakness into a strength, one of the perversities of his new trade.

"Well, can't you use it as a talking point?" Max says.

He suggests the Guru say something like: "My name means 'without sadness', but don't take that too literally."

"And then you go on to make your real point," Max adds.

"My real point," the Guru says. "As opposed to my phony point."

"No, your *talking point.* There's a difference. Think of it as a teaching point."

The Guru signals for more beer, is disappointed to learn there is nothing on tap from Hungary, and orders a Remy Martin instead. Max sticks with beer.

"That's actually a good idea," the Guru says. "It's an opportunity to teach. What do you call it? It's a teachable moment."

"Exactly," Max says, who has orbited the sun enough times to know that students will choose to believe that Ashok the Guru can drive away sadness, no matter how often he denies it.

"Okay. On your advice, I will call myself Ashok."

Max offers a toast, but the Guru demurs.

"Classes aren't going well. It's too early to celebrate," he says. "Perhaps you can come to one tomorrow evening?"

• • •

Max is back in the Guru's place of business at seven the next evening. He takes a seat on a cushion with the others and follows his client's instructions on meditation, just to get an authentic experience. He even meditates for 30 minutes.

Everything seems fine, until it's time for questions.

"So, why would we want to do this every day?" asks a guy in his forties still wearing his shirt and trousers from work. His tone is sceptical and meant to be incisive. A pretty younger woman wearing a rescue-dress with small flowers on it rolls her eyes at him.

"You will help save the universe," the Guru says.

Now it's office-guy's turn to roll his eyes.

The Guru explains that there are two opposing forces in the universe. The first is gravity, which works to squeeze the universe back together into a single point. When that happens there will be another Big Bang, re-starting the cycle of the universe. The opposing force is pain, which is driving the expansion of the universe. Every instance of pain, mental or physical, in humans and animals, drives the universe to expand. Even crushing an insect helps drive the universe apart.

A neatly turned-out guy who looks like he spends his weekends distributing religious literature puts up his hand. "Isn't it a good thing if the universe goes on forever?"

"No, because at some point it will become empty and lifeless. The energy will be spread out too far, it will be too diluted to support life. Too much pain will bring about true death, the death of everything. By meditating, you reduce the amount of pain you inflict on yourself and others."

"When?" office-guy asks.

"When what?"

"When will everything die?"

"I don't know exactly," the Guru says. "About a million years from now."

"Well, the hell with that," office-guy says, standing up. "I'm not going to sit on my butt for hours to prevent something from happening a million years from now. I gotta pay the power bill *next month*."

And, of course, so does the Guru, Max thinks. Three others follow office-guy out of the room.

Max stops taking notes.

The woman in the dress decides to take a shot.

"Don't you get good karma for the next life?" she asks.

She smiles when the Guru replies enthusiastically in the affirmative, but soon learns she has not saved the day.

"Reducing pain in this life brings an amazing gift. And that's why the next life will not be nearly as comfortable for you, but you will be able to do much, much more to alleviate the suffering of others," the Guru says. "Mother Teresa didn't live at the Calcutta Hilton, you know. If you want to alleviate suffering, it's best to go where the most suffering is taking place."

The room quiets. Only the religious guy approves, nodding. A pleasant, studious-looking woman in her middle years stands up.

"So, you're saying the harder I work at making this life better for everyone, the worse my next life will be?" she says.

"You will encounter more suffering, but more importantly, you will better experience the suffering of others. That's true compassion."

The religious guy jumps up: "Yes! That's why suffering makes sense! That's what Jesus was all about!"

There follows some desultory discussion, but the consensus is that it makes no sense to put a big effort into this life so you can experience more suffering in the next. They're here tonight because they want to suffer less and they want it now.

The Guru loses more ground by suggesting that executions might result in a net pain reduction. The trick would be to surprise the prisoner by shooting him in the back of the head when he's not looking. That way he won't suffer the agony of knowing his death is imminent, he stops causing pain in this life, and gets a fresh start in the next one.

"I want to be clear," the Guru says. "I am not supporting

execution, especially if it would cause pain to the victim's loved ones. It would be a difficult calculation. I'm just saying this is how it could be done."

Next, he discloses that, for similar reasons, he is not a vegetarian, thereby losing the woman in the rescue-dress.

And so it ends. Only two prospects sign up for the next class. Max and the Guru wordlessly agree that drinking with the fishes is in order.

• • •

Max barely gets his forearms on the Plexiglas tube before a huge goldfish with O-ring lips takes up his station beneath them. "Take it easy, Max. You'll find a way," it says.

He lets the Guru take a sip or two of Remy before opening the conversation. "Was that typical?"

"Oh-no. That was a huge success by comparison," he says. His voice is full of self-pity unbecoming to a guru.

Max asks if the Guru truly believes all that stuff about saving the universe and backwards karma.

"You're asking if I'm a fraud?"

"Just checking. Nature of the beast and all that. Are there any personal benefits to meditating?" he asks.

"Sure, lots, but if you focus on personal benefits, there won't be any."

"Hmm. If you try for it, you'll never get it," Max says. "It's inscrutable, I'll give you that."

"Is that a key message, old chum?"

"Just fish-talk."

"You know, I appreciate you offering to help, but I can't lie about what I believe. That's not right, not fair."

Max stifles the urge to yell at his client. He dials down his tone and instead beseeches him.

"How did you come to believe in backwards karma? It's the worst motivation for good behaviour imaginable. Worse than condemnation to Hell for bad behaviour."

"Actually, Hell is a state of mind. Even the pope said that."

"That doesn't answer my question," Max says.

"Where does anybody get their beliefs about the afterlife?" the Guru says. "They accept a ready-made belief straight off the shelf, or they make a guess."

The Guru says that his idea just came to him one day. Unlike other beliefs, he argues, his is logical: If the idea is to reduce pain, enlightened people would naturally choose to be reborn where there is more pain to work with.

Once again, Max stares down at his fish, which interprets the gesture as an invitation to speak up: "He's right, Max. Life is good here, but in my next life, I'm going to be human. I've learned a lot in this tube, and I think I can help."

Max is wishing the damned fish would move on when it occurs to him that silence is not the same as a lie. It's his first big insight as a flack, but he suspects it's common knowledge in the field.

"You know, there's nothing wrong with preparing the ground before delivering tough messages," he says.

The Guru signals for more alcohol, which Max now understands to be a sign of agreement.

"So, I could make the karma issue the very last thing in my program, something we don't discuss until they're accomplished meditators and better able to understand."

"Right," Max says. "I wouldn't rush to explain about saving the universe, either, or your possible support for the death penalty. Instead, you explain that becoming ready for certain advanced truths could take years of meditation practice. Not to mention lots of fees. This gives them something to shoot for."

The Guru shoots him a look of disdain at the fees comment, but Max cuts him off before he can speak. "The only thing I know about karma, my friend, is that the power company won't accept it as legal tender. You don't need to be rich. But you're doing honest work and you're entitled to a decent living for it."

The Guru again signals for more drinks before realizing they already have four glasses in front of them.

"Should I continue to avoid discussing any personal benefits of meditation?" the Guru asks.

"I think you're right about that," Max says. "Every spiritual leader offers benefits. But *you're* offering benefits that are available *only* if you *don't* strive for them. It's got mystical 'heft'. And Paul Simon's already prepared them for it: '*... the nearer your destination, the more you're slip slidin' away*'."

"Good lord. Mystical heft. Paul Simon. You are cynical," the Guru says.

"No. I'm practical," Max says. "Will learning to meditate hurt anyone?"

"No."

"Will it help some people?"

"Yes, and the people around them," the Guru says. "That's the whole point."

"Is exploring the cosmic implications essential to helping people?"

"No. It's just something they can pursue."

"So," Max says. "I'm telling you how to effectively communicate something that you believe will reduce suffering. I'm not asking you to exploit anyone."

For a long time, the Guru confers wordlessly with his brandy. Then he orders another round and turns to Max.

"Jeez ... Paul Simon ... really?"

"Sure. Of course, we'll have to work on the wording."

1975

Reporter Gets High on Poorly Aimed Gunfire

A SILENT FORMATION of students barely out of secondary school march up a hill directly toward — again — a Mercedes water cannon. Max hears the aggressive ricochet sound of the Photog's motor drive before he spots him walking alongside the demonstrators, sidestepping to keep an eye on his viewfinder. He is dressed head to foot in Army greens, no doubt in the hope that cops and soldiers hesitate before shooting at him.

The mountain sun paints everything in high contrast. The cobblestones are bright but distinct, as if outlined in pen and ink. Most of the kids wear cheap tan pants or drab tunics, the unofficial uniform of community college students. A few wear toque-like alpaca hats with strings hanging from the earflaps. Some of the girls have shirts or sweaters with beads that sparkle in the sunlight. Almost all the faces have high, strong cheekbones and smooth skin the colour of pennies. Max thinks they could pass for native people in some parts of North America. They march in silence with a lithe and steady gait. There are no chants to hide their fear, which is easy to see in their dark wide eyes and tight mouths. But their shoulders are back and their heads straight, like they're posing for school graduation photos.

They wear white bandanas over their mouths to symbolize state suppression of free speech. Max thinks of the plaza and wonders if they know how brave they are.

He looks uphill, dreading what is about to happen. The black cannon waits patiently, water dripping from its tanks. The Army is absent. Max thinks they've either abandoned shows of co-operation or they're busy in the capital mounting the long-awaited counter-coup.

Max is no tactician, but the positions of the opposing forces make him fearful for the students. The cops can see all the streets and buildings behind the kids, but the marchers can barely see past the cannon and cops in riot gear next to it. A cathedral forms the backdrop. Max looks downslope and is unsurprised to see an armoured personnel carrier slide in to block the way the kids have come. One block farther downhill, the street is conspicuously open.

He cannot understand why the students would put themselves in that position. Perhaps they thought the clergy would emerge from the cathedral to protect them. Max looks up the hill. No clergy in sight.

Max hears the Photog yelling: "Here it comes, man! Here it comes."

The water cannon driver revs the diesel engine, creating a plume of black exhaust.

The Photog takes one look uphill, shoots without looking through the viewfinder, and joins Max on the sidelines. He hands over two rolls of exposed film, as is now their custom.

"What do you think?"

Max looks him fully in the face and for the first time

realizes that the Photog might share part of his bloodline with the kids behind him.

"We're in deep shit," Max says. "We're in the middle of it again."

The Photog looks around and then at Max.

"Jesus, amigo. How does this happen? You're a dangerous guy to be around."

"Some would call it a knack for being in the right place at the right time," Max says, not believing it.

Without ceremony, the water cannon lets loose. Again, the kids go down like dominoes. From the rear, the cops launch tear gas grenades. The foreign correspondents take off downhill. Max doesn't bother taking notes, but the Photog stops every 10 yards or so and fires the motor drive. Max shouts at him as he starts to follow the crowd toward the open side street on the left.

"That's a trap! Don't you remember?"

"Of course I fucking remember! It was your job to make sure this didn't happen again."

Max looks around. "Oh, Christ."

They follow the kids into the side street. Half a block down they encounter a cordon of black-clad cops with rifles and Uzis blocking the way, forcing them into a street on the right. A hundred yards away, an Army troop truck waits for them, blocking the way. This, Max thinks, must be Army's show of co-operation. Out of choices, the kids charge toward the truck. Max has seen something like this before, at a slaughterhouse.

The foreign correspondents scoot into a doorway. The Photog takes a light-reading. "This is going to be bad," he yells.

But the truck shifts into gear and every one of the dozen

or so soldiers in the back turn to face the cops and extend their middle fingers. They hold that pose as the truck drives into an alley and out of the way. The kids charge past. It occurs to Max that few of them even noticed what happened. He and the Photog rejoin them.

And then Max gets a taste of "real action". The cops open fire. For the foreign correspondents, all desire to report on the event is supplanted by the urge to go on living.

In that same moment, protesters and foreign correspondents turn as one, shift into overdrive and accelerate like race cars. The sounds of the shots do not recede but instead surround them. Max's is certain there is a bullet coming his way. Muscles in his back tense up involuntarily to prepare for the blow. Surely to God this can't be the end, he thinks.

A final surge of adrenalin transforms everything. The hardpan underfoot turns into a plush carpet. Running becomes effortless. He can see the rest of the crowd in front of him and feel the Photog just behind him. He can see every pothole and stone miles before he reaches them. Even better, he can see who is going to change direction before it happens and can slip past them effortlessly, like Kareem setting up for the skyhook.

Despite the weight of his armoured camera bag, the Photog manages to keep up as they come upon an open field scarred by a series of ditches. Max clears them easily, hanging in the air for as long as it takes — forever if necessary — to find the right landing spot. One, two, three, four ditches. Max feels no impact when his foot hits the dirt, just a sense of his muscle absorbing the force and straining against the ground for more speed. Now he veers left, away from the demonstrators, and leads the Photog on a long arc through baked farmland and septic fields. He is ecstatic each time his feet dig into the dirt and his strong legs start the cycle again. Ahead, he can see his route to safety, etched in the hardpan.

I'm a fucking gazelle, Max exults. I'm an eagle.

The shooting ends long before Max and his friend stop at the edge of a stream. They lean over, hands on knees, sucking air for several minutes.

"You okay?" the Photog finally gasps.

"Yeah. You?"

The Photog extends his hand and offers the plantation-owner smile: "Yes. And may I say, sir, what an excellent job you did of running away."

"And may I add, your own demonstration of flight was exemplary, encumbered as you were by photographic equipment. It was an honour trying to stay ahead you."

They took a few more breaths. "I suppose this makes us chicken," Max says.

"Perhaps. But chickens who are ... how you say in English ... alive."

"And there's no need to mention our cowardice," Max says. "The Bureau Chief himself said readers want to know about the incident — assuming it's over — not what we did to cover it."

"Precisely!" the Photog says emphatically. "They do not want to know how scared we were."

Max's thoughts goes to his fleeting experience as a gazelle with the eyes of an eagle. The Photog notices.

"You were scared, weren't you?" he asks.

"Yeah, but mostly I've never been so high in my life," Max replies.

The Photog gives him a thoughtful look: "We are more different than I thought."

Max notices they can see the back of the cathedral, which means they can circle some more and arrive at *El Palacio de las Montanas*.

Max stares at the cathedral, noting that no one had emerged from what would certainly be a richly-appointed interior to plead for the safety of their flock.

1954

The Yellow Pencil of Doubt, First of Two Parts

It is the day after Max's sixth birthday and he's attending Sunday school in the basement of the local United Church. A lot of kids are sitting on cheap wood and metal chairs, waiting for the thing to end.

But for Max, this is a special moment. At the end of every class, the teachers give new yellow pencils marked "HB" in gold paint to every student who had a birthday during the past week. These are, without question, pencils from God.

"We celebrate three birthdays today," says the kind-looking woman who runs the class. "Please come up and receive your pencil as I read your name."

Max is already standing when the third name is read out. It is not his. He is still standing when the kids are set free to find their parents upstairs.

He is flushed with embarrassment and, most importantly, alarm. These pencils are awarded by *God*, who knows absolutely everything that everyone is doing at all times. He knows more than either Santa or the Queen. God would not forget to give Max his pencil. God never forgets. Moreover, good behaviour is not a requirement for receiving a pencil, because God is all-forgiving. Max's mind stays with this point: you don't have to be good like Santa insists (although he always relents). Every week Max sees bad kids get their pencils. But on *his* birthday week, Max is denied.

There are only two possible explanations: God hates Max and will send him to Hell when he dies, just like Max's Catholic friend said.

Or ... THERE IS NO GOD.

It's a crossroads: One truth leads to Hell; the other to salvation.

Max frantically reviews the problem one more time and then internalizes the pro-Max conclusion: there is no God, so Max will not go to Hell.

That still leaves a big question: why are so many important people lying to him about this?

1973

If You Go into the Woods Today

It's the kind of autumn squall Max hates most. Rainwater is thick on the asphalt, reflecting every glint of light. Headlights, tail-lights, streetlights, even the moon — now slipping out from behind the storm clouds — dance on the black slick in front of his car. The film of tobacco smoke on the windshield does nothing to improve visibility.

It's Saturday night and he's headed back to the newsroom of the shitty little Sunday Tabloid he works for. He's almost done after four hours of *chiens écrasés*, a.k.a. squashed dog patrol. This means prowling the streets of Montreal with a police scanner screeching beside him, looking for stories, any stories. He has two briefs to bang out and then it's off to the Cat Shack for some beer with the Veteran Reporter and the Copy Editor.

The scanner stops on an exchange about a possible body in some woods. The dispatcher is sceptical. There are a few seconds of useless chatter while the scanner does its thing. Then Max hears a cop ask the dispatcher to repeat the location and — fuck! — it's two blocks away, an empty, double-block lot across from a Canadian Tire strip mall. He doesn't even have to make a turn. In 30 seconds he's pulled up beside the lot.

Max considers waiting for the cops to arrive because they hate it when reporters beat them to a scene. But he'd been to this very spot for the very same reason a week ago and it turned out to be kids screwing around. Someone at a drinking party in the woods passed out so, for a joke, his friends phoned him in "dead" and disappeared. So it's a prank, therefore no harm in checking it out before calling it a night. Max grabs his flashlight, bails out of his warm car and starts down the sidewalk, looking for a gap in this odd square of urban bush.

He finds one quickly, a narrow track matted with wet leaves that branches off into thin tributaries. On instinct Max swings right onto a wider path that seems to head toward a darker part of the woods. The undergrowth is thick but bare, black as charcoal in the moonlight and dripping with cold rain. Max shudders in response to the chill. Branches have soaked his pants with rainwater.

The storm eases a little. He kills his flashlight and stops for a moment, listening for voices or footfalls, but all he can hear is water dripping and traffic hissing by. A little farther ahead he thinks he can see a clearing, likely to be party central. He expects to find the usual crude lean-to or maybe a battered tent but the space is empty. There's a circle of rocks for a fire, but it's obvious nothing has burned there tonight. Max flicks the flashlight on and scans the clearing. He finds a hole in a particularly tangled patch of undergrowth.

That will be the entrance to the make-out space, he thinks and, bending, makes his way through the tunnel. He looks around. Underfoot he finds used condoms and flattened beer cans. Above, the bushes form a canopy, a perfect spot for teenaged copulation.

Max feels the adrenaline before he can process what he is seeing. The scene resembles a diorama from a wax museum. A man in a lumberjack shirt and jeans is lying on the ground, facing straight up. Max swings the light over and sees the man is in his late twenties with black hair in tight curls. His head is large, with weirdly exaggerated features and a day's growth of dark beard. His brown boots are extra large, too. Rainwater from a branch is splatting onto his left eyeball. A deer rifle lies by the corpse's right hand, the trigger guard pinching his thumb. There's an inch-wide crater rimmed with fabric and flesh near the centre of his chest. Max looks at the face again and thinks he sees an expression of shock. It's as if — too late to turn back — the man had spotted something he didn't expect on the other side.

Control your thoughts, Max thinks. The guy got hit in the chest with a 30-30. What do you expect his face to look like?

After just six months as a reporter, Max has it figured out: professionalism and thought-control. That's all you need. Especially thought-control — don't let your thoughts prevent you from reporting objectively. So Max concentrates on "the scene".

There's an open triangular cardboard box next to the gun. Looking past it, Max can see bits of red light from the Canadian Tire sign across the street penetrating the tangle of sodden branches. Fuck. He must have bought the gun at Canadian Tire, carried it in its box across the parking lot and then the street and walked into the woods. Max wonders how long he sat alone with his new gun before pressing it to his chest and pushing the trigger.

"*Bougez pas, mon gars*. Don't move. Police."

The new arrival switches on a strong flashlight and points it at Max's face. His other hand holds a .38 police issue revolver, pointed at the ground.

The cop recognizes him. "*Max? C'est toi?*"

"*Ouais*."

"*Tabernac!* What are you doing?"

The flashlight beam swings from Max's face to the body. Max's eyes adjust and he recognizes the cop, one of a handful of police acquaintances he's made on the job.

"Just doing my job," Max says.

"Ah," the cop says, grinning. "I knew someday you would kill someone just to make a story for yourself. Still, it's a big bust for me, eh?"

"You think it's a murder?" Max asks.

The cop laughs. "Hey, this is not *Hawaii Five-O*. In LaSalle, you find a guy like this, it's suicide. *Point finale*."

"Where's the guy who phoned it in?"

"It was kids. They took off for sure. And you, too. Get out before my partner shows up. He doesn't like it when reporters get to a scene before him."

The cop suddenly shifts his gaze back to the body. He walks over to it and bends down.

"*Chalice*."

"You know him?" Max asks.

"Yeah. Like I know you. From work. I arrested him a couple times for shoplifting. Good guy. Always had something nice to say. Congratulated me on my promotion."

"While you're cuffing him, he's saying congratulations on your promotion?"

"Yep. He had big problems, but he was okay. He was always talking about his plan to go to La Tuque and be a lumberjack."

"Let me guess, he always wore a lumberjack shirt?"

"Yep. Like that one," he says. He goes down on one knee and moves the body's head just enough to avoid the raindrops.

They can hear the cop's partner crashing through the brush, calling out. Max says goodnight, takes about two dozen steps toward the Canadian Tire sign and finds himself on a sidewalk. The transition to normalcy is crazy fast.

It's the homestretch. All Max has to do is get back to the newsroom, file the briefs and then he can head downtown with the Veteran Reporter and the elderly Copy Editor for their ritual post-publication drunk. Max is fond of the Copy Editor, who is his first mentor, and looks forward to hanging out with him on Saturday nights. But recently, for some reason, Max has come to anticipate the company of the Veteran Reporter just as much.

The newsroom is actually the front office of the paper's print shop. The space is drenched with the odour of printer's ink and pulp dust. It's the building's only redeeming quality. That smell has been the elixir of life since Max learned to read, which he did poring over the comics pages in the newspapers. He would spread out the broadsheet pages and kneel before them, examining every pen stroke, no matter how wispy, and sounding out the hand-drawn words of his superheroes. The dusty sweet smell of ink and paper that enveloped him was his invisible shield.

Max now knows that being a newspaperman is what he always wanted. The Dancer was right: physics was a wrong turn.

Five Months Before Now

Loss of a Lifetime

Max and the Wife have decided against eating in front of the television and instead enjoy a meal sitting across from each other, drinking too much red wine. They are hopeful about his worsening memory problems, and talk honestly about his illness and how they'll manage it. He thinks often about how little she has changed. The same brown hair, though now straightened, not curled, and shorter because she'd decided she's too old for long hair. Her cheekbones are still strong. Her eyes say more about her kindness than her age. Her lips, as always, seem barely able to constrain some kind of secret inner mischief. Like the Mona Lisa after three tokes, he used to tell her.

He joins her on the loveseat and they sit quietly for a while. The conversation is idle. She calls him "goatman" a couple of times, and he calls her "cactus." They turn on the TV, but not long after, the Wife says she's feeling tired and wants to go to bed early. Max wants more time to digest the meal and promises to be up soon.

Two hours later, he kisses her cool forehead and goes to his own bed where the Son slept before he moved out. They miss sleeping together, but they have both become snorers.

Max sleeps poorly. At four a.m., he awakens with the familiar sense of doom that troubled him for many years as a younger man. He used to call four a.m. the "hour of the spooks."

He's awake again at seven and goes to check on the Wife. In the dawn light, he can see she hasn't moved since he last saw her. He kisses her forehead.

It is much, much too cool.

1994

We Have a Commodore Here?

MAX HAS BEEN taking angry phone calls from Montreal all morning. It seems the Gauloise-smoking Night News Editor has been catapulted into the editor-in-chief's chair. The callers are indignant employees, certain that this promotion is one of the worst travesties in the history of Canadian journalism. Pickup, an object of derision for more than a decade, has been fired and thus transformed into one of the greats of the newspaper business.

Max suspects the clamour is originating in dayside's charmed circle, a small self-reinforcing group that's been preparing for years to see one of their number get the big office. But they were too busy preparing for power to see the Night News Editor outflanking them via the bargaining committee. Now they've awoken to find a philistine in charge.

The phone rings and it's the Night News Editor himself.

"You're doing a good job in Halifax," he says. "A lot of people thought you'd fuck it up, but you didn't."

"High praise indeed," Max says.

The Owner and the Night News Editor both want Max to return to Montreal and become the managing editor, the

Number Two job. Max is not surprised. Plucking him from Halifax would be unexpected and therefore signal a brave new order.

By way of preliminary negotiation, they go back and forth for a while about what the job would be like, the fabulous food in Montreal, low house prices thanks to the separatists, the effect on Max and his family, etc. Oh, and double his current salary and a reporting job for the Wife.

Then the Night News Editor brings out the hammer. "When the Mother Ship threw you overboard, no one expected to see you again. Now we're ready to take you back, which is unprecedented — *unprecedented.* But this is a one-time offer. If you let us sail by this time, we'll never turn back for you."

• • •

In the Canadian tradition, Max and the Wife take a walk in the snow that evening. The Wife listens and then walks on in silence for a long time.

"You know what, Max? It doesn't make any difference."

"You mean you don't care?"

"Sure I care. But stay or go, all three of us are going to be fine," she says.

But Max has been struggling to reconcile his passion for the Paper, the needs of his family and a chance to play with the big boys again in Montreal. He can't see what the Wife is getting at.

"Look," she says. "We are three little ships travelling the ocean together. My job is to see that all the members of the fleet are as happy and healthy as they can be. I say we can take either direction and we'll be fine. There are pros and cons for everyone, but they balance out."

The metaphor catches Max off guard. He chooses his words carefully.

"But I'm the *captain*, right?"

She brings them to a halt under a streetlight and turns to him. "Well, you're the ranking captain, but I'm the commodore of our little fleet." she says gently.

The commodore role is news to Max, but he feels if there is to be one, it should be him. He test-drives a few arguments in his head. He is the commodore because he'll be the top income-earner if they move? True, but right now the Wife is the top income earner. He is the commodore because he is the man of the household? Nope. That was the Father.

"But am I not the commodore because my job is more important?"

She demurs. Max is exasperated.

"Oh, come on!" he says. "You're arguing that being a flack is more important than news?"

"Okay, I'll give you that one, for old times' sake, but that doesn't make you the commodore. It's a job where you are constantly making little adjustments that the other ships hardly notice. It's a job you grow into."

Max protests: "But we decide things together, like we're doing now."

"Max, you're good at running a newsroom, but outside the office you're not commodore material. For that, you've got to know what's best for others, even if they don't, and you have to know exactly when to take action. And you're a bit passive. So, we're a team of equals but ..."

"... but you're more equal than me."

"Think about it, Maxie. We wouldn't be married if I hadn't seduced you. Are you happy with that outcome?"

"Yes."

"We wouldn't be standing here now if I hadn't got you to man-up back when you were offered this job. Are you happy with that outcome?"

"Yes."

"Well, part of being commodore is knowing what's good for your ships and then making it happen. That's what I do."

"And me?"

"You're Captain Stud Muffin, as well as the officer in charge of morale and inspiration. And you're responsible for keeping the Bad Man away from our ships."

They walk another block. In spite of himself, Max likes the Captain Stud Muffin sobriquet. It takes the edge off not being the commodore.

"Okay. You are and have always been the commodore," he says. "So what do we do?"

"Just like I said. You decide where you want to work. The other two ships will follow your lead."

"Okay," Max says. "I'll make a decision tomorrow."

Max has the feeling that whatever he decides, it will turn out to be what the Wife secretly wanted. He pulls her close and nuzzles her hair, happy to be one of her ships. She kisses him and he likes the way it feels in the cold.

He hears his own voice say "*Stay here, Max.*"

"*No,*" he hears himself reply. "*Not here.*"

He looks at the Wife, who is leaning her head on his shoulder and hasn't heard a thing.

•••

Max leans against the half-height cubicle walls of City Desk, watching the intense chaos that signifies the transition from dayside to nightside.

Sports has arrived and has begun organizing the night's work. Soon they will be loudly demanding to know why the City Editor has reassigned a photographer from one of their stories. There will be an acerbic exchange to iron out the priorities.

The Entertainment Editor, as always, is cajoling the music/theatre writer to get her story filed by deadline. This is a process that will be handed off later to the Indonesian, who will continue demanding copy from her until 11 pm. Max, the Entertainment Editor and the Indonesian meet frequently to "crack down" on her, but they never succeed.

Max suspects there is a good deal of "cross-pollination" occurring in the newsroom, but none of his staff will let him in on it when there's a new affair taking place. However, he can usually tell by observing increases in productivity and creativity. There is a rumour, hotly denied, about the Cartoonist and a general assignment reporter. The rumour is persistent because their colleagues want it to be true.

Bedsides romance, the other factor guaranteed to boost productivity from one end of the newsroom to the other is a juicy homicide. The police scanner blares all day atop City Desk. No one notices it until a note of tension creeps into one of the voices crackling back and forth. When that happens, the background noise in the newsroom drops off sharply and heads pop up, like prairie dogs sniffing the air. Usually it's nothing, but every now and then they'll hear something that cries havoc.

Crime reporter: Where is it?

City Editor: I don't fucking know. Why don't you make a call and find out?

Crime reporter: I want a shooter.

City Editor: You'll get a shooter when I know what the fuck is going on ... hold on ... they're looking for a white van. A lesbian abducted her lover and her child.

Crime reporter: A lesbian kidnapping?

Shooter: Are they movie lesbians or regular-looking?

City Editor: Golly, I don't think the cops have a radio code for "movie lesbians".

Crime reporter: Sarcasm is unbecoming to you.

The Business Editor is polishing his outrage column for the next day. This usually means inserting the clause "and that really burns these business buns." His readers love it.

The copy desk is the domain of the Indonesian after 5 pm. He'll command the group of copy editors, a.k.a "rim pigs", for the next 10 hours as they organize all the stories and pictures into a coherent whole. He is talking to a day-side reporter who wants to know why his story was changed last night. "Because what you wrote was wrong," the Indonesian says calmly.

As Max foresaw, the sports editor has arrived at City Desk to complain about the loss of a photo assignment: "All I asked for was two pictures and you kill one of them. And that one is the HOCKEY GAME for chrissake."

"Use one from another game," the City Editor says. "I keep assigning photos for you and all I see the next morning is the same homo-erotic clusterfuck after someone scores a goal."

"Those are jubilation shots. That's what sports is all about. Max, help me out here."

"Schedule a freelancer for the game," Max tells the City Editor, "but ask for a shot of a player scoring a goal or knocking somebody senseless against the boards. Readers have seen enough jubilation shots for a while."

"Good. Thanks, Max," the sports guy calls as he walks away.

"I want a moratorium on jubilation shots," Max shouts after him.

He turns to the City Editor, who has her head down and her arms up in exasperation, as if someone has just spilled a soft drink on her science project.

"I'll think of something," she says without raising her head.

Max steps back and soaks in the improbable harmony of the whole thing. People stomping back and forth with paper in their hands, pounding their keyboards, arguing, checking the clock or, in a few cases, quietly laying out the pages for the next day. Soon the news meeting will begin and the stories and photos for the day will be prioritized, only to be re-prioritized later should there be a murder or movie-lesbian-kidnapping during the evening.

Somehow — it's never the same two days in a row — all the chaos and strife will coalesce into the next edition of the Paper. The presses will run, trucks will drive away with loads of newspapers, readers will react, and then the whole thing will begin again.

The MBAs and other corporate honchos beginning to take over the news business see only "process" and "product" in all this, but Max doubts any of them have run anything more complex than a lemonade stand. Max believes the jargon helps them sustain the mistaken idea that they belong in news. But you can't monetize commitment. You can't repurpose mavericks into widget-makers. You can't quantify a love affair.

And Max can't bring himself to leave the Paper, at least not before the corporate barbarians come over the walls.

1986

Bastards of the CBC

The Smiling Cobra ardently believes that he is the beating heart of the Paper; that he is adored by every single employee for his generous spirit and overwhelming but gentle intellect. Max knows this because the Cobra has told him so innumerable times, all the while urging him to try to see the Paper through the eyes of a beloved engineer.

Moreover, the only belief he holds dearer than that of his own consequence is the contemptibility of the CBC, infested as it is with fairies, immigrants and haughty intellectuals. Defeat on the baseball diamond by these pansies would be tantamount to being spanked in public by Adrienne Clarkson.

But that nightmare is, now, potentially real because Max failed to consider it when he unilaterally accepted a challenge from the CBC staff to a softball game.

"The softball team is my domain, Max," the Cobra says from behind his desk. "It wears the Paper's uniform, so I make the calls. It's about leadership and morale, also my purview."

"With respect," Max says, "you made us pay for the uniforms and the field rental ourselves, so I don't think that puts a lot of weight in your bat."

The Cobra reacts as if he's been poked by a stick. Then he recovers and the skin of his neck flares into its hood configuration.

"I'll pay for all softball expenses from now until the end of time," the Cobra says, "but there are three conditions: I get to play against the CBC; no women are in the lineup, and the Copy Boy sits this one out."

The negotiated rules require a minimum of three women on the field at all times, so there's nothing the Cobra can do about that. And the Wife, who has been filling in, won't care about giving up her spot to the boss.

The Copy Boy, however, is another matter. He has been with the Paper from the beginning, doing odd jobs and helping out wherever he can. He is difficult to understand because he has cerebral palsy, which has also impaired his motor functions. But his determination to contribute has endeared him to everyone. None of Max's crew would even think of ditching him from the team just to beat the CBC. Besides, the Copy Boy — actually in his mid-thirties — is strong. On those rare occasions when he actually connects with a pitch, the ball is gone, baby, gone.

"Sorry," Max says. "That can't be done. It's just not on."

"I've already talked to him and he agrees with me. This game is too important. He's not retarded, you know, he understands."

"Who said he's retarded?" Max asks, then kicks himself for taking the bait.

"Oh, I think you and your staff patronize his intelligence constantly. Your belief that he can't make decisions for himself about a softball game is another example of that."

Checkmate. Max's distaste for the Cobra's world-view has occasionally led him to underestimate the man's cunning.

"I'm sure you won't mind if I talk to him myself," Max says.

"Not at all. In fact, I encourage it."

The implication here is that speaking with the Copy Boy is something Max rarely does. He leaves the office knowing that he's just had his ass whipped in a game of wits.

• • •

Max finds the Copy Boy helping the Political Reporter retrieve a so-called floppy disc from beneath the heavy end of a steel desk. He does this by getting down on all fours, lifting the desk backhand with his left arm and reaching beneath with his right arm. The reporter, who somehow imagined he would be part of the process, is at a loss for words when the Copy Boy hands him the disc.

"Hi Max," he says, swatting dust from his trousers. "What can I do for you?"

Max has more trouble than most understanding what the Copy Boy says, so they both have to put in extra effort to make their conversations work.

"The Publisher says you don't want to play this weekend," Max says.

"I'm a bad player, Max. We could lose because of me."

"We still win most of our games and sometimes you get home runs. Besides, it's not like there'll be big-league scouts in the stands."

The Copy Boy laughs: "More likely, there won't be anybody in the stands."

"Exactly my point," Max says.

"But the boss really wants to win."

"It's up to you," Max says. "As manager, I'm telling you that we want you on the team, just like always. Just tell the publisher your decision, OK?"

The Copy Boy brightens: "You bet!"

Max experiences the full joy of righteousness on the drive home that evening, but finds the Wife surprisingly hesitant to join in.

"I don't know, Maxie. Not every little wrong has to be righted, you know."

"You've been in communications too long," he says.

But the Wife is unamused and sticks to her guns.

"The Cobra has already humiliated him once over this," she says. "Now, you've set him up for a second humiliation. Believe me, if he loses the game for us, it will be a very bad day for him."

As if the conversation weren't going badly enough, Max remembers that he gave the Wife's spot on the roster to the Cobra. He makes a mental note to tell her before the game.

The Cobra is a repeat visitor in the newsroom for the next two days, gathering each player's statistics and working out a game plan. Max is unhappy at this. Worse, Max's staff likes the unusual attention from the top guy and join in enthusiastically. It's like they're cheating on him. Each time their eyes meet during these visits, the Cobra gives Max a carefully calibrated look as if to say: "Why aren't you helping, Max? We've got a big game coming up."

Game day is perfect. Each bench has a chilled two-four under it and the air is full of the sounds of softballs smacking into mitts and hardwood bats. The Political Reporter has already opened a beer. Max, who has barely retained his position as team manager, surveys the scene and notes that each team has brought a ringer to the field.

The CBC guy is tall and well-built. Tight curls of brown hair form a dark halo around his head. He has a thick beard that almost covers his cheekbones. His eyes are hidden behind silvered sunglasses. Within 30 seconds of his arrival, Max's team has dubbed him the Yeti. But Max isn't laughing because the Yeti is casually swatting softballs out of the park, one after another.

The other ringer, undeniably, is the Cobra. He's in right field with a few others from the team, shagging fly balls. Despite his comic-strip build, he is moving around the field with grace and speed.

Max recognizes this as a sign of a true athlete, someone whose abilities you haven't imagined possible until you've seen them close up. This happened once in Montreal, where Max was playing first base on a team that had mistakenly entered an elite tournament. The first hit that came Max's way was a waist-high line drive, easily within his reach. But the ball was close to breaking the sound barrier. Max, who had no idea someone could hit a ball that hard, calmly elected to watch it go by rather than risk an injury trying to catch it.

"Hey Max! Wake up!" the Cobra calls cheerily from the right field fence and fires the ball toward the edge of the cage where Max is standing. He looks up just in time to see the ball land three feet in front of him and bounce into his mitt. Max has players who can barely throw the ball from base to first. The Cobra flashes a smile and, for once, it appears to be genuine.

"Look alive, Max!" he hollers.

The CBC is the home team, so the Paper bats first. Max leads with the Copy Boy and, on a hunch, pencils in the Cobra as clean-up. This meets with the Cobra's approval. The rest of the lineup is immaterial.

The Yeti is pitching for the CBC. His warm-up throws are low and straight — fastball style. Every other player on the field, with the possible exception of the Cobra, is accustomed to high, looping pitches.

Max walks over to the CBC manager, a well-known on-air "personality" with perfect hair, something regarded in newspaper circles as a tragic defect.

"Sorry, Max," he says. "There's nothing in the agreed rules to stop him."

"Where did you get this guy, anyway?"

"He's the building electrician. I had no idea he liked baseball."

Bullshit, Max thinks.

"Play ball!" the umpire yells, and the Copy Boy lumbers awkwardly to the plate.

The first pitch, like the warm-ups, zooms by the Copy Boy's kneecaps, hard and straight. He does nothing but look at it.

"Strike one!"

"Atta boy! Atta boy!" the Cobra yells. "Wait for one you like! Wait for the one you like!"

In softball, everything has to be said twice.

The Copy Boy lets a second one go by.

"Just make contact. Just make contact," the Cobra yells. Then he turns to Max and says quietly: "Look, he's relaxing. I think he likes fastball pitches because they come in straight rather than falling in front of him."

The next pitch is high and inside. The Copy Boy doesn't flinch.

The following pitch is exactly the same as the first two,

but the Copy Boy makes contact with a ferocious swing that startles all onlookers. The ball heads straight for the Yeti himself, who is unprepared for it, and connects with his ankle.

Yelling and throwing his arms in the air, the Copy Boy ambles to first base.

"I think we just got a break," the Cobra whispers to Max.

"The poor guy's ankle might be broken," Max says, trying to sound concerned as the Yeti writhes on the mound.

"Don't bullshit a bullshitter," the Cobra says.

"Okay. As long as he doesn't die, I'm fine with it."

The Cobra offers his second genuine smile of the day and puts a hand on Max's shoulder as he leans in for a collegial moment.

"He's okay, but he won't be able to pitch off that foot. I don't think he'll be able to field well, either. They'll move him to first base just so he can keep hitting. If he can hit half as well as he did in warm up, that's all they need."

That's exactly what happens, and the new pitcher throws lob balls. The Paper gets another man on base before the Cobra gets his chance. Max marvels at his long torso and wonders if it affords extra strength at the plate.

The Cobra answers the question by blowing the first pitch onto the adjoining diamond and strolling casually around the bases. The overjoyed Copy Boy and the rest of the team are waiting for him at home plate.

Max starts the Copy Boy as pitcher, figuring that all the extra motion entailed in delivering a pitch will drive the CBC batters crazy. It does, except for the Yeti, who is batting cleanup for his team. Injured as he is, he is barely able to clear the fence with his first homer and limps around the bases.

The inning ends when the CBC hits a high fly over the

right fielder's head and the Cobra journeys all the way from left field to catch it.

For the bottom of the second the Cobra, with Max's agreement, moves to centre field, where he can more easily back up both of the other outfielders. Even from there he can be heard chattering at the batters: "Humm-batta! Humm-batta! Pakka-pakka-pakka."

Fortunately for all, only Max realizes that "pakka" is Cobra-chatter for "fudge-packer."

The Cobra and the Yeti continue to exchange home runs. The only thing that varies is the number of runners on base. In the fourth, the CBC batters figure out the Copy Boy and score a couple of extra runs. Max and the Cobra swap the Copy Boy for the City Editor, who had been playing right field in a tennis skirt. This is of no concern because the Cobra has demonstrated his ability to cover pretty much the whole outfield. Max tells him to cheat a bit to the right, just in case.

The Paper is ahead by two going into the last inning. But the CBC scores a run and then gets the tying run on base when the batter is hit by a pitch. The offending pitch has no velocity at all but the batter, a sports reporter, calmly lets it hit her on the shoulder before throwing herself violently backwards to demonstrate an attempt to avoid contact.

Max is furious. He bounds up to the umpire to protest: "She has to make a reasonable attempt to avoid contact!"

"She did," the ump says.

"Yes, but she did it AFTER the ball hit her."

"Way to go, Max. Way to go, Max," the Cobra says.

"Take your base," the ump says to her.

Max is furious. The Cobra sees that, runs in from centre

field and drags Max away before things get out of hand. "Easy Max, baby. Easy Max, baby."

With a runner on first and two out, the potential winning run limps up in the form of the Yeti. Max double-checks the line-up to see if it's possible, and the news is bad. The Yeti, still favouring his ankle, settles in at the plate. Max signals the Copy Boy to take a position at the very edge of the right field fence. The Cobra cheats a little more to the right and backs up.

The Yeti looks directly at Max through his silvered glasses and points with his bat at the Copy Boy, who looks every bit as helpless as he is.

As is customary, the Yeti smacks the first pitch. But the combination of his sore ankle and his attempt to hit the ball to his wrong side sends it high and short. The Cobra, who is way back, starts for the ball, but it's going to be close.

At first, no one notices the lonely fielder out by the foul post. He starts in, shifting wildly from left to right, both of his arms waving randomly in the air, eyes fixed firmly on the ball.

The Cobra is faster, but the Copy Boy has a shorter line to the ball. They are on a collision course. The team yells at them with everything they have, but the two fielders are too focused on the ball to hear.

"I got it! I got it!" they both yell.

The Cobra, being an athlete, finally sees the problem. At first he moves to cut in front of the Copy Boy, but then he realizes it can't be done, and cuts the other way.

Max is marvelling at the near miss when he hears a great howl from the Copy Boy. The howl continues, unbroken, as he races toward his teammates. It takes Max a moment to realize what's happened: the laws of physics and chance have combined to nestle the ball firmly into the pocket of the Copy Boy's glove.

He is still yelling "I got it!" as he crashes into his waiting teammates, who drop everything and carry him off toward a bar down the street.

Max and the Cobra are left to pack up the bats, balls and empty beer bottles. The Wife and the Son pitch in, too.

When it's done, the Cobra is sitting on the bench, shoulders drooping, head hanging. Max, on the other hand, is enjoying the thrill of victory and actually liking the Cobra for the first time in his life.

"C'mon," he says. "Let's go celebrate! You're the MVP! You're the star! Geez, nine RBIs and six homers."

He puts a friendly hand on the Cobra's shoulder, but the reaction is cold.

"No, he's the star," he says, meaning the Copy Boy. "Let him have his glory."

Max protests again, saying it's a team victory.

"Thanks," he says.

Max cannot fathom why the Cobra is so downcast. After all, the Paper won!

"It's Saturday," the Cobra says as he strides away. "I've got a lot of errands to do."

Max turns around. The Wife and the Son are hand in hand, waiting for him.

Max gives them a "what's his problem?" shrug.

"Because you got the lineup you wanted, the Cobra's not the hero today—and he obviously needed that," she says. "You can't edit everything, Maxie."

1995

His Excellency Requests a Favour

"I'M NOT GOING to make His Excellency the Archbishop walk through your newsroom," the Smiling Cobra hisses. "It's bad enough you refused to go to his office."

"We don't have to explain ourselves to police, state, or church," Max says. "If they want to discuss our content, they can come here."

Max loves the walk to the publisher's office. After working almost 15 years in a strip mall, he's delighted by the Paper's airy new building. And the Paper's making money and employing 100 people.

Best of all, the Owner is giving Max most of the credit for the success, making him difficult to fire, something the Smiling Cobra still rabidly desires. Max secretly agrees with the Cobra's analysis of their success: a growing population means a growing newspaper. Nonetheless, he graciously accepts any praise that comes his way.

When Max arrives, he sees that the Archbishop and his Assistant are already present. The Cobra sits nervously behind his desk, which bears a huge new nameplate saying simply PUBLISHER. The Assistant, wearing the requisite black shirt and clerical collar, has turned his chair to face the empty one intended for Max.

The Archbishop is beside him in a well-tailored grey suit. His face is fleshy and heavy-jowled. Oddly, his chair is set closer to the back wall, so that he isn't facing anyone directly.

The Cobra does the introductions, repeating "His Excellency" as many times as possible. The Assistant leans back toward the Archbishop and mumbles unintelligibly. The holy man utters an equally unintelligible reply.

"Max," says the Cobra. "As you know, His Excellency has come here to discuss a serious matter."

"Father Peter," the Assistant says helpfully.

"Ahh — Father Peter," Max replies. "I thought as much."

Max has no idea who Father Peter is.

The Assistant leans toward the Archbishop and mumbles again. His Excellency replies. Max is astonished to realize that the two clerics aren't speaking English, French or the third language that Max would recognize, Spanish. The Cobra nods, apparently believing this is how things are done.

"His Excellency says there is a lot of gossip in Father Peter's former parish."

"*Vous parlez français*?" Max asks the Assistant.

Silence. "*Habla espanol*?" he asks.

"Father — I assume I should call you Father — may I ask which of God's languages you and His Excellency are speaking?"

The two of them confer before the Assistant turns to Max and says: "Latin."

"Have you given up living languages for Lent?" Max asks.

The Cobra, the Assistant and the Archbishop all flush

with anger. In the case of His Excellency, this is an impressive sight. The two holy men engage in an extended conversation.

"The Archbishop is a holy man, Max," the Cobra explains.

"There's no shortage of them," Max says. "What's so special that we can't speak English?"

"First," the Assistant says. "This is not the Lenten season, although we suspect you know that. Second, His Excellency holds a deep distrust of the media, something you have just reinforced. By conversing in Latin, we can deprive you of a direct quote that you could use out of context."

"But your translations are full and accurate, are they not?" Max asks.

The Assistant smiles: "Maybe. Maybe not."

Max switches to French, annoying both the Cobra and His Excellency, but the Assistant doesn't miss a beat. He translates Max's French into Latin.

Got me, Max thinks.

In French, the Assistant explains that any coverage of Father Peter will do great harm to Catholics.

"For Christ's sake," the Cobra says. "Max, Father, whatever, would you please speak English." Max smiles broadly. The holy men stare at the Cobra in silent rebuke. "Oh! Sorry, Your Excellency."

The Archbishop resumes in Latin.

"His Excellency is concerned that coverage of this regrettable matter will undo all the good work Father Peter has done for Nova Scotia and Halifax, not to mention centuries of good work by the Church," the Assistant says. "For example, we fear that the youth and gymnastic clubs Father Peter established will fail. Perhaps even more importantly, we are concerned that publicity in irresponsible journals will unnecessarily shake the faith of some parishioners, which would be very painful for them. Further, it has been dealt with in a most severe manner ..."

Max raises an eyebrow, prompting the cleric to add that Father Peter has been sent to work with the poor under very difficult conditions.

"Where?"

"I am authorized to tell you that he is in Latin America."

The Cobra is again nodding, satisfied at a job well done. Max is feeling less charitable. "I assume that by 'irresponsible journals' you mean this one. The one that I edit."

Archbishop and Assistant confer in Latin. "Yes. That is correct. We believe society underestimates the effect the gutter press can have on people's emotions."

"Quite so," Max says.

"Your competitor would never publish this story."

"They know about it?" Max asks.

"They have known for some time," the Assistant replies smugly. Both of the holy men wear the approving smiles reserved for newspapers that know how to co-operate for the greater good.

Again, the Archbishop speaks through his assistant: "We Christians have a saying: 'It's God's job to comfort the afflicted, and afflict the comfortable.' Are you a religious man, Max?"

"When I was six," says Max, "my best friend explained that we couldn't be friends because I was a Protestant and would burn in Hell. Then there was an unfortunate incident with a pencil. Since then, I haven't been noticeably religious. How about you?"

"There is one more thing," the Assistant says. "Father

Peter is a good man whose fall from grace is punishment enough. And here, I speak only for myself, because it is a difficult topic. It has to be recognized that some young boys have dark hearts."

"What do you mean, exactly?"

"Well, in some cases, they learn how to manipulate human weakness at an early age."

"And ...?"

"They can be seductive. They are often the predators, not the victims."

Max realizes he has been unconsciously measuring the distance between himself and the Assistant. Half a step would put him well within striking distance.

"Yes," he says, hoping the Assistant can hear the malevolence in his voice. "We all understand how seductive these young slatterns can be. No adult could be expected to resist their wiles."

The Archbishop goes red, apparently on the verge of summoning the Devil. He whispers to the Assistant, who relays the message. "You so-called journalists are not careful about what you say and write. You don't worry about consequences. If you are not careful, you may come to regret that."

Max stands: "Indeed. Well, I'll certainly give some thought to everything you've said, including the apparent threat you just uttered. By the way, your 'affliction' aphorism was originally about newspapers before being appropriated by some lay religious writers. And, for the record, I lean toward afflicting the comfortable."

The Smiling Cobra chimes in: "I can assure Your Excellency that you have nothing to be concerned about as far as *this* paper goes."

There follow the ritual goodbyes and a few lame jokes about the rainy weather. The great man and his assistant are at the door when Max asks a final question.

"Your Excellency, I asked if you are a religious man but you haven't answered."

The Archbishop looks at Max as if he has just set his own hair on fire.

"I'm the Archbishop," he says, in English.

• • •

After enduring a warning from the Cobra to spike any story he has about Father Peter, Max heads straight for the City Editor.

"Is Mother Mary here?" he asks. Mother Mary has earned the nickname for her tendency to mother everyone in the newsroom, although she's the same age. She is also the most devout soul in the newsroom, but Hell on wheels if you're an errant priest.

"She's covering the bank robbery."

"Well, when she gets back, tell her I want a story on some local pederast priest."

"Details?"

"All I know is that his name is Father Peter, he's been relocated, and probably worked in or near the city. Oh, and the idiots at the Other Paper are sitting on the story."

1973

Editor in Close Touch with his Emotions

Max pulls into the Sunday Tabloid's watery parking lot wondering if he's emotionally deficient. He practically tripped over a dead body but all he can think of is comic strips he read as a kid and drinking beer after work. He knows he should be more upset. Inside, the makeshift newsroom is lit like Frankenstein's lab with bare fluorescent tubes. Max takes a breath and finds the polluted air to his satisfaction. He locates the Veteran Reporter and heads for a cubicle across from her. He rolls in a piece of copy paper and settles in to write. This is the best part.

"Don't get comfortable," the Veteran Reporter, wearing the usual spotless white blouse and jean skirt, whispers. She is simultaneously hammering away on her typewriter.

A voice like a rusty table saw slices the air from three cubicles away.

"Where the FUCK have you been?" the Editor shouts. The Veteran Reporter sniggers quietly, but keeps typing.

"Dead body in the woods by the Canadian Tire," Max ventures, liking the sound of it.

"It better be a cock-sucking murder."

"Suicide."

"Oh, excuse me, detective, how do you know it's a fucking suicide?"

Max grins. "This isn't fucking *Hawaii Five-O*. You find a dead guy with a rifle in his hand and the box it came in lying next to him, it's a fucking suicide. *Point finale*."

The Veteran Reporter whispers again: "You saw the body?"

"Almost tripped over it."

The Editor cranks up the volume: "Well that's not very fucking good, is it?

"Why not?"

"We don't cover suicides. You know that. What else have you got?"

"Car accident, nobody dead. Robbery at a convenience store, nobody dead, no shots fired."

"Jesus fucking Christ. Two crappy briefs. Nobody dead. Not much of a day, is it?"

"I gave you three stories before five o'clock."

"Well, isn't that just GRAND. We got a guy robbing banks with a machine gun all week and you bring in stories about a 100-year-old woman, a whale caught in a ship's propeller and a strike at a fucking CANDY FACTORY!"

The Veteran Reporter jumps in, still, typing. "You assigned him those stories. It's Saturday. There's nothing new on the robberies, and you didn't assign that to him anyway. And the banks are closed. They're harder to rob when they're closed — even with a machine gun."

Silence. From the cubicle behind the Veteran Reporter, the mild-mannered Copy Editor mumbles: "Too far. You went too far."

Explosion. "Well, aren't we quick to defend our incompetent little friend. I happen to know that our asshole cop reporter was at that suicide HALF AN HOUR AGO because a cop-friend at the station called and told me they saw him running away from the body like some kind of pervert caught in a disgusting act! Never get to a scene before the COPS!"

"Sorry," Max says. "I figured it was kids, so the cops wouldn't care."

"Well, I guess they DO care, because they fucking CALLED ME, didn't they?"

"Sorry."

"I don't give a shit. What I care about is I don't get any copy from you because you spend all day jerking off. What have you been doing for the last 20 minutes? Walking around the woods with your peanut-sized dick in your hand?"

The Veteran Reporter has finally stopped typing and now she's laughing merrily.

The Copy Editor shouts: "Twenty minutes to 10. I need copy now if you want to see it in the paper tomorrow."

"Sorry about your dick," says the Veteran Reporter, who has resumed typing.

1975

Reporter Gets Big Story! (Some May Have Died)

Back at the *Palacio* after dodging bullets Max is still high as he phones in his story.

Being shot at — and missed — is better than anything he'd hoped for on this trip.

"Police opened fire with rifles and machine guns on protesting community college students in this mountain capital today."

"Slow down! Slow down!" the Bureau Chief says. "I'm not Gandalf the fucking Wizard. There's no such thing as magic typing."

"Sorry-sorry," Max says. But he isn't. He can picture the Bureau Chief, the phone jammed between his shoulder and cheek, pounding out the words. Max's words. This is better than sex, he thinks. It's a scene from *The Front Page* — "Hello, sweetheart get me rewrite!" — PLUS sex.

"It's not immediately known whether there were deaths or injuries ..."

"Stop! What do you mean 'not immediately known'? What bullshit is that?"

"Well ..."

"What you mean is, you don't know and therefore I don't know, and that's no fucking good, is it?" The Bureau Chief is shouting.

"Well ..."

"You don't know. Now all I got is another fucking riot story."

"I'll ask around ... hospitals ... cops."

"You do that. Do some reporting. But stay away from the cops," says the Bureau Chief. "They're getting nervous about the Army, and the secret police chief there is a nasty piece of work. *El Mago*."

"Yeah, you told me," Max says.

"Well, I wasn't kidding. He's not afraid to hurt you. How is it you don't know about injuries, anyway? You said you were there."

"We were ..."

"Never mind. Word is, no one seriously hurt. But I don't like reporters who cover stories without leaving their hotel. Finish this and go find out for sure about injuries."

"I don't cover stories from my hotel."

"Stay away from *El Mago*."

"Fuck you. I'll interview him."

Six paragraphs later, he's done. The Bureau Chief will write the background himself, for which Max is grateful because he's only beginning to understand what's going on.

He hangs up, takes a breath, and then nods to the Doorman, who's on the other side of a half-door, waiting at the switchboard. After a minute or so of negotiation with the operator, the Doorman signals him to pick up the phone again. He hears it ringing in his apartment — he's sure he recognizes the ring.

"Maxie?" The Wife's voice is faint. It's like the Doorman has connected him to a different planet.

"How are things, Cactus?"

"Everything's fine, but I miss you." The sound of her voice breaks through the cocoon he has been carefully building since the riot in the capital, and he fights to keep his emotion contained.

They exchange the basics: what's new with her job, the Editor is the same asshole he's always been, they're having a gorgeous spring in Montreal. But the Wife is worried about Max. It seems the Copy Editor had quietly arranged for their service to include the Latin America feed.

"I do read the wire, you know," she says. "You guys were in that riot."

"We watched it from a balcony," Max says. "It was like box seats."

"Bullshit. I saw the photos," she says.

"That was before it got going," he says. "Basically, all we're doing is spending money on travel so we can arrive late for stories."

Max knows the Wife isn't buying that, either, but she lets it go. He tries to reassure her and she warns him to come back in one piece: "Don't let me down. You've got three months left to get this out of your system."

They finish with a few affectionate words and he hangs up. Max has a curious feeling that he is in two places at once, that he is watching himself over his own shoulder. In the next breath the sensation is gone and forgotten.

Max signals the Doorman to put the next call through.

"Oh, Maxie, I wasn't sure when you could call," the Dancer says.

"Every four weeks, right on schedule," he says.

"Everything okay?"

"I'm fine, but it's fucking dangerous here. How are you?"

The Dancer is fine, too, and this time wants his advice on whether to sell her interest in the nightclub.

"They're offering me twice the book value of my share. My board member in Calgary says I should hold out for more."

Max is alarmed.

"What are you thinking of?" he shouts into the phone. "You've told me yourself how nasty these people are. I've written about the things they've done. They're criminals and you're not, and now they've decided you could be a liability. They're being generous because they like you and want you out quickly. Take the offer. No haggling."

"But Calgary ..."

"Calgary doesn't know how those Montreal bastards do business," Max says.

"There could be a lot more money ..."

"Don't get greedy. Okay? You'll take it and run?"

"Okay. I promise. Jesus, Maxie, you sound scared. Be careful."

"I'm not scared. Well, I'm scared for you. Take the offer. Gotta go."

"Wait!" she says. "Your dividends. You want them paid out or reinvested?"

Max is too preoccupied to turn his mind to the matter: "Do what you think is best."

He emerges from the office behind the reception desk of *El Palacio* and pays the Doorman for letting him use the phone. He gives Max a quizzical look.

"Don't get it wrong," Max says. "I am a one-woman man."

"I was more interested in your call to your bureau chief. You seemed very pleased," the Doorman says, having changed into a white shirt and black vest in the unlikely event that a customer shows up in the bar. "May I ask ..."

"I just filed a story to the wire service," he says, unable to repress a smile.

"About the two-headed sheep?"

Max, feeling magnanimous, chuckles tolerantly. "Not quite. There was a riot near the cathedral. Well, not a riot. An attack by the police."

"And you were there?"

"We were right there, man."

Getting high on the experience is icing on the cake. Now he understands that his little omissions are inconsequential. By God, he is a reporting machine. Nothing can stand between Max and a story. The Bureau Chief will see that soon enough.

The Photog is probably on his way back from the airport, having given his film to a pilot friend. They have agreed to meet at the *Palacio* bar, but Max can't wait for him now.

"How many hospitals in this town?" he asks the Doorman.

"Two, but your friend has left a message to meet him at the community college. The students have occupied the cafeteria."

"Shit. How do you get there?"

The Doorman surveys the empty tables. "It is five minutes from here by car. If there is trouble, no taxi will take you. I will be your taxi for five American dollars."

"Deal!" Max says. "But I have to change first."

• • •

Max and the Doorman pull up in a VW Beetle a few blocks away from the community college. Ahead, Max can see a cluster of Ford Escort police cars blocking access to the college.

"The curfew begins at seven o'clock," the Doorman says. "I will finish work and be here — exactly here — at half-past six."

"Got it," Max says as he opens the passenger door. Then he turns back toward the Doorman. "What does *El Mago* mean?"

The Doorman is startled. "That's a person," he says. "A secret policeman."

"So what's it mean?"

The Doorman hesitates. "It means 'The Magician' — because he makes people disappear."

The Doorman is agitated and has more to say, but Max ignores him and hops out of the VW.

He starts walking parallel to the street the police are blocking. He's wearing khaki shorts, heavy hiking boots and a tie-dyed T-shirt. Instead of a notebook, he carries only his folded paper and pencil stub. His Kodak Instamatic hangs from his neck and he's pulled his lengthening hair out from behind his ears. The final touches are his guidebook and a Canadian flag pinned to the strap of his knapsack. He has gone from gringo hack to gringo tourist. Annoying and over-privileged, but harmless.

Max hates the goofy shorts — he has legs like toothpicks — but the disguise is part of being an intrepid correspondent. Heart pounding, he runs crouching from block to block, as if someone might shoot at him, but standing up when he comes to each intersection and walking casually by, looking to see if the police are blocking the way. He does this four times before he comes to an open street. It rises steeply and takes a sharp right to circle around a huge stone building. At the point where the street changes direction is a long stone stairway leading to a balustrade. The building, Max now realizes, is the cathedral.

He is still taking it all in when he sees a familiar metal and glass phallus rise up from behind the stone and then lever downward like a submarine breaching the surface. Right behind it, the Photog's head comes into view, complete with bush-hat. He is glued to the viewfinder behind his most precious and impressive telephoto lens. Max almost laughs out loud with joy and admiration for his formidable friend.

He starts up the hill, Instamatic bouncing on his chest. As he approaches the stairway a dark figure wearing the weird, Nazi-style helmet favoured by the police swings toward him, his right hand resting on his Uzi. Max smiles widely and waves, lumbering toward the guy with an aw-shucks side-to-side gait.

"How's it goin'?" he asks, now a couple of feet away. To his left the dusty street is littered with bricks, stones, cop cars and police. He starts in that direction and the cop immediately blocks his way.

"*No pasa.*" His eyes betray neither hostility nor doubt that the gringo has taken his last step toward the community college.

Max ostentatiously displays a thumb and finger and uses them to delicately retrieve his guidebook from his front pocket. He nods at the blank face of the cop and opens it.

"*Por favor,*" he says in the most engaging tone he can muster. "*Donde esta el churcho*?"

For a long time the guard stares at Max as if he has just stepped from a flying saucer. Then he grins.

"*La iglesia*," he says, correcting Max's Spanish.

"*Si*," Max says. "*La iglesia*."

The guard widens his grin and extends his arm toward the hill.

Max makes a show of laughing at himself and thanks the guy several times. The guard says it's nothing. Max is about to mount the first step when the guard calls out. There is a trace of simpatico in his expression.

"Hey, *turista*," he says. "*Por favor*, be careful. Go away from here."

Max waves his assurances. It occurs to him that underneath the guard's uniform is probably a low-paid family guy who would rather not have anybody's death on his conscience.

At the top of the stairs, in case the guard is watching, Max keeps moving toward the cathedral until he's out of sight. Then, crouching again, he joins the Photog by the balustrade.

The Photog gives him an awkward hug.

"Nice shorts, pelican man. How did you find me?"

Max feigns indignation: "Easy. I'm a trained journalist."

"Trained, my ass."

The Photog says he has come up the other side of the hill because he knew the cops would arrest him if they spotted his camera equipment. He says the street blocked by the guard runs between the teaching building and the administration offices. Near the entrance there's an apartment building. From their perch they can see most of the street but only the roof of the teaching building. The Photog says there are about 100 kids holed up in the cafeteria. So far, they have repelled two tear gas attacks by chucking the canisters back into the street. The Photog has good shots of gas and cops, but none of the students.

"We can't find a better spot?" Max says.

"No, man. I don't want to get my balls shot off. Do you? Oh wait — I forgot — you do."

They wait and listen for something to happen, but aside from the occasional order, there is nothing to be heard. The crisp mountain light is turning to dusk. Max looks at his watch and warns that the Doorman will be at the rendezvous in 15 minutes.

"You're right. Let's go," the Photog says. "It's too dark for pictures and I need to get my film to the airport."

"Good idea, but I'll stay here."

"No-no-no. That is really stupid. If you get caught after curfew, anything's possible."

"I don't care. I'm going to see this through."

"I did not know you could be so stubborn when we started this trip," his friend says. "Stay here. Do not move for any reason. We will come and get you. In an emergency, try to run into the cathedral. Maybe a priest will save you. Maybe not."

• • •

Max feels it's dark enough to safely poke his head all the way above the parapet. A squad of cops block the spot where he encountered the guard. In the last of the light, he sees a black jeep armed with a .50-calibre machinegun pull up. The driver and the gunman wear white kerchiefs over their faces.

The kerchiefs are a bad sign, Max thinks.

The streetlights flicker and go dark. Max can hear combat boots tramping below him, but can see nothing. Young voices begin chanting "*Abajo con la junta!*"

"*Quatro*!" someone says. The word was saw-toothed with rage.

Max sees four muzzle flashes before he hears the gun. The street goes bright orange and maybe half a second later Max hears the gun go off. *Choom-choom-choom-choom*, four times. In the aftermath Max hears brick and glass tinkling to the ground. For the first time in his life, Max hears the sound of adults screaming. The sounds propel him to the ground even though he is well out of the line of fire. Max gathers himself and creeps back to his post.

The same angry voice yells for more shots. *Choom-choom. Choom-choom-choom-choom*. The orange muzzle flashes illuminate the pall of smoke from the previous volleys. Low moans and sobs take the place of the screaming.

Max leans against the stone, facing the church. Combat boots thunder. Orders are bellowed, but Max's Spanish isn't up to the job. He thinks he hears someone ask if there are dead in the cafeteria, but he can't be sure. He thinks he hears someone else say "six", but the Spanish word for it is too easily lost in the commotion to be certain.

It occurs to him that he could go down the hill and try to bluster his way in with his homemade "international press pass" and find out what happened. Or he can say he got lost coming back from the cathedral.

His arms and legs veto both ideas.

"Max, you don't have that kind of courage," they say. "This is where you belong. Up on a hill, looking down at the action."

The struggle between the coward and the indestructible reporting machine with the speed of a gazelle and eyes of an eagle begins. Round one goes to the coward.

So Max lets his head rest on the cobblestones of the church plaza and stares at the sparkling black mountain sky, aware only that he is lost somewhere in the middle of all that, 8,000 feet above sea level, whirling with his planet in a circle at 1,000 miles an hour. It's a beautiful moment, about to be linked forever with Max the Coward.

And so the reporting machine wins round two.

He's starting back down the stone stairs toward the college, rehearsing his lost tourist story when someone grabs his shoulder from behind.

"What the hell are you doing, man?" The Photog's words are urgent, laced with disbelief.

Max spots the Doorman coming up behind his friend: "What's *he* doing here?"

"There is more to him than meets the eye, I think," the Photog replies.

"You should have seen that gun," Max says. "Jesus Christ. Ten shots. It's like a fucking cannon. Somebody's dead for sure, but I don't know how many."

"And you think they are going to tell you? Because I'm telling you, if you go down there, you may disappear from the face of the planet."

Max's mind goes blank for a second. "No. Not this time. This time I'm going to follow through."

"The curfew's on," the Photog says. "File your story and then we'll have a beer."

"I don't HAVE a story. I've got cops wearing bandanas firing a big machine-gun into a school cafeteria. 'And then what happened Max?' the Bureau Chief will ask me. 'Oh, jeez,

I dunno, eh? It was a school night and I had to get to bed. But I'm pretty sure someone must have been hurt.'"

The Photog's voice is flat: "Then you're on your own, for now."

"Where are you going?"

"I'm going to see if we can save your life."

• • •

Max decides to stick with the *turista* bit and casually heads back down the stone stairway. His friend with the Nazi helmet spots him right away and rushes up. At first Max cannot tell whether his expression reveals alarm or disappointment at being deceived. He concludes it must be the former because he protects Max from the view of other cops.

He looks around frantically, then grabs Max by the arm and marches him across the street, trying to make it look like he's merely redirecting someone who's stumbled onto the scene.

"Fast-fast-fast, *Señor*," he says.

They arrive at the door to an apartment building; the guard opens it and all but throws Max into the lobby.

"Go up. Up," he says. "You must stay. Okay?"

Before Max can say anything, the guard hustles back to his post.

Inside Max can see the dim outlines of a courtyard with three floors above it. Everything is tiled and open to the air.

Max figures the guard's advice — "up" — is smart. He climbs the stairs to the third floor, which ought to have a good view of the street. He taps gently on the door of an apartment overlooking the street.

In a few moments he hears someone walking softly to the door.

"*Quien es*?" says a quiet male voice.

"*Periodista*," Max whispers.

"You are a journalist?" the man says.

"Yes."

"Do you have identification?"

Max slides his ridiculous *Prensa Internacional* card under the door. It opens and a guy about Max's age lets him into the apartment, which is dark except for a couple of candles.

There is a dish of untouched paella on the dining table and a young woman, presumably the wife of his host, is on the floor peeking out the window. When she turns to Max he can see that she has been crying.

The introductions are hushed.

"You are *Canadian?"* the man says in astonishment. "This is a crazy night."

The guy says they are both teachers at the community college. Geography for her, math for him. They are less than thrilled to be entertaining a foreign correspondent on this particular evening and aren't sure what to say.

Max asks for a turn by the window. He sees police vehicles everywhere. Cops are running back and bellowing orders and cursing. They have set up a large canvas tent to obscure the college entrance. The opening on Max's side is blocked by a troop transport truck. There are holes in the side of the building, some of them easily two feet in diameter.

"Are there any dead?" Max asks.

The guy translates and his wife responds with a torrent of heartbroken Spanish.

"She says: 'How can there not be dead?'"

"I heard someone say six dead," Max says.

"I did not hear anything like that, nor did my wife," the guy says fiercely.

Bullshit, Max thinks. He spots a phone.

"Can you connect me with the hospitals?" he asks.

After some back and forth, the guy agrees. There are no English speakers at the first hospital but, at Max's urging, his host extracts the information that four wounded students are being treated there. No dead.

At the second hospital they find an emergency room doctor who trained in Miami. Max can hear cries and other sounds of chaos when his host hands him the phone.

"I can tell you with certainty that I have seven wounded students here. I am certain they came from the community college," she says. "A few are very badly wounded. There is a girl who has lost her leg."

Max asks about dead.

"Here, the police don't bring their dead to hospitals," she says. "That's because we don't do resurrections, but we do keep very good records. I don't expect anyone here will die."

Max gets a few details about injuries and hangs up. He gives the couple $10 American and asks if he can use their phone to call the capital. The Bureau Chief takes the new information and tells Max to go home.

But Max has another idea. He thanks his relieved hosts, runs down the stairs and walks calmly toward the troop truck, holding his press card in the air.

"I want to talk to *El Mago*," he tells the disbelieving driver.

1987

Keeping the Bad Man at Bay

It's 2 a.m. Max is awakened by the realization that something in the household is amiss. It reminds him of when the Son was an infant, when he and the Wife worried that he would stop breathing in the night.

The Wife is sleeping comfortably, so he gets out of bed quietly, listening for intruders and sniffing for smoke. Nothing. But when he checks the Son's room, he finds it empty. The boy's jeans and his all-protective Montreal Canadiens sweatshirt are missing from the hooks on the back of his door.

Max refuses to even entertain the possibility that something bad is happening to the Son.

When his search brings him to the ground floor, he sees that the deadbolt on the front door is open. He gets on his toes, looks through the decorative glass and spots the Son. He's sleeping on a lawn chair in his Canadiens shirt, holding his baseball bat in his lap.

Max kisses the top of his head and gently strokes his hair until the boy awakens and gazes at his father with adoring brown eyes. Max wonders how much longer he will be God in the Son's world.

"What's up, buddy?" Max asks.

"I'm guarding our house against the bad man," he says sleepily. "If he comes, I can hit him with my bat, but only if I have to."

Max knows what's on the boy's mind. All the media have been covering the story of a man who breaks into people's houses. Some householders have awoken to find him staring at them in their beds. Most were just robbed, but the police are concerned that the intruder might eventually hurt someone.

At work, Max has taken several phone calls from readers of the Other Paper complaining that the Paper is frightening children with its coverage. They always acknowledge that the Other Paper is carrying the same story, and can never explain why only Max's paper is scaring kids.

The Son read the Paper today and watched the television news. He asked Max and the Wife, separately, about the intruder. They told him it was nothing to worry about, but that apparently wasn't enough.

"I didn't know you were so worried," Max tells him now.

"Just a little bit, Daddy."

"Well, you can't do guard duty on a school night," Max says. "So, let me take you upstairs back to bed, and I'll take my turn guarding the house. Nobody can get past me, right?"

"Oh, I *know*," he says, as if this is knowledge shared by all sentient beings. "But I heard Mommy say you need to rest."

Upstairs, Max puts the little guy to bed and retrieves his copy of *The Handmaid's Tale* from the master bedroom. He wakes up the Wife and explains.

"Oh, Maxie. You'll be exhausted in the morning."

"If I'm not out there, he'll know it and be terrified all night."

It's not clear why the front porch is the best place to intercept the bad man, but Max spends the rest of the night there reading and being grateful for the pleasant weather. He keeps the bat with him.

At 6:30 sharp, seconds after his Garfield alarm clock goes off, the Son is downstairs checking on his father.

• • •

At work, the consensus is that Max should buy a dog. Every boy should have one anyway.

At bedtime, Max again takes up his post on the porch. An hour later, as Max anticipated, the Son comes down to make sure Max is on the job.

"Everything okay, Daddy?"

"All clear, buddy. See you in the morning."

"Daddy?"

"Yep?"

"I don't think we need to guard the house tomorrow."

"Why?"

"By then, the bad man will know that you live here," the boy says, punching his right fist into his palm. "And once he knows, he'll stay away."

"You sure he'll know?" Max asks.

"Ohhh ... *he'll know* alright." The Son gives him a hug and charges back up to his bed.

And Max plunges back into his book, grateful for the privilege of doing his fatherly duty but alert for signs of the bad man.

You never know, he thinks.

1995

Holy Threat

HAVING LOADED THE dishes into the "marriage-saver" and sent the Son upstairs to do his homework, Max uncorks a bottle of Bordeaux and sits close to the Wife on the loveseat.

"You know, they make red wine in places like Chile and California. Even in Nova Scotia," she says.

"Oh," says Max. "I can re-cork it, if you like."

"I didn't mean that." She holds out her glass.

"When the French run out of wine that I like, I'll shop around," Max says. "But so far, so good."

"Max, I'm a little bit worried about something."

The Wife tells him that the Archbishop took her aside after a university board meeting that afternoon.

"And was His Most Venal Excellency his usual slithery self?" Max asks.

The Wife says he praised her for being so careful in her writing in news releases and other communications items.

"He said I was precise and careful about how it might affect others," she says.

Max, on the other hand, is quite careless, he had told her.

"He said your 'musings on abortion' are very harmful. He said he's worried about the effects they might have on my career if they became a board matter."

Max gets the Archbishop's point right away.

"He wants me to spike a story on a pederast priest," he tells her. "But I've never written about abortion. He could be referring to the miscarriage column, but that's crazy. It was a long time ago."

The Wife wearily covers her face with her hands. "The word 'abortion' was in the headline, wasn't it?"

"Sure."

"Well, all he has to do is wave the clipping in the faces of the board members," she says. "Once they see that word in large type, you can stick a fork in my job. The board doesn't like controversy. Peace over principle."

"Why wasn't there an uproar when the column was published?" Max asks.

"Because it was innocuous and because back then people like university governors didn't read the goddamn Paper."

"Sorry. Didn't see that coming."

"Not your fault. Have you got a plan?"

"Maybe," he says. "But you may not like it."

She kisses him lightly on the lips.

"Fuck 'em if they can't take a joke. Do it."

"What about your job?"

"We're white and middle class. We won't starve."

The Wife refills her wine glass and bangs the bottle down on the counter like a movie cowboy. "What the world needs, Max, is an H-bomb that only kills shitheads. Maybe every 10 years or so we could set some off. There would be a few bright flashes, and a bit of a mess to clean up, and then the rest of us could get on with being human for a while."

Max kisses her forehead and she responds with a long hug.

Max hears his own voice in his head: "*Here. This will do. Let it be here.*"

• • •

The next morning, as always, Max heads straight for the City Desk hoping it has found some fresh news for him. The City Editor is wearing a puffy, flowered dress complemented by fire-engine red hair.

"Uh, you're not wearing a crinoline, are you?" he asks, immediately regretting it.

The City Editor pretends to be making notes, reading aloud as she goes.

"And then he asked if a crinoline might irritate, quote, my long, smooth thighs ..."

"Okay," says Max. "Let's start again. I see that, as always, you are appropriately dressed this morning."

He asks how Mother Mary is doing on the Father Peter story.

"She's stuck," is the answer. "He appeared in provincial court at seven a.m. last week and received a discharge on a complaint of simple assault. He flew to Toronto the same morning, but that's all we've got."

"He was in court at seven a.m.? How is that possible?"

"Court is in session whenever it wants to be," she says.

Max retrieves his contact book from his jacket pocket and shows her a long international number.

"Let me see if I can help. Would you please ask reception to set up a call for me to this number?"

Being the City Editor, she is not satisfied that she has all the information that is her due.

"London? What's up?"

"Does anyone around here just do what they're asked?" Max says.

The City Editor reminds him that he does the hiring and firing and, besides, it's the nature of the journalistic beast. Max looks skyward.

"It's called the Western Centre for Counter-terrorism."

"Ooh. Anyone in particular, or just the nearest counter-terrorist?"

"Just tell them it's Max calling for *El Mago*."

Now he has her full attention. The smart-ass banter is gone. Max heads for the office.

"Wait! What's going on? This sounds great. Come on, tell me. Please! Yes, I *am* wearing a crinoline. Please!"

"Sorry," Max says, waving his hand without turning around. "I've already said too much. It's a matter of provincial security."

"There's no such thing as provincial security," the City Editor says.

"There is if you're in the loop," Max says and disappears into his office.

The day's off to a good start, he thinks.

1961

The Yellow Pencil of Doubt, Second of Two Parts

Max is watching the Canadiens on television with the Father the night before his confirmation as a United Church member. He suddenly remembers his sixth birthday, when God failed to arrange for his Sunday school pencil. He recounts the story, making sure there's an edge to his voice.

"I'm not sure you've got the right interpretation when you say it means there's no God," the Father says.

Max has another problem: during his final Confirmation class, it emerged that the New Testament is supposed to be true. Max thinks the stories are clever, but they seem made-up to him. "I thought they were more parables," he says.

Before his father can field that issue, Max produces another.

"What about Communion?" Max asks. "If Jesus and the Disciples drank wine at the Last Supper, why do we drink Welchade at Communion? And why do we want to drink someone's blood?"

"We drink grape juice because United Church members are not supposed to drink alcohol, even though they do when they're not in church," the Father says. "It's called hypocrisy — you say one thing and you do something different. And it's not actual blood; it's a symbol."

"I thought it might be something like that. But if we can have Welchade instead of wine for Communion, why can't we have Ritz crackers instead of bread that someone squeezed flat? And if grape juice and squeezed bread are symbols, doesn't that mean we *would* drink Jesus's blood and eat his flesh if we really could? I mean, the French kids actually believe that's what they're doing, like it's some kind of magic. Does that mean they're cannibals?"

"So," the Father says, "I get 12 weeks of silence from you about Confirmation classes and, the night before the big day, with the whole family coming, you come up with this. Actually, including the pencil business, that's six years of silence from you on your own religion."

"I needed to think it over."

The Father looks around to ensure they're out of earshot. He scratches his head, then looks to the Habs for salvation, but the game's in intermission.

"When you didn't get your pencil, what did you think?"

"I thought the whole thing was just a bunch of bullshit," Max says angrily.

"Watch your language. And what do you think now?"

"The same," Max says. "And I don't like making crappy plaster praying hands at Sunday school. That's for morons."

The Father sighs. "I guess we're making progress. It took a war for me to figure it out, but you got it without firing a shot."

"It?"

"Yeah. It *is* all a bunch of crap, Max." The Father pulls his wallet from his back pocket and produces a five-dollar bill, a small fortune. "Here's something for all the Confirmation classes you endured."

"And I don't have to say a bunch of things tomorrow that I don't believe?"

Max's father pulls out another five: "This five is yours if you do everything on cue tomorrow and look like you're excited. It's very important to your mother and her family."

"You want me to lie in front of everybody?"

"Do it, and we'll never bother you about going to church again."

Max vows to himself that after tomorrow he will never again darken the doorway of a church.

1995

The Campaign: "Pilot" Is "Plot" with an "I"

***A private pilot** from Maine whose engine failed over Nova Scotia says he owes his life to a runway under construction near Kejimkujik National Park.*

The amateur aviator was certain he would crash into the woods when he spotted the runway, where he was able to land and repair the plain ...

Coincidentally, Max is circling the typo when the City Editor, wearing a yoga outfit, walks into his office.

"I just got off the phone with some guy at the flying club. He says no way there's a runway where that pilot says."

"That's because it's new, right?"

"He says no. If there was a runway under construction, the flying club would know," she says. "Apparently, pilots are big supporters of runways, so they're consulted before one goes up."

"It could be private."

"Doesn't matter. Their members are everywhere. They would know."

The provincial election campaign is on and Max has 52

ridings to cover with fewer than 20 reporters, not to mention all the bullshit stories associated with the leaders' race. He does not have the resources for a wild goose chase.

"Sorry," he says. "No sale. Maybe after the election. Nobody's available right now."

"How about the News Weevil?"

Max is aghast. In this newsroom, calling in the News Weevil is the equivalent of diving off the edge of a quarry without checking the depth of the water below. You could get killed or have an invigorating swim, but once you jump your fate is out of your hands.

"Please, Max," she says. "I'll triple check everything he turns in."

"Oh, I'm not worried about accuracy. It's just that while getting the story he'll find a way to piss off every cop, firefighter, widow and orphan in the province — did I ever tell you that on my second day here I had to take an angry call from Desmond Tutu's office? I mean, we pissed off a living saint."

"Max, you've mentioned that at almost every news meeting for the last 14 years," she says.

"That's a gross exaggeration. It was a very stressful incident, though."

"But the Weevil was still in high school. Put it behind you, Chief. I swear, I'll take care of every call before it gets to you."

Solely because of the City Editor's excellent instincts, Max approves taking on the News Weevil as a freelancer. The City Editor clasps her hands in front of her chest like she just got the best Barbie accessory ever, and almost skips out the door.

"Hey!" Max shouts. "Remember, if he fucks up, you wear the whole thing."

"I know, I know!"

Of course, they both know who'll really wear it.

"And don't call me Chief!"

• • •

No one knows how the News Weevil got his name. The Proofreader thinks it's because his ax-shaped head resembles *Diaprepes abbreviates* (citrus root weevil) and he once provided a picture to prove his point. Max thinks it's because, if you find a weevil in your pantry, you might as well set the whole place on fire.

The Weevil was once assigned to write a story on the province's progress against racism. In the process, he alienated minority leaders so much that Max had to convene a meeting with them with the help of mediator. But no one at the meeting could think of anything the Weevil said or did that would explain the problem. The mediator finally concluded that the Weevil's eagerness and intensity were coming across as prosecutorial. The story was re-assigned and Max paid the mediator to coach the Weevil on his tone.

The Weevil is standing before Max now, his thin shoulders supporting two bags of hardware. He's young — raw — and his face does in fact seem to terminate in a fine edge running from his forehead to his chin. Thick blond hair sprouts from the centre of his scalp like ornamental grass.

"A pilot let you take all that gear up with you?" Max says.

"Yeah, but I had to leave most of it in the rear compartment. That's why I couldn't call you."

The gear includes two cameras, one of them a large-format Hasselblad, with two to four lenses for each.

"You don't think the Hasselblad is over the top?"

The Weevil, who regards Max as his mentor, looks hurt: "Chief, this is for aerial photography. Superb detail." The Weevil habitually calls Max "Chief" and doesn't seem to hear his boss's demands that he stop. Invariably, this inspires staff to pick up on the *Get Smart* theme with straight-faced references to the "cone of silence" or the "shoe-phone".

The Weevil's kitbags also contain a pager, walkie-talkie, light metre, range-finder, portable police scanner, waterproof pen and notebook, waterproof film canister, and a cellular telephone the size of an army surplus field radio.

Max wants to know what he found.

"Chief, it's just a black strip at the edge of a circular clear cut. The pilot estimated the length at 8,000 feet—I'll know for sure once I soup the shots from the Hasselblad because I know the altitude and the focal length of the lens, so then it's easy to calculate ..."

"Let's cross that one when we come to it," Max says. He begins herding the Weevil out of his office toward the darkroom.

"You're right. Sorry about that. But 8,000 feet is longer than the Halifax airport. And here's the thing: the pilot figures it's only 50 feet wide."

"So what?"

"Well, that's really narrow."

They've made it as far as the darkroom door.

"Hmm. What do you think it is, then?" Max asks.

"I think it's the Hell's Angels. They're building a landing strip for drug shipments."

Max points to the darkroom: "Well, we won't know anything until you get your film souped."

The Weevil pivots and is gone. Max turns to the City Editor. "I thought we agreed you would run interference for me."

"Sorry about that, Chief," she says, grinning evilly. "I thought I had him pinned down and then the Batphone rang." The Batphone has a secret number that bypasses the Paper's switchboard and goes straight to City Desk. It's for important calls, newsroom staff only.

"Well, there really is a landing strip," Max says. "The Weevil thinks it's an airport for drugs."

The City Editor snorts. "The mainland is bristling with defence radar. Why would you build a landing strip in the hope you can get past it when you have 4,500 miles of poorly guarded coastline to work with?"

Max smiles. "Maybe it's for one huge shipment, like a 747. You unload it and get out before the cops arrive."

"The wing span of a 747 is about 200 feet. How wide is the runway?"

"Okay, it might be a little narrow for that," Max says. "Let him work on it, though."

Max suspects that everyone, including him, is secretly fond of the News Weevil. He's a comic-book expression of their inner news-geeks.

• • •

Max and the Wife are spooning contentedly in the marital bed. Max is considering whether to execute one of his masterful foreplay moves when the phone rings. Given the hour, it has to be a wrong number, a death, or the biggest news story in a generation. Heart thumping, Max grabs the phone.

"Chief?" a hushed voice says. "It's me." That would be the News Weevil.

"Why is it you?"

"I've been going over the Hasselblad photos and saw something I missed earlier."

"Why are you whispering? Is the SS outside your door?"

The Weevil pays no attention and continues whispering. "Chief, you can see people on the runway."

"You couldn't see them with your eyes? I mean, you were in a Cessna, not a reconnaissance jet."

"It was cramped in the passenger seat and it's a big camera, so I kinda snapped the shutter without looking."

"Okay, but so what?"

"Chief, the blow-ups show they had tools — they're still building the thing."

The Wife reaches behind her back and begins searching for something. She finds it. "Hmmm."

"Can't this wait 'til tomorrow?" Max says.

"I don't think so," the Wife says.

"But Max, I thought you'd want to know right away," the Weevil says. Max can tell his feelings are hurt again.

"Let's deal with it tomorrow," Max says.

"Okay, if you say so," the Wife says.

"Not *you*," Max says.

"What?" the Weevil says.

"First thing tomorrow," Max says before hanging up.

"If not me, then *who*," the Wife says, having managed to roll on top of Max without letting go of the object in her hand.

1995

Beloved Cleric Treated to Scenic Tour

"HEY, MAX, HOW'S it goin', eh? It's been a long time."

It's the unmistakable Ottawa Valley accent of El Mago.

"It has," Max says. "But I've been following your career closely ever since that day when you decided not to dump me in the ocean. How are you?"

"I'm doing great. There's a lot of money in counter-terrorism and the future is very bright. You should join me here, Max. I'm expanding fast and I could use a guy like you."

Max finds himself liking the prospect of money, and helping to catch bad guys would be good. But, then, El Mago himself is a bad guy.

"Bring your lovely wife, too," El Mago says. "She's an excellent writer. I could use her help writing proposals."

Max says he'll think about it, and turns the topic to Father Peter.

"Piece of cake, Max. Your city editor told me all about him."

"She did?"

"She was very smooth. I couldn't believe she got past the switchboard to me. Anyway, she told me the whole story."

"She did?"

"Yes. Luckily I still have connections with my former colleagues in several countries and they had no trouble tracking him down. He's already been for a helicopter ride."

Max swallows hard as he pictures Father Peter rocketing into the ocean. His remorse is immediate and powerful. He has started a chain of events that resulted in the cruel death of someone he has never met. Sometimes, he says to himself, you're just too smartass for your own good.

"Jesus," he says. "I didn't want him killed. I just wanted to know where he was."

El Mago enjoys a hearty laugh. "That's old school, Max. They just took him up over the jungle so he could see how big it is. It's vast, eh?"

"Big-time. Not the ocean?"

"The jungle was closer. They took his clothes off, showed him how the helicopter door works and talked about all the animals there and how there wouldn't be a trace of him left once the beasts found his body. They are confident he won't be a problem anymore."

El Mago gives Max the cleric's phone number and predicts it will be a co-operative interview. He also passes along his colleagues' gratitude for the tip, along with some of their names and numbers.

"It's a get-out-of-jail-free card, Max, in case you return to your old beat. How did you wind up in Halifax, anyway?"

"I pissed somebody off."

El Mago laughs again. "Imagine that! Anyway, come to London and make some real money."

"I'm making good money," Max protests.

"I am told you are making poor money, my friend, even for your business. *Hasta la vista.*"

PRIEST QUIETLY SHIPPED SOUTH AMID ABUSE ALLEGATIONS

A well-known Halifax area priest has been quietly moved to a remote mountain parish in South America after complaints of inappropriate behaviour involving altar boys.

The beloved "Father Peter", also known as the "pop pastor" for the alcohol-free dances he organized for preteens, among other youth projects, expressed "deep regret" for his actions in an exclusive, detailed interview ...

• • •

Max begins his day as usual, listening to a litany of complaints from the dayside crew about nightside as he makes his way across the newsroom to his office.

O Max, nightside knows nothing about apostrophes.

Pray for us.

O Max, nightside screwed up my lead again.

Pray for us.

O Max, you won't believe what Business has done.

Tell me it's not actionable ...

"Tell me it's not actionable," says Max.

"No. They screwed up the stocks pages again. Geez, you seem kinda jumpy."

"You know I hate lawsuits before lunch," he says.

Har-har.

"Any reaction?" Max asks the City Editor.

"A little," she says. "The Cobra is bouncing off the walls. He told everyone who was here that this means the end of the paper and it's your fault. Also, you're an arrogant prick, blah-blah. Nothing new there. Oh, and clean out your desk, you're fired."

"The Archdiocese?"

"They'd like you to call," she says, handing him a message slip. It's from the Assistant.

Max steels himself for a blast, but the Assistant is icy-calm.

"You know, Max," he says. "I told his Excellency I was pretty sure you would run that story, but I assumed one of your miscreant reporters would call him for comment first."

Max knows that ethically he's on swampy ground with that decision. He tries to block doubt from creeping into his voice.

"Normally, I would have done that," he says. "But your boss would have called my publisher to have him kill the story. Now he's just going to kill me."

Max waits.

"You and all the other so-called journalists are nothing but snivelling shites," the Assistant says, abandoning calm. "You love to talk about the public's right to know and comforting the afflicted and all that crap. Well, it's BULLSHIT! All BULLSHIT!" Max is certain he can hear the sound of spittle hitting the Assistant's mouthpiece.

"The truth is you're failures, every one of you. You haven't got the brains or determination to make something of yourselves, so instead you spend your days barking and nipping at the heels of those who have."

It occurs to Max that the man of God may have hit on something.

"You may have a point there," Max says. "But it doesn't change anything."

"What?"

"I said, you may have a point."

Max waits again. And waits. He waits still longer. He can sense a fresh round of rage building at the other end of the line.

"His Excellency wants a word with you," the Assistant finally croaks.

Max hears the sound of a speakerphone being slid across a desk.

"Eat shit," says the Archbishop. "You sheepfucker."

"Thank you, your Excellency. Will you be having my wife fired?"

"Not today, asshole. But there'll be another time soon."

Max is feeling shaky but relieved as he strolls out of his office. Five of his beloved "miscreants" are hanging around City Desk. They are visibly worried.

The City Editor looks at him: "The betting back in Montreal is that you'll survive this because whether or not to tell the Cobra in advance was a judgment call. But the Owner says your judgment was extremely poor. You should have told him. The consensus is you should keep your nose clean for a while."

Max ponders. "Okay. I'll go see the Cobra, then."

Eyes widen in alarm. They know it's bad timing. If Max shows up in the Cobra's office now the publisher will redouble his efforts to fire their editor and might succeed. The former crime reporter and now Political Reporter finally speaks up.

"Great job, Max. You deserve a nice lunch," he says.

"But I just got in."

"Let's have lunch anyway, a long one. I'll smother you with fulsome praise for your courage. You always like that."

"Come on, Max, he's right. You *know* you love that," the City Editor says. "Get out of here until things cool down a bit."

Max nods and starts for the door. The Political Reporter starts right away: "There are lots of big talkers in this business, Max, but you're the real thing ..."

"Oh, please."

1973

Cat Shack Routine Ignored —What's Going on Here?

The Cat Shack is the opposite of trendy. Everything about it is either cheap or beaten up. If you sit too close to the washrooms, you have to endure the rotting-pine smell of urinal cakes. It enjoys a loyal clientele.

Max gets there around eleven. But somehow, even though the Copy Editor had to stay behind to edit Max's stories, he's managed to get to the bar first and order a round — six glasses of draft. He's got his pipe going, sipping draft and looking contentedly around the bar. He's technically retired but it's obvious he enjoys his Saturday nights working at the craft he loves and then drinking hard with his two young friends.

Max is pulling out a chair when the Copy Editor utters a name and motions toward a middle-aged man buying drinks at the bar. "If you ever commit a crime and everybody knows you're guilty, that's the man who'll get you acquitted. I can introduce you."

"No thanks, I don't plan on committing any crimes."

The Copy Editor chuckles and puts a wooden match to his pipe, something Max thinks he does so often that he inhales more sulphur fumes than tobacco smoke. He is a caricature of a kindly old professor, thinning gray hair combed straight back, a grey moustache and heavy-framed glasses. He wears a tweed jacket with leather elbow patches. Max pegs his age at somewhere between 60 and 80.

"Look around," he says. "And tell me what you see."

Max sees four women, including the Veteran Reporter (how did SHE get here so fast?), dancing in a circle in front of the DJ. He accurately relays this to the Copy Editor, who says "hah!" thereby creating a fragrant cloud of smoke that lingers around his head. His voice is a vintage wine for the ear: warm, avuncular, with a hint of fondness and a strong note of nostalgia.

"Well, given sufficient time, and if you keep looking, you'll eventually see about six gentlemen at various tables staring at the dance floor. This is their technique for picking up strange women at a bar. Hah! As our esteemed Editor would say, they are sitting around with their dicks in their hands. Metaphorically, that is, though I venture to say it's an accurate prediction of how their evenings will end."

Max thinks it over. "You're saying he's right about my reporting?"

The Copy Editor looks over his glasses at Max. "I had the pursuit of the fair sex in mind but, yes, your reporting would improve if you looked around a bit instead of just showing up and taking notes. I have high hopes for you, and you're a good writer, but your reporting, not to mention your powers of observation, remains mediocre."

The word mediocre stings. Worse than being called an asshole.

Max's attention returns to the dance floor. The Veteran

Reporter, like many women journalists, is wearing a shapeless skirt and boxy blouse. Both seem designed to hide interesting curves and or anything else that might garner attention. Max approves. Using sexual attraction to get stories would be unprofessional.

The skirt, however, does appear a little tighter than he's used to seeing, and so does her blouse, and he's never seen her dance before. Her exertions appear to have caused the second button on her shirt to pop open. Max wonders how old she really is.

He turns back to the Copy Editor and discovers that another round of beer has arrived. Max gestures toward the Veteran Reporter and asks: "How old do you think she is?"

"Hah!" comes the reply, this time creating a puff of smoke worthy of a locomotive. "Precisely my point about observation." Mysteriously, the pipe goes out. The Copy Editor fishes a wooden match out of his jacket pocket, strikes it against the metal rim of the table and inhales a lungful of sulphur. He leans back, apparently satisfied about something. "You should take a look," he says.

After two more songs the Veteran Reporter shows up at the table. She grabs a brimming glass of draft and takes a long drink. Max notices that the glass looks big in her hand. He has always thought of the Veteran Reporter as a large woman.

"Gawd," she says to the Copy Editor. "I'm gone for 10 minutes and you order two rounds. I'll never get through this."

"I believe the record indicates otherwise," he replies. "Besides, it's watered down."

"Yeah," says Max. "That's what they mean when they say 'two-for-one' here. It takes two beers to get the effect of one."

Max braces for the comeback. The Veteran Reporter, in addition to knowing everything there is to know about news, is smart, and her words can pack a punch. She's the only staffer who can get away with standing up to the Editor. Much of the time, come to think of it, it's in defence of Max.

Not always, though. So Max tries to focus, prepare himself for a verbal tussle.

But instead the Veteran Reporter guffaws. Then she looks him straight in the eye and allows her features to soften for a moment. Something's different, Max thinks.

"So," she says, "did you really almost trip over that guy?"

"What guy?"

She fires off a look of disbelief. "The suicide, you clod. You tripped over a dead body two hours ago and you have to be reminded? You stoned or something?"

"Oh, him. Yeah, one more step and I'd have kicked him in the shin."

The Copy Editor re-lights his pipe yet again: "Good thing you didn't. Cops notice that stuff. It would be a long time before you got near a crime scene again." Then he does an odd thing: he glances at the Veteran Reporter's chest and nods to himself.

"Why don't we cover suicides?" Max asks.

"The theory is ..." He pauses while wreathing himself in smoke, a prerequisite for any serious pronouncement. "The theory is that it encourages other people to follow suit."

"You mean kill themselves."

"Yep."

"Well, they wouldn't if they saw what I saw," Max says, noticing what could be a look of approval on the Veteran Reporter's face.

The conversation moves on to a selection of the usual topics: The Editor, the mayor, journalistic ethics, Mao, official corruption, the Mob, David Bowie and, of course, crappy reporting in other papers — always a high-priority topic.

The Copy Editor lumbers toward the can. Max figures there must be an intercom in the *pissoir* because the bartender shows up from the other end of the room with four more beers.

"How does he do that?"

"Beats me," the Veteran Reporter says. "He gets the Nobel Prize for Surreptitious Beer Ordering."

The Copy Editor returns with a bombshell announcement: he's going home to his girlfriend.

Girlfriend?

"Say hi for me," the Veteran Reporter says, unconcerned.

Max is speechless. Never — never — have the three of them failed to close the Cat Shack on a Saturday night. Never— never — had it occurred to him that the Copy Editor would have a girlfriend.

The Copy Editor reaches awkwardly for his raincoat. The Veteran Reporter makes room by moving her chair. As she does so, Max again notices the open expanse above the buttons of her blouse and the curve of what could well be a breast. It has never occurred to Max that the Veteran Reporter might have detectable breasts as if that, too, would violate some professional code. He notices a small silver pendant at the base of her throat. As if to reinforce the point, it's the gender symbol for female.

The Copy Editor slips on his coat and drops his pipe into a pocket. He puts on a serious expression.

"Remember. If you want to sell newspapers," he says,

"don't fuck with the crossword." He chugs his last glass of beer and slams the glass on the table. "And?" he asks expectantly.

The other two chime in, raising their glasses: "And don't fuck with the comics."

This is the benediction that signals the end of a Saturday night, except this time the Copy Editor is alone as he weaves his way toward the parking lot. Max is still shocked. The Veteran Reporter doesn't seem to mind the change in routine.

"He has a girlfriend?" Max says.

"What? You think Copy Editors don't mate?"

But Max doesn't really hear. This is the first time he's ever been alone with the Veteran Reporter and he's not sure how to handle it.

NOW

Visit to a Holy Place

MAX, THE GURU and his two-and-a-half ton Town Car rolled confidently across the harbour bridge. The Guru was on the phone, explaining to the Beacon Arms that he and Max were going for a drive.

"A fire? At the supermarket?" he said. "Really? Well, there was some commotion when I picked Max up, but he was outside. Of course they can talk to him but his memory isn't what it was. I'll call after we finish our ride. Bye for now."

"Who wants to talk to me?" Max asked.

"The cops. There was some kind of fire at the supermarket."

"I have a vague recollection of something like that," Max said. "When did it happen?"

"About the time I picked you up," the Guru said.

"Did you know you can buy a beer and a lunch in that store, but you can't drink the beer?"

They left the bridge behind and headed for the highway to the Annapolis Valley.

The car's enormous engine took to the divided highway like a stallion that's escaped the barn and spotted a willing mare on the horizon. Cars in the slow lane fell behind them like Tim Hortons cups in the wind.

"Max, old chum, what are you going to do?" the Guru asked.

Max felt calm and safe, relieved of the burden and confusion caused by having to fact-check his every thought. He slipped gratefully into a soothing oasis of clarity.

"Well, I'm going to keep looking for the Wife as long as I can still form the intent," Max said. "I don't know what the hell is happening to me, but it's obvious this part of life's journey is downhill for me. It's not going to end well."

"It's nothing to be alarmed about," the Guru said. "And I doubt it will end badly."

Max looked at him as if he were crazy and said as much. "However, you now have my attention which, no doubt, was your purpose."

"You are transitioning out of this life, just as you transitioned into it. If you can hang onto that idea, it may help you into the next one."

"So, have I lived this life well enough that I can expect the circumstances of the next one to be more difficult, at least according to you?" he asked.

"Yep," the Guru said. "But you'll suffer less, and so will those you're able to help."

This idea is one of the few that Max has been able to hang on to through his ordeal, which he thinks is ironic given that he has never understood it.

"So I should give up looking for her?" he asked, speaking of suffering.

"No. The main thing is to *allow* yourself to be anywhere you turn up. I think you've been fighting it. That will just cause suffering."

Max sighed. "I can't recall the details of where I've been, but I'm awfully tired. I'll admit to that. What if I find the Wife?"

"You'll know what to do," his friend said.

As the Guru knew well, Max was a firm believer that his existence would end six feet under. Period. And that he definitely preferred that fate to the Guru's notion of afterlife.

"There's nothing to transition into," Max said.

"I don't think you mean that."

The Guru reached 'way over to his right and popped open a glove compartment big enough for a large loaf of bread. Inside was a collection of 8-track tape cartridges.

"They came with the car," he explained as he steered back into his lane. "Getting pretty rare."

Max slid a cartridge into the stereo and heard Gary Puckett singing *Woman, Woman.* He popped it back out immediately. "Reminds me of her," he said. "This isn't a good time for that."

His next try was Steppenwolf cranking out *Born to Be Wild.*

The Guru rolled down all four motorized windows. Max played rhythm on the dashboard. Both accompanied the band on vocals. The engine took the speed up a notch or two.

Get your motor ru-nnin' ... lookin' for adventure

They crested the hill that offered their first view of the valley and Minas Basin. They could see part of the quilted farmland, framed by copper cliffs and the sea. The water tugged at Max.

"There are places in the world where the energy of the universe is more concentrated," the Guru said as they took it in. "This is one of them."

They drove on toward the energy, across the valley floor and up the North Mountain where, on this day anyway, everything changed. The sky darkened and below to the south they could see the shadows of clouds slipping over the fields.

A light mist rolled in during their descent to the far shore, where the wind was whipping whitecaps from gunmetal waves and driving them hard into the rocks. They continued until the road ended in a small parking lot. They had been here together many times before. The Guru led the way to the trailhead and started into the woods. The ground was wet and the tall trees were dripping.

The trail was rough in spots and featured some steep grades, so there were muttered profanities and some puffing. But otherwise they were quiet, content to experience their surroundings. Max called it "forest bathing" and regarded it as a spiritual pursuit, nothing less.

They neared the end of the trail two hours later, half an hour longer than it used to take. Max was completely free of the internal stresses of his predicaments and his head was clearer than it had been for a long time. The vegetation overhead began to thin out and the ground beneath was dappled with sunlight.

They had walked the shaft of an arrow that jutted far into the Bay of Fundy. They emerged from the woods onto a three-sided meadow that narrowed almost to a point. The sea was on all three sides, hundreds of feet straight down. Below, currents merged and parted randomly, angrily tearing at the rocks in their paths. They were restless, powerful and hungry.

The sky ahead was dominated by a squall line a few

degrees below the sun. The water changed from grey at the horizon to sparkling blue nearer the cape. The wind, as always, threatened to pick them up and toss them into the currents.

They walked ahead to see the Split: what at first appeared as a single meadow revealed itself to be the tops of two sandstone formations. The second was a pillar, seemingly close enough to jump to until your mind recalibrates and you realize that it's really half a city block away.

The Guru said: "This was the place where Glooscap, the first human being and protector of the Mi'kmaq, smashed a massive beaver dam separating the waters of the basin and the Bay of Fundy. Cape Split is one of the remnants of that feat. For my money, it's one of the holiest places in the world, right in our back yard."

They found a spot out of the wind and the Guru produced a bottle of wine from his knapsack.

"The doctor says I'm not supposed to drink this," Max said accepting a plastic cup brimming with Beaujolais.

"I heard," the Guru said. "Can you feel the energy here?"

"We're radios," Max said, earning a quizzical look from his friend.

"We're all tuned to the energy around us. No one disputes the existence of that energy, but we're all tuned to it differently, so we express it differently. That's the difference between you, me, and a salamander or a tomato. That's why I can travel in time. It's just a matter of tuning."

"Max. A radio? Really?"

"I'm having a good day," he replied. "I can't remember your name, but I recognize you. I can't name this place, but I love it like no other. And I can *also* remember your own personal theory of existence, which is pretty fucking cock-eyed itself."

The Guru smiled and poured some more wine. Max heard the half-empty bottle make a pleasant clinking sound against what was obviously a companion vessel.

"Max, you are a mischievous man to go provoking a venerable and infallible guru such as myself."

Max saw that his friend was grinning. Their gazes met and they laughed until the Guru's eyes grew teary.

• • •

With a mixture of dread and confusion, Max allowed the Guru to escort him back up the path to the Beacon Arms. The sight of Purple Hair reassured him for some reason. She bolted out from behind the reception desk and gave him a long, wordless hug, pressing her face into his chest. Max squeezed her back.

"I told your colleagues Max was safe with me," the Guru said.

"I know," she said. "I missed him, that's all. All these cops and arson investigators got me worried. I just wanted to see him again."

She told the Guru that in the end investigators decided to drop the matter, including the idea that the Guru had aided a fugitive. Max stood quietly, taking in all the excitement and emotion.

"You know," he said to them, "I can't shake the feeling that — somehow — all this has something to do with me."

1 9 9 5

The Campaign: And They're Off!

Max looks around the Cobra's new office. It is a monumental step up from the large supply closet he occupied in the old building. One wall is a long curve, with a window of glass blocks specially shaped to match. He has decorated the sill with his most expensive Formula One models. The teak desk is ornately yet tastefully carved. It is said to have belonged to a former premier and obtained quietly from the government surplus disposal agency. The wall opposite the grand desk is lined with books purchased wholesale by an interior decorator. This, Max thinks, explains the presence of the complete works of Pierre Trudeau, or any books at all for that matter.

To the side is another "bookcase" that's really the door to the publisher's plush new private bathroom. It swings open and the Cobra emerges. As usual, the toilet is still flushing.

Max fears there's another clash about the Archbishop on the agenda.

"Just had a meeting with the Premier," the Cobra says. "He's calling the election tomorrow, and he doesn't want any trouble from you."

"Tough shit," Max says, relieved.

The Cobra's hood flares. "He's the head of the province, for Christ's sake."

"True, but he doesn't edit this newspaper," Max says calmly. "I do."

"No, you don't," says the Cobra. "I do. You report to me."

Once again, Max explains that he's answerable to the Cobra only on business matters. If the Owner decides someday that he doesn't like Max's work, he — not the Cobra — will fire him. Max knows this is not 100 per cent true, despite the Paper's success. If the Cobra makes enough noise, then the Owner will swing his axe. The question is: whose head will be on the chopping block?

"The thing is," Max says. "The Paper has been in the black since I became editor and the Premier actually worries about what we're going to write. The Owner likes that."

In response, the Cobra grabs a sheaf of paper from his desktop and waves it at Max.

"Have you seen the demographics? Our readers are all conspiracy theorists and Buddhists."

"Bullshit," Max replies. "But, that said, there's nothing for them in the Other Paper. And why shouldn't Buddhists and conspiracy theorists have a paper of their own as long as they help pay our bills, which they do?"

The Cobra stands up and glides the length of the Formula One display, slowing twice to adjust one of the cars. In time, he slides outside Max's peripheral vision. It's game on: will Max turn toward him to hear what he says next, or will he wait him out?

It's a busy day for Max, especially now that he knows the Premier's going to drop the writ, so he swivels his chair around to face his tormentor. The hood, made more obvious by more than a decade of comfortable living, expands dramatically. The Cobra's beady eyes converge on Max. He smiles and licks his lips.

"Max!" he says sharply, and then allows his voice to descend to a low monotone. "You don't have the professional training that we engineers use to understand the order of things. The Premier is at the top. He tells me what he wants, and I tell you what I want, which is the same as what he wants. That's democracy."

The Cobra's hood deflates as he relaxes and slithers back to his desk. He looks at Max intently, trying to discern whether his words have had an effect.

"Message received and understood," Max says.

"And?"

Max raises his eyebrows, expels a breath and shrugs, as if to say that no one really knows.

"Well, let me be clear. I don't want to see another story about Father what's-his-ass."

"Why not?"

"Because bad news makes people vote against governments, and the future of this province depends on the Premier and his party."

Max remarks that the economy has stagnated under the Premier's leadership and the provincial debt has set a new record.

"That," the Cobra says, "was necessary for the strategic positioning phase of the economic plan. Now we are positioned for a new era. If the Party is defeated now, it will all have been for nothing."

Max surmises that the Cobra has just explained the broad outline of the re-election campaign.

"How can you say something like that," Max asks, "and then tell a Rotary Club luncheon that you're non-partisan?"

"Because I *am* non-partisan. I support the party in power, no matter who it is."

"Of course," Max says. "Anything else would be irresponsible."

For Max, one of the joys of working for the Cobra is that he's deaf to sarcasm and irony. Still, on this occasion, his boss senses that something is wrong.

"Let me be even more blunt," he says. "Any story about the election campaign that you like, I don't want to see in the Paper."

Max clicks his heels sharply, bows slightly, and strides purposefully toward the door.

He heads straight to the City Editor from the Cobra's office.

"I need Mother Mary to get something new on Father Peter," he says.

"Max, that story's dead," she says, brushing aside a lock of neon green hair.

Max raises an eyebrow.

"However, I can see that you have a brilliant master plan too complex for me to understand. I'll get her on it."

Max walks the ten feet to his new office, which has a single window overlooking the parking lot. The "restful" motif has already been fouled by piles of paper and sticky-note mosaics. For reasons unknown, one such note reminds him about the election call. He grabs his phone.

"City Desk."

"I forgot to tell you the preem's going to drop the writ tomorrow. Get someone to start work on the government's shitty economic record. Um, please."

"How do you know that?"

"If I told you, you wouldn't respect me in the morning."

"As opposed to now? Do you want an election story for tomorrow?"

"No. I can't trust my source that much."

1995

Service with a Smile

Max is feeling "goodish" as he pulls into the parking lot at the Paper. At home the previous night, he got a call from Montreal saying that he would keep his job despite the Cobra's latest allegations of insolence.

"The Owner thinks you're an aggressive prick, but your boss is an asshole," the Montreal Daily's new Editor-in-Chief says. "If he keeps it up, you could be the publisher in six months."

"Really? But I thought the Mother Ship would never turn back for me."

"This isn't turning back," he says. "You'll always be in the minors. But listen, there's one thing the Cobra does right: he knows how to get along. We want you to work on that."

"We?"

"Yeah. Me and the Owner."

As Max strolls into the lobby at the Paper, the receptionist nods toward a nondescript man in a London Fog raincoat.

"You have a visitor," she says.

It doesn't feel right. Max's stomach begins churning.

Usually these morning visitors bring banker boxes of paper documenting Workers' Compensation abuses, certain that Max is duty-bound to set it all right with a series of blockbuster stories. This guy is travelling light, though, and seems sensible.

"Are you Max?" says the guy says as he stands up, his voice friendly and free of guile.

Max realizes the guy is a bailiff, but greets him with a friendly handshake. There's no point in antagonizing people who are just doing their jobs. The bailiff recognizes the gesture and smiles with relief.

"I just need you to sign here, acknowledging you have received this Notice of Intent," he says.

Max doesn't have to look to know he's being sued for libel. He doesn't care who. He signs the notice and slides it into a jacket pocket.

"Listen," the guy says. "There's something going on with you at Bentley & Steele. There was a kind of excitement when I picked this up, like there's more to come."

"Thanks," he says, not feeling especially grateful.

Max heads for the newsroom without reading the document. Bentley & Steele is the Party's law firm, which tells him all he needs to know for now.

•••

The City Editor is styled in punk today, complete with black army boots and fishnet stockings with big ragged holes in them.

"Anything going on?" Max asks.

"Nah. We need a murder," she says. "You know we're being sued, eh? The liquor board chair."

Max closes his eyes. He hasn't even looked at the document yet, but the City Editor knows who the plaintiff is.

She answers his question before he can ask it: "I know because I dated that process server for a while."

"I wouldn't have thought he was your type," Max says.

"That's how you find out what your type is — you try them on for a while," she says.

The law requires a plaintiff to give newspapers seven days' notice before he can sue for libel. That's the Paper's opportunity to apologize, which usually kills the suit.

The chair of the liquor board is one of the province's many "fine men", men who have been steered to wealth or influence by a grateful political party. They are presumed to be above reproach but, when caught, are judged to have "suffered enough" merely by virtue of their arrest and are usually given suspended sentences.

Max gets the Lawyer on the phone. She, of course, already knows about the notice.

"He's claiming that your editorial said he's unqualified to be the chair," she explains.

"He's not qualified, but we didn't say that," Max says. "We just said the board needs new leadership. I could have said he's still working on his high school diploma. Anyway, it's opinion.

The right to express an opinion is the standard defence for claims like this."

"You're right," the Lawyer says, "and eventually we'll win."

"Eventually."

"Yeah. But our legal bill will be $60K or higher before it's over."

Max knows this is chump change for the Board Chair,

but serious money to the Cobra, who, in the first place, never sees any point in defending a libel suit. His motto is "apologize, apologize, apologize."

"You mean *your* legal bill," Max says sourly.

"That's not fair, Max."

"Sorry. Bad day. What do you recommend?"

"Our best strategy is to stall until election day and hope he loses interest," she says. "But rest assured that meanwhile he'll be doing everything he can to goose up your costs."

"OK. I'll go tell the Cobra."

"He already knows."

Good news travels fast.

Half an hour later, the Cobra's assistant hand-delivers a memo.

Max:

"Regretfully, I have no choice but to document the libel suit you have attracted from the chair of the liquor board.

"This is typical of what has become of your carelessness about defamatory content and an apparent disregard for our legal budget. Our insurer has already inquired about our ability to manage this liability.

"Please do your best to ensure this does not happen again."

It is copied to the Owner and the message is clear: The Cobra thinks he's got Max in his crosshairs.

• • •

The Wife agrees.

They have just finished dinner and the Son is upstairs doing his homework and/or trying to download dirty pictures. Max knows because he heard the modem squawking when he picked up the extension.

Max and the Wife are in their loveseat, feet resting on the coffee table, something that is normally verboten. A spare bottle of French Merlot stands at the ready, even though it won't help Max's stomach.

The Wife has placed a pillow over her midriff to hide yet another imaginary fat dome. Even in a terrycloth robe, she looks good. She is old enough to be maternal and young enough to be sexy. Her fingers continue to be the longest and most delicate Max has ever seen. Her wine glass seems more like an accessory than a drinking vessel until she drains the last ounce and holds it out to Max for a refill.

The university administration, and therefore the Wife, knew about the lawsuit almost before Max did. Max is puzzled until she reminds him that her board, except for the Archbishop, is composed almost entirely of Party members. The other parties "have" university boards of their own.

"The vibe was strange," she says. "Finally the president called me into her office for a private briefing. The Archbishop is making noises about the so-called abortion issue."

"I can't stand this — these partisan pissants beating up on me."

"Hang in there," the Wife says. "The threat's almost always worse than the reality."

Max opens the backup Merlot and they sip in silence for a while.

"Okay," the Wife says. "I think I can get you something on Bentley & Steele if that helps, but it won't come from me."

"Hmm, my own Deep Throat," Max says, sidling closer.

The Wife cuddles up. "I mean it literally. Like Watergate. We will never discuss this again. But you'll recognize it when it shows up."

Max, of course, is focused on the carnal meaning of Deep Throat.

1995

A Quiet Talk with Sergeant Fury

FOR THE FIFTH day in a row, Max wakes at 4:08 a.m. This is not his alarm sounding. It's when his roiling bowels wake him up. He cannot begin to fathom how his insides know the time so precisely. Only their two hungry cats can match that feat. Max pops a couple of Pepto-Bismol and tries to sleep, but his mind is back at the Paper. The Wife reaches out and strokes his back. He takes an assortment of meds each day before going into work now, but by lunchtime his intestines feel like they're infested with a colony of crayfish trying to claw their way out.

Breakfast is soda biscuits, which do not promote stomach acid. Lunch is two tuna sandwiches, whole wheat bread, heavy on the mayonnaise. These are the two daytime foods that don't stop partway down his oesophagus, inspiring the muscles to cramp painfully around it. When that happens he feels like he's swallowed a softball. He was sure he had cancer until a suite of tests came back negative. "Are you experiencing any stress?" the specialist asked.

A little, yeah.

Max's beloved newsroom hacks know Max is under

pressure and are trying to do their bit to help. The result is that only the most egregious errors and omissions by night-side are brought to his attention during the morning litany of complaint. This has the opposite of the intended effect because now there are no easy answers to start the day off. Worse, sometimes the rite is ignored altogether, which makes Max feel out of touch or, on his worst days, that he has lost the respect of his staff.

This is one such morning. The staff is oddly silent and the City Editor greets him by awkwardly motioning toward a large man sitting on a small chair outside his office.

"Max," the City Editor whispers, "it's ..."

"I know him," Max says, his gullet filling with partially-digested soda biscuit.

He's a police superintendent, known as Sergeant Fury since the day when as a rookie he fired a shotgun through the windshield of his own squad car at a bank robber who was pointing a pistol at him. The effect was so spectacular that three other robbers, poised to run, chose instead to hurl themselves to the ground.

Even before Sergeant Fury's ears stopped ringing, cops and robbers alike knew there was a new sheriff in town. Armed bank robberies dropped off sharply.

And Sergeant Fury's visage had come to match his moniker. Roughly the size of a restaurant refrigerator, he has a perfectly square head topped by black hair and punctuated by a Hitlerian moustache. He has Rocket Richard's thousand-yard stare.

Max and Sergeant Fury have met a few times at "functions", where they enjoyed sharing their distaste for such events and making jokes about low-grade criminals. Max isn't fond of cops in general, but he admires Fury's ability to rise through the ranks in a society where standing out is eventually punished.

Sergeant Fury gets up and offers a hand the size of a catcher's mitt.

"Max, it's great to see you," he says heartily. "I hope I'm not intruding, but I was down the street on other business and I was hoping you could help me with something."

Bullshit, Max thinks.

"I'll do the best I can," Max says, trying to sound relaxed, and escorts the big man to his office door. "Just give me a second and I'll be right there. Make yourself at home, but don't overdo it."

Max tells the City Editor to make sure there's a photog around, just in case he's arrested. She points to her go-to shooter, who is sitting at the copy desk a few feet away, already getting a light reading on Max's office door.

Churn-churn-churn.

Neither Max nor Sergeant Fury enjoy pleasantries, so once the door is closed they get down to business.

"Max, I'd like to know a little more about how newsrooms work," Sergeant Fury says. "I know you're busy, but I'm sure you of all people know *you have no obligation to talk to me.*"

"I do know that," says Max. "How can I help?"

"Just the other day, the department's media relations guy was saying how little our officers know about newsrooms. And I thought, he's right. Why don't I drop by and talk to Max. There's a guy who'll talk freely and won't lawyer-up like some assholes would, *even though it's his right.*"

Max realizes that Fury is sneakily advising him of his Charter rights. He grabs one of the Pepto Bismol tablets lying loose in his desk drawer.

"Pepto?" he asks, holding it out for Fury.

"No thanks," he says. "I'm a Kaopectate man."

Max looks at his guest, who starts to tug nervously at his ear. Something is definitely up.

"You haven't referred to my right to free legal counsel yet," Max says, "but I'm sure you would have gotten around to it. That means I'm being treated as a suspect in something. Are you going to detain me in any way?"

Sergeant Fury smiles. "C'mon Max. It's *certainly true that you have a right to legal aid*, but I don't have anything like that in mind."

Max laughs: "Okay. Now you've covered it. What's up?"

"The chief justice has asked us to investigate a possible contempt charge in *R v Spadinsky*," he says. "The police chief wants to keep it high-level, so here I am."

Max is familiar with *R v Spadinsky* because he fought and lost against a publication ban in the case.

The defendant, Spadinsky, has quite literally been a pain in the establishment ass for some time, being an expert in spankings and other domination services. But she's also mouthy and something of a city hall gadfly, so someone decided to charge her with operating a common bawdy house.

Her defence is that she doesn't perform sex acts in her "dungeon", therefore it is not a bawdy house. As part of that defence, she advised the court that she would be presenting videotapes of herself and her clients going about their business. This prospect likely caused considerable alarm in a variety of social circles and much speculation in newsrooms. In any case, the judge accepted the Crown's request that the identities of the men in the videotapes be suppressed. For the greater good.

When Max asked the Lawyer to fight the ban, the Cobra

countermanded him, so he went to the courthouse and intervened himself from the public side of the bar. He made a hash of it and annoyed the judge. Other journalists accused him of showboating, but he got his objections on the record.

"But we've been scrupulous about the ban," Max tells Sergeant Fury. "Actually, we have no choice — we don't even know who these people are. And I don't care. But if it's illegal for Spadinsky to be there, it must also be illegal for her customers. They're found-ins. What's saucy for the goose, is saucy for the gander, if I may say so."

The massive cop grins: "I don't disagree. But the court is concerned that your descriptions of the tapes are so detailed that the clients will recognize themselves, which violates the ban."

"That's crazy. It could hardly be a surprise to them," Max says.

"Again, that's not the point. As part of my investigation, I have to know who is responsible."

"What exactly do you mean?"

Sergeant Fury selects a copy of the Paper from the pile on Max's desk and points to the first byline he sees.

"This is called a byline, right?" he asks. "And it tells us the name of the writer responsible for the story, right?"

"Not exactly," Max says. "Stories get changed all the time without telling the writer or changing the byline. And memories fade quickly, so it would be pretty hard to determine who might have changed any particular story and what they did to it."

Max is well pleased with himself. If they can't tell who did what, they can't charge anyone.

Sergeant Fury leans back and strokes his chin.

"Let me put it this way, Max. If there's a pattern in the

ban being violated every morning in this newspaper, who would be responsible for correcting that?"

Max clears his throat of regurgitated soda biscuit: "That would be me."

"And is it possible that an editor like yourself would direct his staff to come as close as possible to violating a ban without crossing the line?"

Max raises his eyebrows, expels a breath and shrugs, as if to say that no one really knows: "Jeez, look at the time. It's been very pleasant, but I'm afraid I gotta go."

"Well, I wouldn't want to *detain* you," Sergeant Fury says, extending his hand. "At least not yet."

As they walk into the newsroom the photog gets four quick shots, just in case.

Sergeant Fury turns back before leaving: "I'm sorry, Max."

Back in his office, Max knows that if he crunches any more Pepto Bismol his stomach will turn to concrete. Instead, he closes the door, eats four soda crackers and speed-dials the Lawyer.

"The cops are investigating me for contempt of court," he tells her.

"That's interesting. Spadinsky?"

"Yep. But I'm ... in the clear, right?"

"Max, it's contempt. The judge can hang you by your thumbs if it suits him, but jail's more likely. Did you say anything?"

Oops, Max thinks. "Jail?"

"It's a possibility. Did you say anything?"

"A little, maybe."

"Shit. Can you come over this afternoon?"

1995

The Campaign: Cartoon Shocker Boosts Soda Biscuit Sales

Max arrives for work thirty minutes early, catching dayside unprepared, and makes it all the way to City Desk without fielding a single complaint.

The City Editor crushes this small triumph.

"There's something you should see," she says, handing him a note. "Nightside left this for you."

"If it's for me, why have you got it?"

Max sees the City Editor actually blush for the first time since they met.

"It was dropped off at my place last night," she says.

The City Editor's outfit makes her look professional and attractive. There is nothing in her hair-colour or jewellery to suggest wacky or wild. Her only jewellery, in fact, is a modest string of clear glass beads. The effect is unprecedented.

"It was dropped off, you say," Max says. "Interesting use of the passive voice. It's like Nixon saying 'mistakes were made'. True, but it doesn't tell us who made the mistakes or what they were."

Max pauses for effect.

"Was it the Indonesian who dropped it off, by any chance?"

"Do you *have* to call him that?"

"Aha! So it *was* him. Where can I reach him?"

"I'm sure he's at home," is the answer. Her tone is a trifle arch.

"Excellent," says Max, taking the note and starting for his office. "And here I was thinking the two of you would never get together. Finally, some good news."

The City Editor calls him back to the City Desk: "Don't forget to read the note. It's really important."

"Yep."

"And Max ... do you think I'm making a mistake?" The tough-babe façade is gone for a moment.

"You mean with the Indonesian?"

She rolls her eyes: "Yes. I mean the Indonesian, as you insist on calling him."

"Well, it's hard when your shifts don't line up," Max says. "But I was thinking it's time we moved him to dayside anyway. I need someone to handle the morning complaint-litany."

"What about the Cobra? He's not still after him?"

"Water under the bridge," says Max.

"And you're not worried about conflict of interest between me and him?"

"On the contrary. Productivity will shoot up, and nobody has to be murdered."

"Although a homicide is always welcome," she adds.

The City Editor returns her gaze to her computer. She's extremely happy with the way her day has begun. Her expression is identical to one Max often saw on the Wife, a long time ago.

Max is happy for the City Editor and the Indonesian, so he saunters into his office. He closes the door and opens the note from the Indonesian: "Max, those three assholes in the composing room who call themselves the Collective were bragging last night that it's their job to ensure you don't slip anything past the Cobra."

Better get your game-face on, Max, he thinks. He picks up a fat envelope from his incoming mail tray. The return address bears the imprint of the despised law firm, Bentley & Steele, and the words "delivered by hand". This is never good and, indeed, the first page is headed by the dreaded phrase "WITHOUT PREJUDICE".

The words are supposedly intended to protect the contents of the letter from becoming evidence in a trial, but Max has always suspected the secondary purpose is to scare the crap out of people like him.

Max feels something gurgling below his beltline. Mission accomplished. Another day, another $60k, he thinks.

This time his tormentor is the Premier. He and the opposition leader both appeared in a cartoon in the Paper the previous day. The Premier wants to deregulate gasoline prices, saying it will reduce costs for drivers. The opposition leader vigorously opposes the idea, saying "regulation always means high prices". The Premier instantly called his opponent's position irresponsible. The news cycle was half over before the Political Reporter parsed their statements and realized they had said the same thing.

This is juicy chum in the water during an election campaign and the feeding frenzy was intense and gleeful.

The Cartoonist's contribution was to draw the two politicians sitting unsteadily on the ground with a jerry can marked "high-octane gasoline" between them. The implication is that they've been sniffing gasoline. Lest anyone miss that point, the cartoonist has drawn a word-balloon with the pair simultaneously saying: "We gotta cut back on this this stuff."

Alas, it's also chum in the water for Bentley & Steele.

The phone rings and it's the Lawyer.

"So, where are you planning your vacation this year?" Max says.

"Well, I was thinking Florida, but now I'm looking at the Riviera and then Greece," she says.

"So, you've seen the latest from Bentley & Steele?"

"Yes. They're suing, of course. And the Human Rights people ... Max, something's wrong with the line ... I can't hear you."

Max has karate-chopped the speakerphone button, sending the apparatus six inches into the air. Nonetheless, when it comes down the speakerphone is engaged, allowing him to continue the conversation with his forehead on his desk. From this vantage point he can speak to his feet.

"I'm ready now," he tells her. "Go ahead."

"The Human Rights people say the opposition leader looks like an African Nova Scotian in the drawing and it's hate-speech against African Nova Scotians because there are no African Nova Scotians running. It's bullshit, of course."

"Sixty thousand dollars worth of nonsense."

"For the libel case, yes. We've got more options with Human Rights. Their big hammer is wasting your time. I suggest you agree to their mediation process."

"Oh, good," says Max. "Because, if there's one thing I've got, it's time, right?"

Max wishes he'd had the discipline to eat soda biscuits for breakfast instead of bacon and eggs.

• • •

Stomach churning, Max pulls into his driveway. The cats, who routinely rush out to challenge the familiar sight of his car and then flee in terror, are already stationed where the gravel meets the lawn. They calmly hold their position.

They are furry lawn-Buddhas sleek in the evening sun, watching small grasshoppers jump in front of them. Every few seconds an insect hops too close, provoking one of the cats to snap its jaws on the flying morsel, making a hollow crunching sound. This is followed by thoughtful chewing, and a thorough licking of the chops before the ready position is resumed. Nothing in the mien of either animal suggests anything out of the ordinary.

Max leans against the fender to watch for a while. The animals give him the slow blink of feline welcome and resume the feast.

"This is life, Max," the laid-back one says between grasshoppers. "Sometimes, all roads seem to lead to Hell. But other times, on a warm day, fresh delicacies just jump into your mouth. Either way, everything is fundamentally okay. Just *be*, Max."

But the neurotic one wrecks the moment: "Max, these are great. You really should really try some. You won't be able to get them in jail, you know."

1995

The Campaign: Flacks' Night Out

STANDING IN THE centre of a hotel ballroom, drink in hand, Max is miserable. He is surrounded by hundreds of people murmuring like extras on a movie set. "Rhubarb" is what the extras actually say, over and over again, a friend in the film business told him once. For Max's purposes, the ballroom crowd might as well be doing the same, because he goes deaf in crowds.

The men are all puffed up in tuxedos or expensive suits. Penguins fluffing their feathers. They exude a certainty that they are the right people in the right place. Movers, shakers, power brokers. They talk loudly and laugh even louder at any provocation. You could slaughter a lamb on the stage and they would still be laughing, Max thinks.

The women, who likely have been preparing for weeks to fit into their favourite evening clothes, seem largely ignored. Except for two.

There are two notable clusters of men, each surrounding a woman. One Max knows to be the Wife, although she is too short to be seen in the group. She is wearing a strapless green gown with her dark brown hair styled high, but not too high. She is glowing because on this evening she will receive the Communicator of the Year Award. The men are attracted to her like mutts. A few are curious about her professional ideas, but Max knows that most are wondering what might happen if Max left the party early or, even better, passed out drunk in the men's room, or was hit by a bus. Would any of these events propel the distraught Wife into their arms, they wonder.

The Wife pokes through the crowd to point out Max. She waves her "stay where you are" wave. Max is fine with that. A couple of the men turn toward Max to check him out and assess their chances with his wife. He waves to them, thinking "hands off, slime balls. She's mine."

Max looks around some more.

There is a half-cluster of fawning silver-haired men and women around the Archbishop. Nothing interesting there.

But he notices the head of glorious red hair at the centre of the other, slightly older man-cluster. That hair, too, is piled high. Max can see it clearly.

One of the men detaches himself from the pack and walks confidently over to Max.

"You must be Max, spouse of the guest of honour," he says, and introduces himself as the CEO of GCPR, a public relations firm.

"We've got a small but rapidly growing communications and public relations firm. I'll be blunt: I've heard a lot of good things about you and I like your paper. You should join us — I'd love to work with another member of the advisory board."

Max is stunned. It has never occurred to him that he would ever meet another member of the Dancer's advisory board.

"You're on the advisory board?" is all he can manage by way of reaction.

"Yep. I'm at her table tonight."

"She's here?"

"Maxie!" someone say behind him. He sees a red-haired woman head peek out in his direction from inside the circle of would-be hound dogs.

The mongrel horde parts, and Max recognizes the Dancer.

"Maxie! It's been so long. You stay right there!"

She pats the hands of a few of the grey-templed executives and busses a couple of clean-shaven cheeks before making a beeline for Max.

They have talked many times since that memorable meeting in Montreal, but there's been no face-to-face. The Dancer is older, of course, but as sexy as a barn fire. Max notes that her backside has not fallen, despite her pragmatic prediction of 25-plus years ago.

She, too, is wearing a strapless green dress, but hers is sequinned and considerably tighter than the Wife's. Max's special male sense makes him wish the Dancer and the Wife weren't wearing strapless gowns of the same colour. Actually he wishes the Dancer was wearing a muumuu. He thinks this is not the best time for them both to be in the same room.

But Max is surprised by how good his old friend's embrace feels. He holds her tight for a moment. Despite himself, he is flooded with warmth and near tears. My two favourite women in the world are here together, he thinks.

In the grip of knee-jerk male guilt, Max's next thought is that it might be wise to somehow keep those friends separate. But that horse is out of the barn. About half the room heard the ruckus when the Dancer spotted Max; the half that included the Wife and her gang of two-legged sniffers and snorters. She is making her way over.

Max knows that matter-antimatter explosions are the most powerful imaginable, but he's sure they won't come close to what's about to happen.

But, inexplicably, there's a look of recognition on the Dancer's face.

"You're Maxie's wife?" she says.

"Jesus," says the Wife. "You're his *friend*?"

The Dancer nods yes and the two perform the double cheek-peck.

"You two know each other?" Max asks, feeling oddly disappointed.

The Wife explains that they are "acquaintances", having met at PR conventions. But, perhaps luckily for Max, they never had a chance to "really sit down and talk."

"That dress looks fabulous on you," the Dancer says. "You'll have to tell me what you're wearing to future events like this. I don't think I'm up to the competition."

The Wife is smiling broadly.

"Oh, I don't know," she says, pointedly looking the other woman up and down. "I think you're holding your own."

Then she adds: "You don't look anything like the pictures."

There's an awkward silence.

"Oh, you mean the Montreal pictures — the trial," the Dancer says. "That was Maxie's idea. He told me not to run from the cameras, but to make sure no one would recognize me after the trial was over. He told me to put on some weight and dress like a madam from the movies. I stayed behind with my lawyer after court and changed into a wig, put on a ton of make-up and put out some cleavage for the media. I thought of bringing a whip, but I wasn't sure Maxie would approve."

"You never know," the Wife says, holding his gaze for a long moment. "Maxie's full of surprises."

Har-har-oops, Max thinks.

The Dancer says she got into real estate after the publicity died down. Now she has a holding company with several businesses.

"Real estate? That wasn't Maxie's idea, was it?" the Wife asks.

"It was. He said all the house-hungry baby boomers made it a sure thing. He also suggested I change the company name from Goldpussy to Golden Cat."

They both look at him fondly, although the Wife seems a little perturbed by something. The wait staff are ringing small bells, the first warning that dinner is on the way. The Wife says the Dancer "must come to dinner", etc., but the answer is a genial "no" disguised as a "maybe".

"I travel a lot. I have business interests here, but I don't live here. Not anywhere, really. More important, Maxie is a business advisor."

"Yes, absolutely."

"And normally I have a rule about separating business and friendship. I know you understand."

Max has never understood it. But he nods knowingly.

The Wife laughs. "You're every bit as smart as Maxie says."

The Dancer reaches out and touches the Wife's bare arm.

"I wonder if I could ask something. After this party's

over, could I have Maxie to myself for a couple of drinks? No funny business, of course. I'm too old for it."

The Dancer fires a look at Max to see if he got the reference before she goes on: "We just haven't seen each other in a very long time and I'm leaving first thing tomorrow."

Max does indeed get the reference and winces, but the only thing to do is watch and listen. His fate is out of his hands.

"Well, I'll need Max around for the post-event back-slapping," the Wife says. "But then I can take some dessert home and wait in bed for him there. I want something in exchange, though."

She whispers to the Dancer, who laughs and whispers something back.

"I had no idea," the Wife says.

She turns to Max: "Don't worry, we're not talking about you."

Yeah right, Max thinks.

"Well, that's good," he says. "I was thinking I might need a therapist."

How can the Wife and the Dancer be getting along, Max wonders. Have they been swept up by the manufactured goodwill of the event? Aren't these events bullshit in every respect, or is there something wrong with me?

• • •

The awards are over and only stragglers remain. The Wife, as usual, picked the perfect moment to quietly depart. On his way to meet the Dancer, Max encounters a drunk car dealer, a major advertiser in the Paper.

"That's some fine woman you've got there," the dealer says. "Yep, that's a woman who actually deserves to be on that pedestal, or podium. Or whaddever."

"Missed the whole thing," Max lies, wondering how he can end the conversation civilly.

"Well," the guy says. "You should have been there. I tell you, that's one fine piece of female you got there. She's not this year's model, if you know what I mean, but she's got that classic appeal. Stylish and comfortable."

"Tell you what," Max says, fishing his keys from his pocket and holding them up. "Here are the keys to my house. Why don't you try her out? You know, kick her tires, take her for a spin around the bed."

The major advertiser lurches. "You're kidding, right?"

"Oh, no, of course not, but fair warning: don't engage her turbo — I doubt you can handle that much woman."

As Max walks away, the dealer shouts: "Everyone knows your wife makes twice the money you do, asshole."

• • •

The Dancer is waiting for him in a piano bar across the street from the hotel. Campari and soda await him on the table. They talk for a while, a bit about their lives, a bit about business, a bit about their odd relationship.

The Dancer confirms Max's suspicions that her encounters with the Wife were not coincidental: "Her name was on the attendees list and I saw a chance to see what she's like."

Max wonders why she has refused to meet him face-to-face over all these years.

"Sometimes a kiss is not just a kiss," she says.

Max is still puzzling over that remark when she gets to her key message: he is in trouble.

"Nonsense. I'm not in trouble," says Max with mock casualness. "Let me put things in perspective for you. I find it helps to make a list. Let's see. I've got two libel suits, a human rights complaint, the Archbishop is trying to get my wife fired, and the cops are investigating me for contempt of court. So, you see, I'm not in trouble. Once you organize the issues, you realize there's really no problem."

She touches his cheek and looks him in the eye: "You don't deserve it, Maxie. But you're not careful about your enemies."

"It's the job," Max says. "If you aren't making enemies, you aren't doing it right."

The Dancer grimaces.

A waiter, seemingly unbidden, plops a Scotch beside Max's half-finished Campari and withdraws.

"So," Max says. "I'm paranoid AND people are out to get me?"

She doesn't laugh. "People here don't like you, Maxie."

"What's not to like? And how would you know?"

"I have a business here. I speak to people, and they tell me what's on their minds. Your name keeps coming up."

"My name? That's crazy. I'm below the radar for those people. Do you know how obscure the Paper is?"

"It's not obscure in Halifax," she says. "This is serious. They don't see you as a force of progress."

Max sputters out a rapid-fire defence. "Progress? That's the last thing they want. Why don't they just have me fired if they're so powerful?"

"Because someone in Montreal likes you and your enemies don't have much clout there," she says. "They're making progress, though."

This is bad news. Max has always presumed that fighters of the good fight — e.g. Max himself — would eventually prevail, in one way or another. The Dancer is bringing a different message.

"You could have told me this by phone," Max says.

"You wouldn't listen to me that way," she says. "The truth is that you need to focus on a graceful exit."

"No way," Max says. "The Paper is my life."

Silence ensues. Max knows what's coming: she gives him the same crazy-woman stare he got the night they met in Montreal.

"Really, Max? It's not your family, for example?"

Fuck. Max has imagined many ways this conversation might go, but this isn't one of them. Worse, he is beginning to think the Dancer has it right. The lawsuits, the human rights complaint, a contempt investigation, the Wife's job. The most likely conclusion is that he'll leave the Paper wearing the scarlet "A", for Asshole. He'll have to hope the Wife keeps her job and supports the family.

The Dancer digs into her purse and pulls out a jeweller's box and hands it to Max.

Inside, Max finds two gold cufflinks in the shape of large staples.

"This is your welcome aboard gift from Golden Cat Public Relations," she says. "Just call when you're ready."

She hugs him, hard: "You're everything I thought you were, Maxie, including your lack of greed. And you're kind. I'll always have your back."

He returns the hug. When finally he looks at her, he sees that she's worried about him and his heart sinks.

"Don't worry about me."

"Why is it inconceivable that someone should worry

about you? I decide who I worry about. And I worry because I know what makes you tick. So does your spectacular wife."

"She's worried, too?"

The Dancer treats him to another crazy-woman stare.

"Okay," Max says. "I get it."

• • •

At home, the Wife is waiting for him, as promised, in bed with a creamy dessert purloined from the banquet.

"Are you worried about me?"

"Yes."

"Okay. I accept that."

"Very generous of you."

"Did you like her?" Max asks.

"She's classier than I expected. And smarter. She says you're one of her key advisors," the Wife says. "Why didn't you tell me about all the advice you give her?"

"We just talk a few times a year. I've *told* you that," Max says. "It didn't seem important. It just seemed like it was a leftover from a previous life."

"I hope I'm never one of your leftovers," she says.

"I didn't mean it like that. She's my second-favourite woman in the world, but she's in another ..."

Max can't find the right word, so the Wife finishes his sentence for him: "She's in another compartment, right?"

Max elects not to engage with that idea.

"Is it true you told her to invest in Microsoft?" the Wife asks.

"She was going to put it into Commodore."

"Why didn't you invest in Microsoft?"

"I don't trust the stock market."

Max changes the topic: "Ever heard of Golden Cat Public Relations?"

"Absolutely," the Wife says. "They're shaking things up in the sector."

Max nods.

"At the awards, what did you whisper to her that made her laugh like that?" he asks.

"I asked her how she keeps her butt from falling."

"Surgery," Max says, again thinking back to the long-ago conversation.

"No."

"Really? What did she say?"

"Can't tell you. It's a gender-security issue and you don't have clearance."

1995

The Campaign: Enough!

"DO YOU REMEMBER that car dealership jerk from the awards ceremony?" Max asks the Wife.

"He swings a heavy bat in this town."

"A car dealer?"

"Car dealers have lots of money, Maxie. That makes them leading citizens."

"Well, he's one of your fans. He says you're stylish and comfortable. He also said I make half the money you do."

The Wife nods her agreement.

"What part are you agreeing with?" he asks.

"All three," she says, pecking his cheek and moving on toward his earlobe. "You know what my salary is."

"The next day he threatened to pull his ads from the paper if I didn't quit and said I'm holding back your career," Max says. "The Cobra had to talk him down."

"So what?"

"I should quit, I guess," Max says. "I don't want to hold you back."

"You're going to take advice from a car dealer?"

Max gives this a few moments' thought.

"Have I ever told you," he says, "that you're stylish, yet comfortable?"

"I'm glad you feel that way," she says. "Because His Excellency finally did it — sent an informal note to the university president saying he's concerned that I may have had an abortion."

"The sheepfucker," Max says. "I've had enough of this crap."

"About time."

1975

Reporter Meets El Mago, Gets Even Bigger Story

MAX SITS IN the blackest darkness he has ever experienced, trying to estimate how long it has been since his arrest outside the community college. The APC they tossed him into stank of body odour and diesel. The ride was rough; seemingly every pebble jarred his bladder another notch toward urgency. When the APC stopped, Max was blindfolded by sweaty hands and walked to his cell, his feet only occasionally touching the ground. In the short time between the removal of his blindfold and lights out, Max saw that he was in a genuine dungeon, complete with arched roof and chains anchored in a stone wall. His escorts laughed and killed the lights when he asked to pee.

"*The Wife is not here*," his own voice says in his head as he relieves himself against a wall. "*We're not even married yet*."

Max's experience of breathing gains new prominence. Sometimes a breath reassures him that he is alive and will find a way to stay that way. Sometimes he feels like a man underwater breathing through a pipe, not sure how far the intake extends above the surface.

Max notices a hollow feeling just below his sternum

that signals irrevocability, like the one he gets when he realizes that he can no longer control his skis and that only luck and the laws of physics will determine whether or not he slams into a tree. This is Max now, waiting to see whether a tree is around the corner.

He hears footsteps and sees a flashlight bouncing on the wall opposite his cell as someone makes his way along the paving stones. The flashlight arrives and turns directly on him. Max is blinded.

"Do you know how to make someone disappear?" says the owner of the flashlight. "One method is to fly them to a remote spot over the ocean, remove their clothing and drop them alive into the water. Alternatively, there is the jungle. In either case, you then burn all of their belongings. And then you make sure you have a reputation for barbarity, so the missing person's friends don't come looking for him."

Silence.

"This isn't just death I'm talking about," says the voice. "It's the end of your existence. In time, no one will know you ever walked the earth."

The light disappears.

Sometime later, Max has no idea how long, the overhead lights come on and a guard leads him down a low passage. Lighting comes from an electrical conduit running down the centre. There are low cells like Max's on either side, again with arches of brick. It could be a tourist attraction, he thinks.

The guard leads him up a flight of stairs to an ordinary-looking office door marked "*Sala de medicos*" — Doctors' Lounge.

"Is this *El Mago*'s office?" Max says to the guard.

The guard is slow to answer, but finally nods.

El Mago is waiting for him behind a steel desk painted a mouldy green that could have been anywhere in Max's high school. He rises, hand extended, and gives his prisoner a strong handshake. Max, who is beginning to collect himself after his purgatory, figures the sudden contrast is meant to disorient him. It's working well, but even more confusing is how good-looking the guy is, something Max never admits about other men, even to himself.

El Mago is fortyish, sporting a spectacular head of silver hair set above a pair of expressive black eyebrows. The face is intelligent and open. There are laugh lines starting around alert blue eyes.

Moreover, there is something oddly familiar about the accent.

"Come on in. Have a seat," he says in a warm, soft-spoken tone that Max thinks might actually be genuine. "I hope you like *café con leche*."

Max is not especially fond of it, but decides that a windowless room in a Secret Police building is the wrong place to take a stand.

"*Muchas gracias*," Max says.

El Mago nods graciously as he passes Max a large cup brimming with coffee and milk.

"I thought so," he says. "You are a true traveller, someone who knows that even a couple of words in his host country's native language can open doors and start friendships."

"Are you the guy with the flashlight from a few minutes ago?" Max asks.

El Mago chuckles. "Yeah, sorry about that. I realized too late you might find that upsetting."

Max doubts it was an oversight.

Another friendly chuckle. "Well, try some of that coffee."

Max does. As usual, it's too milky, barely hinting at the heavyweight caffeine punch Max yearns for. He looks at the cup's inscription: "National Press Club, Ottawa, Canada's Capital."

El Mago notices Max's reaction and laughs again, like they are old friends looking at old yearbooks.

"I was wondering when you would notice," he says.

Finally Max realizes that the mysterious accent he's been hearing isn't an accent at all — the guy's speaking Canadian.

"I learned to speak English in Ottawa, eh?" tilting his head to ensure Max gets the cultural reference. "I spent two years training in counter-insurgency with your RCMP's Security Services. I still have a lot of friends there."

"The RCMP does counter-insurgency?"

"You bet."

"And you got this cup at the National Press Club?"

"I was an associate member, yes," El Mago says. "About half a dozen of us were members. In addition to hacks like yourself, the place was full of politicians and diplomats, some of whom were intelligence officers or outright spies. So, it made sense for us to know who was talking to whom. And, of course, journalists and politicians are always happy to share their inside knowledge over a drink."

"I used to go there, sometimes," Max says.

"So I'm told," El Mago says. "That's why I thought you would like that mug."

Max has read that psychopaths are charming. The two chat for a few moments about the Ottawa Rough Riders and marvel that Latin Americans are able to afford soccer stadiums triple the size of Lansdowne Park.

"I'm sorry I never got to see Russ Jackson play," El Mago says.

Bullshit, you whacko, Max thinks. "Me, too," he says.

El Mago offers Max a flour-covered roll and some butter.

"So, Max," he says helpfully. "My officers say you demanded to talk to me. May I ask why?"

"Well," Max says, retrieving his pencil and emergency note pad, "I think you would make a pretty good story. Perhaps we can begin with you telling me your real name."

El Mago smiles ruefully. "You know, it is a standing joke here that everybody knows where the secret police building is, so how can it be secret? The truth is, we are not secret about *where* we are, just *who* we are."

Max recalls the lack of a name on the office door. El Mago continues.

"No one inside this building uses my name or rank. Or outside, for that matter. That's because we're fighting the war that the Army won't fight. The insurgents would gleefully kill my family if they knew where to find them."

"Does your war include killing school children?"

El Mago purses his lips and turns his head sideways a little. "You're a brave man, Max, asking me a question like that on my own turf."

Max gets the point. He tries and fails to keep his hand steady as he reaches for a sip of coffee.

El Mago keeps going. "This building was once a mental hospital. You spent the night in a tunnel between the admin building and the treatment centre. The worst patients — the ones that they didn't want the public to see — were kept there."

"What's at the other end of the tunnel now?"

"Headquarters for the regular police, which is where I start my day. Then I take the tunnel to work. The Maoists can stake out the secret police building all they want, but they'll never see anyone go in but substaff and, of course, decoys. But Max, my point is this. The book at headquarters already shows that you were released almost as soon as you arrived."

"You're trying to frighten me," Max says. "It's not working. How many kids were injured in the shooting?"

"The shooting was a lesson that had to be administered."

"How many were hurt?"

"Eleven."

"That's the same as I said in my story."

"What you put on the wire isn't good enough for you?" El Mago says.

"It's just suspicious. How many dead?"

Max wondered why El Mago's eyes seemed so blue all of a sudden, then realized that it was his face turning the colour of clay.

"You should take a fucking walk outside the city," he tells Max. "Talk to the farmers who've had their crops and livestock confiscated by these terrorists. Talk to the women and girls who've been raped. Ask about their missing sons or the ones whose heads have been delivered to their doorsteps in burlap bags."

El Mago is standing now.

"These 'kids' you talk about give these killers support with their demonstrations. Aid and comfort. The response must be harsh, for the sake of the country."

A moment of silence.

"So, how many kids died last night?" Max asks.

"Do you know how easy it would be to sneak you out of here and dump you 200 miles over the ocean? It's EASY! I thought I made that clear. You'll be fish food, Max. You'll finish up in a can of anchovies. And being disappeared is worse than death for people like you. Terrorists, journalists, crusaders of all kinds; disappearing off the face of the earth is the worst possible fate. Would you rather be Max who died defending free speech, or Max the guy who walked away from a police station toward the whorehouses and never came back?"

Max struggles to keep his voice steady. "Is that what you're going to do?"

El Mago expels a tired breath and looks at the ceiling.

"No," he says. "I am going to call your babysitters in the Army to come and get you. Now is the time for me to start improving relations with them."

With that, he grabs the phone on his desk and quietly issues some orders. Max is reasonably sure he's telling someone to send for the Army.

"Six," El Mago says, hanging up.

"Six?"

"Six died last night, versus 33 innocent people who have died since I was assigned to protect them."

"Can I quote you?"

"Then I could be fish food, eh?"

"Good point," Max says. "Well, I don't need to quote you. You've just confirmed what I thought I heard an officer say last night. Couldn't be sure, though. One last question: what will you do when the number of dead children equals the number of dead peasants? Thirty-three, right?"

El Mago drops the last trace of gentility and shoots him a murderous look. Max can see that he might be regretting the decision to let him go.

"You just took a big chance on your weak Spanish, Max," he says.

He lets that sink in.

"I'll stay in touch," El Mago says. "We could be valuable to each other some day. If things go the way I expect, I'll be starting a career with Army Intelligence any day now."

"Really?"

"The signs of counter-coup are everywhere. But the Army can't fight the Maoists without my help. It's either that, for me, or a swim in the ocean."

• • •

Twenty minutes later, Max is in an Army staff car with the Doorman at the wheel. He's surprised to see the sun already well up in the sky. Time flies when you're having fun, he thinks.

"It is good to see you, Max," he says. "We were not sure we ever would."

Max takes a moment to savour the feel of the sun on his face.

"Me, too."

He notices the Photog's absence.

"He is at the base," the Doorman says.

"So, you're in the Army?"

"Like your friend said, there's more to me than meets the eye. I can take you back to the *Palacio* to write your story."

"Six dead," Max says.

"He told you that?"

"Can't say."

"For him to tell you that means he's got big friends in the Army. After you write your story, I have another, much bigger story for you."

"You do?"

"I will take you back to the capital, courtesy of the Army, where you will interview a certain general."

"What general?"

"The general who found a basket of eggs with his morning paper today," the Doorman says. "You are about to get a *scoop*!"

"What exactly do you do for the Army anyway?"

The Doorman turns to him with a wide smile: "Intelligence. But I am studying my true passion — public relations!"

1995

The Campaign: Bentley & Steele's Problem

Max strides into the newsroom, noting that the City Editor is again professional-looking in a slim grey skirt and a new hairstyle that highlights her strong cheekbones. She flashes him a big, winning smile.

"Jesus, Max. It's crazy this morning. A car accident, a fire and a bank robbery by a guy wearing a fucking OJ Simpson mask," she says. "The photogs are bitching like crazy. I mean, isn't this what we pay them for? Isn't this what those assholes *like* to do?"

"So, we're off to a good start," Max says. "Anything else?"

"Yeah. You'll love this," she says waving a brown envelope at him. "It's an actual brown envelope. The real thing. Just like in the movies, eh? Someone slipped it under the front door last night."

Max looks inside. It's a printout from the business registry showing Bentley & Steele's corporate status is "inactive" because they failed to renew the rights to their name.

Max smiles.

"How long did it take them to notice?"

"About two months," she says. "I called the registry.

Bentley & Steele sent someone down with a cheque two days ago."

"So, no harm," Max says.

"No harm, but what kind of law firm can't manage its own registration? The public should know, don't you think?"

"Definitely. It's an outrage. Get the story all teed up, but don't call Bentley & Steele until I give the word."

Max surveys the City Editor's new look, looks her in the eye and raises his eyebrows.

"Everything's different when somebody wants you," she says.

• • •

"You were right, Max," Mother Mary says.

"Those are words we need to hear more often around here," he says.

He can see Mother Mary nervously writing that in her notebook.

Her face is too worn for someone still in her twenties.

"I was at the county courthouse looking for lawsuits involving the church and Father Peter," she says. "But they said they wouldn't give me anything unless I had the surname and address of a plaintiff and the year the action was filed. It was bull, but they wouldn't budge."

So Mother Mary asked them for a copy of the local phonebook and used the information to fill out request forms.

Each slip forced a clerk to go back to the filing room and retrieve a file, if there was one.

"I was getting really angry," Mother Mary says. "So I said to myself, I'll do another 50 like this and then I'll call you to get a lawyer in."

"You could have done that right away."

"Yeah, but it would have been at least a day before one could get there. Anyway, finally I heard this big 'slam!' on the counter and it was seven civil cases — against the church. In one of them, the church says it was the boy's own fault because he seduced Father Peter." Her face is grim.

Max says she should track down the family and get a reaction.

"They are furious, but they wouldn't let me talk to their son," she says.

"You mean you've already talked to them?"

"Got pictures of the parents, too."

Max tells her to write it up, but not to call the church until he gives the word. Mother Mary starts out but turns at the doorway.

"I don't know if I believe in Hell anymore, but I did when I was a girl. I used to worry about who would go to Hell, because there were people I loved who sinned and didn't tell the priest. But now I know who's really going to Hell, and I'll go there, too, just so I can stoke the fires under their feet."

• • •

Max is headed for the news meeting when the wire guy calls him over. He points to a story on his computer screen.

"Hey, Max, is this your friend?"

The Photog has been shot in the occupied territories and taken to a hospital in serious condition. Max skips the news meeting and puts in a call to the Bureau Chief, now working in Paris.

"Yeah, it's him, Max."

"Jesus. What happened?"

"They're saying it was a stray bullet," the Bureau Chief says, "but it went right through his camera and hit him in the face. Sounds intentional to me."

He adds that the Photog has a chance of surviving, but others in the local press corps doubt he'll ever be the same.

"It's pretty bad, Max."

Max can't work, so leaves the Indonesian in charge and heads home early. But being home is no help. At a loss for something to do, he goes into his office and just sits.

An hour later he feels something give way in front of him. It's so subtle and sudden that he stops to reflect, to be sure it happened. It's like a string has broken, letting something go.

Not too long after, the Bureau Chief calls to say the Photog has died.

"I know," Max says.

• • •

Max and the Wife are enjoying a late Sunday afternoon on the deck when the phone rings. Incredibly, it's a ham radio operator.

"I don't get much call for this these days," the guy says, "but I picked up a walkie-talkie signal way out in the woods. He asked if I could connect him with you."

This could only be the News Weevil.

"Thank you," Max says. "Can you patch him through somehow?"

"Roger that. Here you go."

There follows a rush of static and then the hushed tones of the Weevil: "Max, Max, Max. This is me. Over."

He is following marine radio protocol, despite the fact he's connected to a landline. Max is looks at the Wife and rolls his eyes: "Weevil, this is Max. Go ahead on this channel."

"Weevil? What's Weevil? Over."

"Ahh ... it's a code name."

"Good idea, Max. Over."

The Wife has figured it all out. She dashes into the house and comes back with another phone so she can eavesdrop.

"Weevil, what's your twenty?"

"Chief, you have to say 'over'."

"Over," says Max.

The Wife is bubbling over with mirth.

"Chief, I am in the woods next to the runway. There are workers painting stripes on it. Over."

"Weevil, why are you in the woods ... uh, over."

The Wife has now moved on to tears of laughter.

"Max, they said they would beat me up if I didn't go away. Over."

"Weevil, maybe you should leave that location and talk to some of the nearby homeowners."

There follows a good half-minute of silence before Max catches on.

"Over," he says.

"Chief, I've done that already. Got pretty much the same response. Over."

"Weevil, they threatened to beat you up? Over."

"Chief, roger that, and a woman threatened to shoot my gonads off with a 12-gauge shotgun. As you know, at that range a 12-gauge would blow out my entire pelvic region. Over."

"Roger, Weevil. Recommend full retreat at this time. Over."

"Chief, roger that. But in case I'm killed, you should know something. Over."

"Weevil, no one's going to kill you. Over."

"Uhhh roger, but with respect, that's easy for you to say when you're in Halifax. Over."

"Weevil, you seem petulant, but your point is taken. Over."

"Chief, the thing is, it's not a runway. It's a highway. It's got pavement markings, a culvert and a 100km/h speed limit. It also has a big green overhead exit sign but with just an arrow. No words. Over."

Max has had enough of protocol.

"Where the fuck does it go?"

"That's the thing, Chief. It doesn't go anywhere. It doesn't start anywhere. It's just there."

Max gives the Weevil a heartfelt attaboy and tells him to get out before he gets beaten up.

Then he turns to the Wife: "Do you get it?"

"Yep."

"The fucking thing is a vote-creation program. It's about votes. That's why they keep piling on the pressure."

"I get it. And I love the way you say 'roger'."

"You didn't say 'over'."

"Umm, over."

"Roger that, and come over here."

1995

The Campaign: The Ride of the Valkyries

For the first time in months, Max's insides aren't torturing him. He feels a freshness, a lightness of being.

He calls the City Editor into his office and asks her to close the door.

"What?" she says. "After all these years, *now*?"

Max ignores her: "You and the Indonesian don't seem to mind spending time together."

The City Editor looks skyward.

"So I have a job for the two of you," Max says. "Two days from now—a week before election day—I want three stories on Page 3: the road to nowhere; the archdiocese's seduction defence, and Bentley & Steele's failure to maintain their registration. All edited and ready to go."

"Can't be done," she says. "The Collective will tip off the Cobra. He'll kill the stories and fire you. Maybe all of us."

"The Collective will never know," Max says. "Just quietly get those stories ready for publication. Leave all the stuff on my desk and I'll come in during the night and get it camera-ready."

"You don't know how to do that," she says.

"How hard can it be?"

• • •

Two days later Max arrives at the newsroom at 3:30 a.m. to get the page ready. He finds a large envelope pinned to his office door. It's hard to miss because taped to it is a black-and-white photo of dog feces, the ones deposited so long ago by Big Mac. There's a sticky note from the City Editor: "Max, we never had to use this to fire the prick, but I've kept it for some reason. Thought it might cheer you up. *Nil bastardo carborundum*."

Max's recognizes the phrase: made-up Latin for "don't let the bastards grind you down."

When he finally opens the envelope, Max finds his Page 3. Except for gaps where reaction quotes will go and a picture of the Premier, the page is ready for the presses. It seems the City Editor and the Indonesian have been busy.

With his work done for him, Max has time to go home and resume his sleep. But first he spends an hour in the pressroom, admiring the machinery and inhaling God's own elixir of ink and paper dust. The sun is rising when he finally steps outside.

• • •

In the afternoon, the Cobra slithers into Max's office. Max is editing letters to the editor and doesn't notice him.

"You've been a bad boy, Max," he says.

Max snaps his head up and sees the Cobra's hood has already flared. He's ready to strike.

"I thought I told you I don't want to see that stupid 'road to nowhere' story in the paper," he says. "But I have it on good authority that you're working on it, and maybe some other stories that I might not like."

Max makes a show of checking his notes: "I said only a fool would run it without you seeing it. That's all. And I believe that if we get the story, you'll be bowled over by it."

"Really?"

"There are few things I'm certain of," says Max. "This is one of them."

Finally, after all their years together, the Cobra strikes. In a flash, he bends forward at the waist and stops with his face millimetres from Max's.

"Well, don't try anything smart-ass, Mr. Editor. This is my paper and nothing happens here that I don't know about. Nothing."

He rears back to the strike position and Max looks him in the eye.

"I can say with 100 per cent sincerity that I stake my job on it," he says.

Max watches him depart. It's those little legs, he thinks, that let him walk without moving his head.

• • •

An hour later, the City Editor is in his office to say the News Weevil is on the Batphone and wants to talk to him.

"Why the Batphone?" Max inquires. "I have a phone right here on my desk."

"You have to ask? It's not enough that I tell you it's the Weevil?"

Reluctantly, Max trudges after her to the Batphone. She asks him to be quick because there are serious journalists who use that line.

"Chief," he whispers. "It's Weevil. I'm in the legislature library."

Max explodes: "Why are you fucking WHISPERING?"

The newsroom goes quiet.

"Because I'm in a library."

Max can feel his intestines waking up. He takes a breath.

"Okay. Point taken. Why are you calling yourself Weevil?"

"It's a great nickname, Chief. I want to keep it."

Max allows his head to free-fall to his chest. The Weevil continues.

"It's in the Premier's riding."

"What is?"

"The runway. The road to nowhere."

"But it's not. We triple-checked that."

"Yeah, but our map was from before redistribution. There was a delay printing the new one," the Weevil says. "We never checked the actual report."

Max wants to kick himself. The Paper was focused on the big picture, i.e., the game of transferring voting power from Halifax to the outback. They—Max—forgot the details.

"The Premier's new riding lost a sliver on the east and added one on the north," the Weevil says.

"And how did that work out for him?"

"The eastern section voted heavily against him in the last election, but the polls in the north are pro-Premier. This gives him a better cushion."

"Especially if the area has road-building money coming in," Max says.

"That's right, Chief," the Weevil whispers. "Everybody loves a new road. Even if it doesn't go anywhere."

Max goes to see the City Editor, but she cuts him off: "I know. We'll fix up Page 3 and keep it hidden. It's kinda fun sneaking in here at night. I mean, you know." She has a sly look on her face.

"Spare me the details," Max says, but he's already looking around the newsroom to see where an enterprising young couple might "do it."

• • •

Max's revenge is at hand. He and the Wife are watching *Apocalypse Now* on the VCR when the Indonesian calls. Max cradles the phone against his cheek while he opens a third bottle of Côtes du Rhône. The Indonesian is reading from notes prepared by Max.

"Hello, Max. I'm calling about a large brown envelope I found on my desk when I came in tonight. On the outside, it says to call you at midnight."

Max motions to the Wife. He returns to the phone and confirms that the Collective has gone home.

"Good. Now, for the record, have you ever seen this envelope or its contents before?"

The Indonesian is a famously honest man, so his answer is a long time coming.

"No," he says.

"Correct. That is because I myself secretly set the type and made up the page for the camera. One moment please ..."

Max mutes the phone.

"This is the last chance to call it off," he tells the Wife.

"You can call it off, or you can live with yourself," she says. "Do it."

Max returns to the Indonesian, speaking slowly and carefully: "I am instructing you to take that page, for which I have sole responsibility, to the press crew and have them substitute it for the current page three. You can do this, or you can pack up your personal belongings and go home — for good. For greater clarity, if you do not do it, you are fired immediately."

The Indonesian clears his throat: "Max, I do not wish to be fired and, after reading the page, I can see no reason why I would not follow your instructions. Therefore, I have no choice but to do as you say immediately."

Thirty minutes later, the Indonesian calls to say the presses are running.

1995

The Smell of Napalm in the Morning

It's a week before election day. Max is staring at page three, thinking about the nice job the City Editor and the Indonesian did putting it together. The road to nowhere story was so outrageous that the Other Paper had no choice but to assign reporters to it. The other media picked up the signal and followed suit.

"I and my colleagues have nothing to apologize for," the Premier is telling the broadcast hacks, over and over. "This government is not afraid to help Nova Scotians. That is all I have to say. What I *can* tell you is how much I wish the newspaper that published the so-called story had given us a chance to comment. But they wouldn't have a story if they did that, would they?"

As well, all the competing media jumped on the priest story because the church is now officially a target. And they all hate Bentley & Steele, so that was a no-brainer.

But oddly, even though he came in early just for that purpose, Max hasn't been fired yet. The phone rings and it's the Lawyer. The Cobra must have asked her to do the firing.

"I've been taking calls all morning," she says. "The libel actions and the contempt investigation have been dropped.

Human Rights is backing off, too. I'll have to dial-down my vacation plans, but I'm happy for you."

Max needs a moment to absorb the news.

"You don't find it all a bit strange?" he asks.

"Nothing about your Paper surprises me any more. Bye, Max."

In his fevered fantasies, Max's private homage to *Apocalypse Now* never got past Robert Duvall extolling "the smell of napalm in the morning".

Now, Max thinks, this could truly be "the smell of victory."

He calls the Wife at work.

"Everything okay?" he asks.

"Definitely. A courier just delivered a note from his Excellency — copied to the board chair — praising my work."

Max asks what she thinks is going on.

"Maybe they're trying to get you to drop your guard. Maybe someone will shoot you in the parking lot tonight."

"Yep. That's it. You'll miss me, then?"

"Oh, terribly. Gotta go, but while I still have you on the line, do you have that car dealer's number by any chance?"

"He's not nearly enough man for a woman like you," Max says.

• • •

Max is as fond of the City Editor as ever, but their meetings have been duller since she started dressing professionally, swearing less and making fewer suggestive remarks.

"This came for you," she says, pulling a video cassette out of a courier package, popping it into Max's VCR and hitting play.

"Don't let me hold you up," he says. "Feel free to play it."

She hands him the sealed envelope that came with the cassette.

Onscreen they see a colour image of a naked white man, middle-aged with a considerable paunch. He's on his hands and knees atop some kind of bench about four feet off the ground.

"Excellent definition," the City Editor says.

A skinny woman with breasts held up by a pointy half-bra enters the frame wielding a ping-pong paddle. She lines it up with his backside.

Whack!

Max and the naked man flinch in unison.

"Is this one of the tapes from *R v Spadinsky*?" Max asks.

"Well, it's not Mr. Roger's Neighbourhood."

Whack! The young woman strikes an especially effective blow. The man groans. "Now shush," Spadinsky urges him. "This is what you signed up for."

Whack! Whack! A deeper groan.

"Ewww," the City Editor says. "I hate it when they dangle like that. I like 'em high and tight, you know?"

"Of course," Max says solemnly. "Everyone says that."

There's a break in the action. The naked man turns his head back to face Spadinsky.

"Recognize anyone?" the City Editor asks.

"Well, it's not his best angle, but is this ...?"

"You bet it is," she says. "Wait 'til Mother Mary sees this."

Whack!

"Make friends with the paddle, your Excellency," Spadinsky says, coaxing him on.

"There was a note taped to the cassette," the City Editor says. "There are four other names on it, all of whom you'll know."

Max scans the note: "Well, certainly they've all been bad boys. Very bad."

Whack! "Oh!"

"Take that you nasty little boy!" the City Editor barks to the screen.

Whack!

"Should I put the Weevil on it?" she asks.

"No. It's their private lives," Max says. "The important thing is that they believe we'll use this stuff, if they're not careful."

"Well, why did you fight the ban then?"

"It's what we do," he says. "Anyway, the Spadinsky case is toast."

Max has no doubt the tape explains all the conciliatory phone calls and other positive news this morning.

He opens a sealed envelope that came with the package. Inside is a card with the words GCPR in gold across the top. And below that the words "Communications and Public Relations Consultants."

There is also a handwritten note:

> *Max—Found this in our office yesterday. No idea where it came from. We felt the ethical thing was to send copies to all those depicted. (No, I don't mean you're one of them. Maybe next time.) We just thought you might be interested. And remember, our invitation to join our rapidly-growing firm remains open."*

It was signed by the CEO.

The City Editor leaves and Max calls the Dancer's special number, which turns out to be a satellite phone.

"Maxie!" she shouts. "Sorry it took so long to answer. The concierge had to bring it to me. You should be at this party. No one's wearing any clothes. You'd love it!"

Happily, the party turns out to be in Milan.

"Where did you get the tape?" he asks. "I thought you were out of that business."

"I don't know what tape you're talking about," she says. "But if I did, I would say that selling real estate, a person meets all kinds of people."

They chat for a bit, but the Dancer has to go: "It's cold just standing around."

The City Editor knocks on his door: "The Crown just dropped the Spadinsky case."

1995

The Campaign: *Sic Transit Maximus*

It's a week after Operation Apocalypse Now — election day. Max is watching the television coverage in his office. An hour in, CBC declares the Party and the Premier re-elected for the fifth time. Unprecedented, they say.

Everyone's reporting that the Premier's popularity actually shot up after the road-to-nowhere story.

Max looks up to see the Cobra standing in his doorway.

"Max, I'd like you to meet your replacement," he says.

Beside him is Big Mac — Amhuinn Maolmuire Maceachthighearna — older but no less hairy.

The Cobra looks like he's found a sunny rock to relax on. Max knows his days at the Paper are over.

"Aye, that's him," he says to the Cobra, pointing to Max. "He fired me because I'm from Cape Breton."

Max rises and extends his hand: "Actually, I said Cape Bretoners move too slowly in the winter because the cold makes their blood thicken up. Still, it's close enough for the game we're playing, right? How's your dog?"

"I'm afraid he's passed, but he sired a sturdy lass that's waiting in my car."

"We can't have an editor who's biased against Cape Bretoners," the Cobra says.

"You're right. I might as well be a racist," Max says.

Big Mac lunges toward him: "You *are* a racist — are you sayin' Cape Bretoners are not a *race*?"

"Never mind," Cobra tells Big Mac. "Max, we'll need a cover story for your departure that won't embarrass the Paper."

"I'll have that by tomorrow morning and I'll be gone by mid-afternoon."

"Good," the Cobra says. "In case you wondered, dickhead, I don't like being underestimated, either."

• • •

Max calls the Dancer's special number again.

"I want to join the firm," her tells her.

"That's *wonderful.* I just *knew* you would," she says.

She starts talking madly about the arrangements, including the $500,000 price of buying a partnership. Max breaks into a sweat. He doesn't have that kind of money.

"Of course you do," the Dancer says. "Your shares of Golden Cat Enterprises are worth twice that. We'll just do a swap."

To Max, this does not seem possible.

"Maxie, every year for more than two decades I've called to ask you if you wanted dividends or more equity," she says.

That was because, until very recently, Max assumed the Dancer didn't have much money and needed the cash. He didn't want to put her on the spot.

"That's what I thought," the Dancer says. "You're so adorable that way. But I did tell you I'd make you rich. And it hurt that you never asked. Oops! Gotta go — partner!"

2005

You Think You're So Clever and Classless and Free

The emcee calls Max to the podium to accept his award as Halifax's Communicator of the Year. The crowd is still applauding a ludicrously expensive video about his career. Spotlights are lurching drunkenly across the crowd.

Max grabs both sides of the lectern, looks out at the room and waits. Just as the rhubarbing begins to decline, but not before, he looks over at the Wife and then speaks.

"Now," he says, and the noise drops immediately. Max knows he has the crowd on his side. They're dying to laugh or cry with him, as required.

He realizes that he's back a bit from the microphone's sweet spot. This is confirmed when he sees the sound technician getting ready to adjust the gain. He moves in a little.

"Now," he says, getting the resonance he wants this time. "If I had said ... a decade or so ago ... that tonight I would be accepting the Communicator of the Year award ... how many people here would have bet against me?"

On cue, the Wife extends her lovely arm and almost the entire room follows suit in a crescendo of warm, boozy laughter.

So, Max says to himself, this is what it's like inside the tent. God, what bullshit.

1973

Seduction Truth Revealed!

"HERE. THIS IS the place," Max's own voice says in his head.

He is disturbed by the voice on the one hand but, on the other, he has the feeling the voice is speaking some kind of truth. Then the voice and the memory of it are gone.

• • •

Without the avuncular presence of the Copy Editor, Max and the Veteran Reporter sit in silence at the Cat Shack for almost the entire length of *You Are the Sunshine of My Life*. The Veteran Reporter is watching the dance floor. Max uses the opportunity to discreetly "take a look", as advised by the older, wiser Copy Editor.

Obviously, she has no grey hair. God, he thinks, she's kind of elegant and, at most, maybe three or five years older than me, not 10. For the first time since they met, Max tries to check out her breasts. His angle is awkward, but he is able to confirm actual cleavage.

Without shifting her attention from the dance floor, she asks: "Are you done, or would you like me to take my shirt off?"

And just like that, he's been exposed. A full-blown chauvinist caught ogling a professional colleague and mentor.

"Done what?"

The Veteran Reporter swings around and faces him full on. There's no escape. Max is inclined to turn away, but knows he can't without looking like a fool. It's like he's a *Star Trek* character locked in a force field.

"Done checking me out."

Max decides to roll the dice. "It's the most rewarding thing I've done all day," he says, and waits for a blast.

She takes a long pull from her draft glass and leans toward him.

"How is it you can trip over a guy who's just shot himself and then write two news stories before the hour's up? You see bodies all the time?"

"First one," Max says, "and you're right. I don't feel a thing. I think I must be some kind of sociopath."

"Well, then you've made the right career choice. So tell me the whole story from the sociopath point of view. I've never met one before."

Max starts his tale with the police radio call and moves quickly to the spookiness of the woods. Finding the body, he says, was like an electric shock. He describes how he had the reaction before he even understood something was wrong.

"How did you know he was dead?"

"It was the crater in his chest. Hardly any blood, just a black hole with edges surrounding it."

"How big was it?"

"Jesus, I dunno. I guess I could have stuck my thumb in it."

Max describes the rest of the scene, the horrified look on the guy's face, which Veteran Reporter describes as a "bit melodramatic". Nonetheless, she's listening carefully. He tells her the saddest thing was seeing the empty rifle box.

"Why?"

"Don't know."

"So here's the question I ask all sociopaths: Why did it take you twenty minutes to do a five-minute drive? WERE you doing something perverted in the woods like the boss said?"

Max knows she's making fun of him, but gives a straight answer.

"I drove to the Canadian Tire parking lot and had a couple of smokes."

Max tells her he imagined the guy's route across the pavement from Canadian Tire to the woods. He could see him carrying the rifle box, hunched over against the rain, his giant head covered by a toque, and his giant boots anchoring him to the ground. Like a walking question mark. How was it possible to form and maintain so much self-destructive intent? Go to the store, buy the gun, buy some ammo, carry the box across the parking lot — careful crossing the street! — walk into the woods, find the right spot, load the shiny new gun, lie on the wet ground, put the muzzle to his lumberjack shirt and then reach up to jab the trigger with his thumb.

It was a lot to take in, so Max needed some time in the parking lot before he got back on the road.

The Veteran Reporter is smiling again, just like she did when the Copy Editor decided to leave them alone in Cat Shack. They drink and work their way through the usual topics twice more.

Now the DJ gets to his favourite part of the night—when he pretends he's working for a radio station. He lowers his voice an octave and leans into the mike: "And now, we'll slow things down for the lovers out there, and perhaps even some new lovers who've found each other at the Cat Shack tonight. We'll see you all next Saturday. Until then ... the night is ours."

Usually this is a signal for the last round, but that doesn't seem right without the Copy Editor there, so Max reaches to unhook his jacket from the back of his chair. The Veteran Reporter has a different idea.

"C'mon," she says. "Let's dance. I've never danced with a sociopath."

Max has the idiot-thought that it might be unprofessional, but gets it under control. She looks him in the eye.

"You can do this," she says. "It's only four songs: *Woman, Woman; Killing Me Softly with His Song; When a Man Loves a Woman*, and *Midnight at the Oasis*."

How does she *know* that?

"Dance with her," the voice in his head says.

Intrigued and unwilling to hurt her feelings, he agrees. She grabs Max's hand and leads him to the dance floor.

The Veteran Reporter maintains what Max judges to be a professional distance as they begin slow dancing, her left hand on his right bicep. Seeing her this close, he thinks he's beginning to see the Copy Editor's point. Max has created an image of her as an aging amazon, but up close it's different. His hand covers most of her back, which feels supple. Max can see the top of her head, which is covered with brown hair in long curls, not wild tangles. He wonders if the Veteran Reporter's hair has always been shiny or is it just tonight. He's astonished to notice that her skin is perfect. He wonders if she might be a *lot* younger than he assumed.

Max starts to get a shaky feeling in his chest but, just in time, his thought-police regain control of the riot in his body. Why do people think *Woman, Woman (Have You Got Cheating on Your Mind)* is romantic, he thinks. Gary Puckett is singing about his woman cheating on him. How can that be romantic?

Next: Roberta Flack, *Killing Me Softly With His Song.* Once again, it doesn't make sense. What's romantic about killing? The Veteran Reporter slides her hand from his bicep to his shoulder, moves a little closer, close enough that his skin tingles. How would I describe her smell, if I had to, he asks himself. Max's mind races through his favourite smells. Cinnamon? No! Vanilla? Jesus Christ, vanilla? No, she smells ... good. You're going to be a big-time writer and the best you can come up with is GOOD? But good is all he can think of. Just really good. Roberta sings "*strumming my pain with his fingers.*"

Percy Sledge steps up with *When A Man Loves A Woman.* Well, this makes a little more sense. THIS is romantic. Max is just starting to wonder if the Veteran Reporter might be the same age or younger than him when she closes the remaining gap between them. Apparently there is a notch below his right shoulder where her cheekbone fits perfectly. The thought-police are about to compare the whole thing to a space-docking but can't because she has already completed the manoeuvre. The presence of breasts is re-confirmed, as well as thighs. Max is overcome by an urge to hum to her. They are weightless inside a capsule of scent and body heat.

It's too much for the thought-police, who stagger out

the door, leaving Max to fend for himself. Max thinks of her irresistible voice, which he now realizes he could hear over the din of a thousand newsroom typewriters, even over the buzz of his own thoughts. He thinks of all the times she made him laugh with her clever comebacks, how much he likes it when she teases him. She's just so ... nice ... he thinks. Max hums to her. Percy sings *"If she plays him for a fool; He's the last one to know; Lovin' eyes can't ever see."*

The Voice is back: "It's the Wife, dummy. Relax."

Percy's almost done, which is a problem because something has asserted itself. If they have to make their way back to the table now, it will reveal itself as a sturdy tent-pole rather than the tiny legume described by the Editor. Max feels like he's fourteen again, walking between classes with his three-ring binder held awkwardly over his groin. It's not a good feeling. "Are you sure there are four songs?" he asks her. "Yes," she breathes into his ear. "Do you want to sit down ... for some reason?"

Mercifully he doesn't have to answer because the DJ segues from Percy Sledge to Maria Muldaur singing *Midnight at the Oasis*. What will she think if she notices it, Max wonders, as Maria urges him to "*send your camel to bed ... Cactus is our friend.*" He is miserable. He has just realized how fond he is of the Veteran Reporter, and now he is in danger of revealing himself as, well, unprofessional. They dance like this for a while.

Maria sings "*I can be your belly dancer, prancer, and you can be my sheik.*" Suddenly there is a minor commotion between them, as if the Wife has tripped. As they rearrange themselves, the tent-pole has miraculously moved to a position more or less flat against his belly. This gives him hope of making it back to their table without attracting attention. They dance. It is pleasant. Maria sings "*you won't need no camel, no, no, when I take you for a ride.*"

The Wife presses herself against him, humming, with his predicament firmly sandwiched between their bodies. The shared knowledge of its existence can no longer be denied.

Maria sings:

Come on, Cactus is our friend
He'll point out the way
Come on, 'til the evenin' ends.

"Maxie," the Wife's unmistakable voice whispers into his ear.

She's so young.

"I hope that cactus is for me," she says.

But Max's lust for her is overpowered by an inexplicable feeling that he has arrived somewhere. Again, he hears his own voice: "*Here,*" it says. "*This is where it ends.*"

Max squeezes the Wife tightly, allows his eyes to close, and lets his mind rest.

Acknowledgements

Andrew Safer for his generous help.

All who toiled at the passionate and fearless *Halifax Daily News*.

And, of course, the folks at Guernica Editions.

About the Author

Bill Turpin has worked most of his career as a journalist, first in Montreal and more recently Halifax, but has also afflicted government and the communications world. He is currently living off his wits while studying to be a gadfly. Turpin is married and the father of two cats. *Max's Folly* is his first novel.

Printed in July 2016
by Gauvin Press,
Gatineau, Québec